The Return
of the Hippy

The Return of the Hippy
A Novel of Hope

by David Luddington

Mirador Publishing
http://www.miradorpublishing.co.uk

First Published in Great Britain 2010 by Mirador Publishing

First edition: 2010

ISBN : 978-0-9567111-2-0

Mirador Publishing
Mirador
Wearne Lane
Langport
Somerset
TA10 9HB

To My Sarah

Who provided the magic tin in which to keep my dreams

Chapter 1

It all started with a painted tobacco tin. I don't smoke now, and haven't for some years. Part of maintaining control of my life you see. How can you expect to be in control of anything when you're always gasping for your next nicotine fix?

I like to be in control. Or I did until I saw the tobacco tin. As these things go, this was not particularly unusual. It bore the painted image of an Indian, or Native American as we're supposed to say now. In the clouds above him drifted a faint picture of a bear. Everything had a purple tinge, a dream-like quality. I used to be big on Indians in my hippy days. But that must be... oh, twenty-five years ago now. I had a dream-catcher once, long before anybody knew what dream-catchers were. Nowadays of course they're made of plastic and you get them free with a Happy Meal.

Anyway, the tobacco tin. I was on holiday in St Ives with my adoring family. At least holiday was the official line; unofficially I was suffering what they call 'executive burn-out', or Post Credit Crunch Trauma as the psychologists had taken to labelling it lately. Either way, moving billions of pounds of other people's money around the world's money markets in an attempt to outrun the approaching tsunami of world debt had finally taken its toll. Normality started to escape and I had got to the point where I didn't know which way was Tuesday any more.

It was peeping inside Pandora's Box that finally melted my sanity like a pat of butter left out after a sunny picnic. In the world of the money movers we held a pact. Nobody was to look inside the box. It would ruin everything and send the world into oblivion. But I had peeped. I had seen that all it held was fairy dust. Fairy dust and little promissory notes from people with no money but big dreams of owning their own property. The box was a myth perpetuated on the fantasy that if only we all kept selling it to each other and nobody actually looked inside then the magic money bubble would continue to grow. Then I had dared to peep and the madness escaped.

Sam, my wife, had first noticed that I was acting 'a bit odd', as she called it, and insisted I take some time off. I didn't consider my actions 'odd' at the time, and I'm sure I had a very good reason for burying the television set in the garden. It's just that I can't remember what it is now.

Getting away like this though had made me feel like a freed prisoner. My working life had always been spent mainlining coffee whilst watching a screen in a sealed office then coming home late to another sealed room with a plasma screen on the wall and a gin waiting on the table.

The tin had drawn me like a magnet; it was nestling on a shelf amongst a pile of incense burners, Chinese stress balls and sweet smelling joss sticks. Just one of a number of shops that littered Cornwall's seafronts. It was obvious the tin wasn't really for keeping tobacco in.

I could almost smell the sweet scent of the treasures that ought to lurk within the tin. My mind was already crumbling the pure black resin onto the tobacco. That was when Sam crept up behind me.

"What are you looking at, Tony?" she asked.

She might just as well have shouted "Boo!" for the effect it had on me. My fight or flight mechanism couldn't decide which to trigger, and so opted for twitching all of my muscles simultaneously. The tobacco tin I had been holding somersaulted lazily through the air before breaking the nose off a glass dolphin.

"Hell, Sam! Why do you keep creeping up on me?"

It seems that everybody's creeping up on me these days. Why can't people walk normally like they used to? So I can hear them coming.

"I'm sorry, love, I didn't mean to startle you."

She knelt down in front of me to retrieve the dolphin's nose. Her roots needed doing again. Her once, waist length blonde hair was now a short perm in Wella Chestnut. I don't know why she does that.

"You will have to pay for that, you know!" Now the shop assistant had crept up on me. I started and turned to see her pointing at a cardboard notice that informed me in an annoying little rhyme that if I broke it then I was to 'consider it sold'.

"You're not supposed to touch you know." She had an accent that belonged at the opposite end of the M5 motorway.

"That's not actually the case," Sam said as she straightened up. "You see, as a point of law, you have a responsibility as a shopkeeper to exercise due and reasonable care over the placement of your goods within shop premises with public access..."

And on and on...

It had seemed a good idea at the time, marrying a law student. After all, you never know when you're going to need some legal advice; especially with the way things appeared to be going at the time. I could hear her droning on, but I shut out the words. This was a familiar scene. Overcooked food, overcharging window cleaners, and once even a Girl Guide selling yellow dusters.

The shop assistant stood dropped jaw in front of Sam as she received her lecture on the finer points of the Shops and Retail Premises Act. I pulled a twenty from my pocket and pressed it into the girl's hand. She had suffered enough.

"It's all right, I'll pay for it," I said to Sam. "I quite fancied that dolphin anyway."

"You don't have to you know. You shouldn't let these people get away with it." She made it sound as if we were standing by watching the Great Train Robbery in progress. "What do you want that thing for anyway?" She pointed at the tin. "It's just more junk!"

"Where are the kids?" I asked, hoping that if I could trigger her maternal instincts I might not have to explain what I wanted 'that thing' for. I didn't even know myself.

Could I buy my youth back again in a painted tobacco tin? Perhaps that's why antiques are such big business.

"I think they went next door, into the amusement arcade," she said.

"Well you go look, I'll pay for this. Catch up with you there."

I collected the freshly bagged tin and dolphin with the broken nose, and while at the counter, I noticed a few more treasures. A second transaction secured me a carved wooden box to keep my joss sticks in, a yin yang medallion on a leather string and a good-luck crystal. Shopping had never been my strong point; I'd always relied on Sam for that. Food, clothes, household equipment, holidays. In fact, just about everything. Sam always said I was too naïve to make a good shopper.

The amusement arcade was a maelstrom of flashing lights and electronic noises. Despite the non smoking signs it still stank of cigarette stale cigarette smoke. I wondered why they called it an amusement arcade. The look on the faces of the punters as they shovelled money into the machines was far from amused. Eyes set in grim determination as if by the power of their will alone they could influence the spinning wheels.

Simon, at thirteen the elder of my two children, came running over as soon as he saw me.

"Can I have some more money please, Tony?" he asked. He had taken to calling me Tony lately. He'd decided that as we treated him so badly he must be adopted, and therefore he didn't need to call me dad any more. His logic was that no loving parent could possibly ask their own flesh and blood to put out the trash on a Sunday night.

"What did you do with that tenner I gave you earlier?"

"Oh, come-on, don't give me a hard time. I only want a fiver that's all. I'll give it back to you later."

"And how are you going to do that?"

"I keep winning on the machines!"

"Well, if you keep winning what do you need more money for?"

"Because I put it back in again!"

"That's not winning. That's called losing."

"Yes, but I've won loads of money."

I could be having this conversation for the rest of my life. Five pounds seemed a small price to pay to finish it, so I relented. The note was snatched from my grasp so quickly that it left me with a burning sensation on my fingertips. He seemed to melt back into the kaleidoscopic hellhole that masqueraded as value-for-money entertainment.

Within seconds, Natasha was tugging at my sleeve, informing me it was unfair that just because Simon had spent all of his money, he was given some more, whereas she had been a good girl and kept her money but now she was being refused more. Oh, the logic of a six-year-old. Now I was ten pounds down.

My ears felt like they were bleeding from the noise and my eyes had difficulty focusing as the coloured lights flickered and beckoned the unwary.. I found Sam arguing with an attendant over a stuck crane machine. I waited for a break in the haranguing then told her I would wait for them in a cafe a few doors up.

The inside of the Cafe Oceanic contrasted strongly with the exterior. From the outside it bore all of the hallmarks of Ye Englishe Tea Shoppe. However, once inside, that image was quickly dispelled. Halogen spotlights illuminated a Formica counter leaving the rest of the interior in shadow. Ridiculously tiny cane tables were scattered over a polished pine floor. The tables were of the four-legged variety and therefore guaranteed to wobble no matter how many folded napkins were stuffed under the legs. Why can't all tables be made with three legs? Three legged tables don't wobble.

A highly polished and unnecessarily complicated espresso machine took over the whole of the counter at the far end of the Cafe. The owners of this place had clearly gleaned their knowledge on the layout of coffee bars by watching re-runs of Frasier.

I sat down at the nearest empty table and surveyed the menu. It seemed to consist entirely of things to put inside of baked potatoes. You had to marvel at the imagination of people who could construct such delicacies as 'Pilchards with honey' and 'Garlic peppers'.

A waitress crept up on me and made me jump.

"What can I get you?" She wore patched, flared jeans and purple tie-dyed T-shirt. Her waist length, sun-bleached hair was plaited and beaded Bo Derek style.

"I'll have a coffee please."

"What sort?"

"White please."

"Yes, but what sort? Where from?"

My mind froze. She was talking gibberish. As far as I could see, there was only one place she could get the coffee from. And that was from the coffee machine, unless I was missing something here.

"Over there?" I suggested, pointing at the bar, knowing I was making a fool of myself, but not quite sure why yet.

Her eyes narrowed as if studying me. I realised they were quite beautiful. The slightly annoyed wrinkle perfectly set off an unnaturally sharp blue. Then she smiled.

"No, I meant what country do you want your coffee from?" She pointed at a chalkboard. It contained a list of most of the countries of the Southern Hemisphere. My coffee drinking was usually limited to white, three sugars, served in a plastic vending cup.

"Umm, do you have any Nescafe?"

"I'll see what I can do." She smiled again and leaned over to wipe the table. It wobbled as she did so. Her hair flopped forward and the beads pattered across the plastic surface. I caught a strong smell of Patchouli oil. I drew the scent deeply through my nose, savouring every trace of the hypnotic aroma

My eyes followed her as she headed back to the counter. I couldn't help it. Superbly rounded buttocks filled her jeans to perfection and rolled from side to side as she walked. Perhaps that's the attraction of the Chinese stress balls. Maybe they fill some deep Freudian need.

I opened the little plastic bag that held my treasures and spread them across the table. I wanted to admire them before Sam came. She was very down-to-earth and I knew she would be quite scathing about my purchases. Especially as they seemed to serve no useful purpose whatsoever. I examined the tobacco tin. The Indian's enigmatic face stared out at me. His eyes seemed to hold a strange blend of sadness and wisdom. I prised open the lid and my distorted image shone back at me from the highly polished interior.

The waitress tried to sneak up on me again. But the scent of Patchouli gave her away, and I looked up just as she arrived. She placed the coffee cup on the table. The table was clearly not up to the job and promptly wobbled, causing coffee to spill over into the saucer. She nodded towards the tin.

"What're you going to put in that, then?" Her eyes made contact with mine. A smile flickered across her lips, as if to say she knew what I ought to be putting in there but did I know?

"I don't know. What would you suggest?" I asked. Why did I say that?

"Some Moroccan would look nice." She raised one eyebrow, quizzically. She was testing me. Well, I may not know my coffee, but I do know my cannabis. Or at least, I did.

"I thought some Acapulco would look good. Any idea where I might find some?" What was I doing?

"I'll see what I can do for you, sir," she said, with feigned servitude.

She headed over to a table that lurked in one of the darker corners. Two youths sat there. They wore blue jeans and identical, army-surplus green fatigue jackets. A German badge on the shoulder indicated which particular army they were surplus from.

There was much whispering and pointing in my direction. They were clearly eyeing me up in an effort to establish whether I was a member of Her Majesty's Constabulary. Though one would hardly have thought that my attire of Marks and Spencer's khaki slacks and Fred Perry T-shirt would be suitable disguise for a member of the drug squad. It appeared they agreed, and one of the youths ambled over to my table.

"Cool, man!" he said as he sat down.

At least the language hadn't changed in the last twenty years.

"Far out!" I returned and gave him the two-fingered peace sign. He looked at me strangely.

"Astrid tells me you're looking to score? What're you looking for, a teenth?"

Oh dear, more gibberish.

A few more misunderstandings, the passing of a fifty pound note, and I was the proud owner of what I hoped was not a bag of hedge trimmings.

All I had to do now was to keep this from Sam.

Chapter 2

I hid my contraband on top of the wardrobe in our bedroom. I had decided that the less Sam knew about this the better. She had never shared my interest in illegal substances when we were younger, so I saw no reason why I should expect her to start now.

We were staying in a cottage that overlooked the cliffs to the west of St Ives. The cottage belonged to my boss, Grahame. He had lent it to me to 'hasten my recovery'.

It was his habit to give away weeks in the cottage as a prize to the brokers. All they had to do was to make £1,000,000 profit for the firm and they were allowed to stay for a week in his cottage rent-free. At some stage he had read a book on motivation.

To further motivate us, and to add to the joy of the stay, it was his custom to come down for an evening and treat the lucky winner to a meal. Tonight, he was extending that little treat to me.

When I returned to the lounge Sam was lying back on the sofa watching a fuzzy Jerry Springer on a tiny TV.

"Are you ready yet, Grahame will be here soon."

"I only have to change my shirt."

She peeled her gaze from Jerry and turned to look in my direction.

"You should put a tie on, love. You know what Grahame's like."

Yes, I did know what Grahame was like. Even though we worked in a stuffy, overheated and windowless office he still insisted we all wear ties. I'm sure the tie is a symbol of oppression, a nod in the direction of slavery. How can you ever be free when you start the day by tying a noose around your neck?

A tie, white shirt and red braces. That was the uniform. I'd grown tired of arguing with Grahame about the logic of this, when the only outside visitors we ever had were the computer repairman or the girl who sold sandwiches at lunchtime. All the dealings were now done over the telephone or via computer terminal.

I went upstairs again to select my noose. I chose the Bart Simpson one. It looked innocuous enough at first sight, row upon row of little Barts. But right in the middle, if you looked carefully, one of them was dropping his trousers and pointing his naked buttocks outwards. It summed up how I felt.

As I was removing the tie from the wardrobe, I felt an overwhelming urge to gloat over my hidden treasures again. Is that why dogs keep digging their bones up? I stood on the edge of the bed and retrieved the tobacco tin from its hiding place. I'd swear the Indian looked happier now he was guarding something worthwhile. I popped the lid off the tin and extracted the little plastic bag. I still wasn't quite sure why I had bought the stuff, or even if I'd had any intention of using it. But then events sometimes have a way of taking control of themselves.

I extracted a large pinch of the sweet smelling vegetation and brought it to my nose, inhaling deeply. There was no mistaking that smell.

And that was how I nearly got caught. The pinch of cannabis was in my right hand and my left was clutching the little plastic bag, when the door clicked open.

My left hand reacted rationally, and stuffed the plastic bag into my pocket. It was my right hand that let me down. An autonomic response from my student days clicked into action and deposited the handful of greenery into my gaping mouth.

The door pushed open.

I chewed frantically.

I swallowed.

The dry, bushy stuff remained in my mouth absorbing the last of my saliva and stubbornly refusing to respond to my manic chewing.

Sam stepped in through the door. She instantly assumed her concerned look when she saw my startled expression.

"Are you all right, dear?" She was probably wondering if I was safe to be left alone with the television set.

I nodded. I was beyond speech. My cheeks felt like they were bulging outwards and I tried my hardest not to look like a guilty hamster. Her eyebrows dipped into a V shape as she studied me.

"Are you sure? You look very pale."

I nodded again. My mouth felt as though it had the best part of a tree inside it. And a very dry tree at that. I tried swallowing again and managed to dispose of some of it, but then a branch became lodged in my throat and started tickling. I was now desperately trying to resist the urge to cough. I knew that if I did so, Sam would be picking little bits of cannabis out of her hair for the next twenty minutes. I felt my cheeks start to turn red and tears came to my eyes.

With the final, supreme effort I managed to send most of it on its way towards my digestive system.

"Sorry, dear," I mumbled. "I've got a bit of a frog in my throat."

"There's a mouth-wash in the bathroom if you want a gargle. And I should do your teeth while you're in there, you've got a bit of..." She tapped her teeth with her forefinger. "I don't know what that is. What have you been eating?"

I ran my tongue across the front of my teeth and realised with horror, that a piece of greenery had become lodged there.

"Oh! It must have been that prawn and lettuce sandwich that I had earlier." It was clear that she didn't believe me, but she wasn't going to push it.

"Well hurry up and get ready. The table's booked for eight. Grahame will be here any minute."

She bustled out of the room. I rushed into the adjoining bathroom and drank the best part of four glasses of water in an effort to wash the last of the bush away.

I did my teeth, and with a final check in the mirror ensured that all traces of my snack had been removed.

"How is the old Bugger then?" Grahame's booming voice drifted up the stairs. I couldn't hear Sam's reply but I could imagine her expression. I steeled myself and put my smile into position before setting off down the stairs to enter the 'Jolly Zone'.

He must have heard me coming, as he turned to face me before I'd even hit the bottom step.

"Aha! There you are! How are you, old boy?" He grabbed my arm and started pumping furiously, patting my shoulder with his free hand. For some reason the image of a water pump came into my mind. The ornate, garden variety, with a long wrought iron handle. Maybe if I held my left hand out, water would start to dribble from my fingers. I suppressed an urge to giggle.

"I'm fine, thank you."

"Well, that's good then! Soon have you back in the fold." He was staring at my tie. I don't think he'd ever seen the Simpsons and it was obviously a complete mystery to him as to why Bart should be dropping his pants. I think Grahame has the Financial Times piped directly into his frontal lobes.

He looked as if he were about to make a comment, but then I guess he figured that it was just one of my little eccentricities and thought better of it. Grahame has never understood frivolity. To him, the world was just one big pay-cheque with the payee name blank. You had to go out there and do battle with everybody else to be the first to write your name in the box. Frivolity consisted of a carefully planned party with a precisely timed strip-o-gram to celebrate the end of the financial year. The measure of a man's success was how much stuff he had accumulated. Fast cars, yacht's, even a racehorse named 'Dow Jones'.

"Can I get you a drink, Grahame?" I asked.

"Good show! I thought you'd never offer. Got any shampoo? I fancy a Bucks fizz."

I looked at Sam, "Sam?"

"Yes, I bought some earlier." She disappeared into the kitchen.

"I'll go help her." Not that I didn't trust Sam, but I didn't. Her family was from genuine aristocratic stock, and to her, putting anything other than an olive into a glass of champagne was an executable offence. Goodness knows what she'd put in it if left to her own devices.

She was standing by the kitchen cupboard with a packet of bicarbonate of soda in her hand.

"He'll notice that." I said.

"Bloody philistine wouldn't notice if I put chilli powder in it." She slammed the packet down onto the kitchen table and yanked open the fridge door so hard that everything inside it rattled. "He couldn't tell a Bollinger from a Bordeaux."

"Did you actually buy any champagne?" I asked.

"Yes, I found this in the supermarket." She pulled out a bottle of sparkling Italian wine that proudly proclaimed to be manufactured in the 'methode champagnois'. I took the bottle from her and surveyed it. The label was in a mixture of European languages and told of its 2009 vintage.

"Good year! I've got socks older than this."

"You've got socks older than me! Anyway, he won't care what year it is. As long as it goes pop when it opens."

I gingerly prized the wire cage from around the end of the bottle and started pushing the cork. If it was a pop he wanted, he'd certainly got his wish. The cork exploded from the end of the bottle like a Scud missile and embedded itself into the door of the cuckoo clock.

"Good show!" I heard Grahame call from the lounge.

"See! I told you that's all he wanted," Sam said.

"I thought we'd go Indian tonight," Grahame said as I returned with the drinks. I had a mental picture of us all dressed up in loincloths and feather head-dress, carrying bows and arrows. For some reason I was feeling very visual tonight. I struggled with the image for a while trying to understand what he meant. I was fairly sure he didn't really mean fancy dress. I realised that he was still talking.

"...the Taj Mahall, down on the quay..." he was saying. Of course, Indian food, that's what he meant. What's the matter with me? I recalled my earlier snack. Oh shit!

"Okay! Right! Good! I'm in the mood for a curry." In fact at this moment, I was in the mood for anything. I was starving.

"So, how's Ffiona?" Two F's Ffiona was Grahame's wife. His 'first wife', was the way he always introduced her. Keeps her on her toes you see, he would explain. I'm convinced Ffiona only had one F before she'd met Grahame. But then I don't think that Grahame was born with an E on the end of his name either. He's probably under the impression that the further up the social ladder you move, the more extraneous letters you can insert into your name.

Another badge.

"She's at home nursing Tricksie."

Tricksie was Grahame's near-tame Rottweiler. I couldn't ever remember coming across a dog with a more inappropriate name.

"Just had her spayed," he continued. "Dangerous Dogs Act and all that nonsense."

"You could say the judges are up to their old tricksies again then!" I said. I don't know what made me say that, but it immediately struck me as being outrageously funny. My insides began to vibrate as the laugh spread through the whole of my body. When it reached my lungs, it exploded out in a loud guffaw that disintegrated into paroxysms of giggles. I was well pleased with myself. It that was certainly one of the best jokes I had cracked in many years, although strangely enough, neither Grahame nor Sam seemed to find it funny.

They both looked at me with the kind of expression that was usually reserved for double glazing salesmen explaining they were in the last week of their special offer. They obviously hadn't got the joke, so I proceeded to explain it to them.

14

"Tricks, Tricksie, you see your dog's called Tricksie, up to their old tricks. Sort of a play on words you see..." No, they still weren't getting it. We all three stood in silence for what seemed like many minutes.

Grahame was the first snap out of it. A momentary closing of the eyes, a flick of the head and he seemed to shake himself free of his puzzlement.

"Right! We'll make a move then, shall we?" he said. "Where are the kids? Are they joining us?"

"They're upstairs, playing on the Playstation. I'll go get them." Sam ran upstairs calling out the children's names.

Grahame offered to drive, and we all clambered into his Porsche Cayenne. It was brand-new and still smelled of the plastic that had been used to cover the seats. Sam sat in the front and I sat in the back between the children. As we drove through the narrow St Ives streets, I could see Grahame was well pleased with himself. The extra height clearly made him feel superior. He kept complaining of 'Bloody tourists' as other cars wove in front of him. I found myself becoming increasingly annoyed with him. I tapped him on the shoulder.

"Hey, Grahame,"

"Yes," he answered.

"What's the difference between a Four-by-Four and a hedgehog?"

"Tony! Sam snapped.

"What?"

"Why don't you tell him the one about the fishermen instead?"

"No! Come-on Grahame, what's the difference between a Four-by-Four and a hedgehog?"

"I don't know," Grahame said.

"Well," I paused for dramatic effect, "with a hedgehog, the pricks are on the outside!"

I laughed until the tears started to run down my cheeks. In fact, I was laughing so much that it didn't dawn on me for a while that nobody else was laughing. Sam and Grahame stared fixedly at the road in front of them. Even the children were looking po-faced. Definitely a sense of humour shortage around here tonight. If this carried on, it promised to be a mind numbingly boring evening. So, I suppose it was going to be up to me to liven things up a bit.

The narrow streets twisted and turned in front of the Porsche. Pedestrians dived for cover into shop doorways, for there was little doubt that Grahame would have mowed them down had they remained in the road.

The Porsche was equipped with a set of menacing bull-bars on the front. They must have been an optional accessory as I couldn't believe that Porsche would willingly weld what appeared to be an iron gate to the front of their flagship model. I'd heard that bull bars were designed for pushing Kangaroos out of the way in the Australian outback. What they were doing on the front of this vehicle was beyond me. There were very few kangaroos in Knightsbridge, which is where Grahame spent most of his time

A Four-by-Four Porsche must be a marketing man's worst dream. I mean, who do you aim your advertising at? Farmers who want to get out to the cows really quickly? I suppose there may be some mountaineers who want to do nought to sixty up the side of Everest in under four point two seconds. My mind was wandering. I felt a tug on my sleeve.

"Are we there yet?" Natasha asked.

"What's up, Love?" I asked.

"I'm hungry, Daddy."

"So am I," I admitted.

"Won't be long," Sam said from the front.

"Tell you what," I said to Natasha conspiratorially, "I'll get us a snack."

"Oh yes please!" she said.

Simon gave me one of those disapproving looks that he'd learned from his mother. I held my forefinger to my lips, "Shush."

He frowned.

I tapped Grahame on the shoulder.

"Can you pull over at the Late Store? I need some bits and pieces."

"What bits and pieces?" Sam asked.

"Just things. Things. You know, just things."

Natasha sniggered.

"I could use some petrol anyway," Grahame said. "This thing's attempting to drink Saudi Arabia dry."

A few minutes later we pulled into a garage. While Grahame filled the tank, I went off into the shop to see what goodies I could find. When Grahame had paid for the petrol and returned to the vehicle, I was already in the back going through my purchases with Natasha.

By the time Grahame had the engine going I had opened the packet of Maryland chocolate chip cookies, and before he had left the forecourt of the garage, we had managed to spill the family size packet of M & Ms all over the back of the Porsche. Little chocolate beads crunched underfoot and rolled around with every corner. I gave up trying to retrieve them as it was making me feel sick, Grahame's swerving and my head between my knees in search of the brightly coloured chocolates. Tricksie could have them next time she took a ride in here. I felt another laugh welling up inside of me at the thought of the good joke I'd cracked earlier about Tricksie's name. I barely managed to suppress it.

I tapped Sam on the shoulder.

"Do you want some chocolate cake, love?"

"What!"

"Chocolate cake! I bought some chocolate cake at the garage. Do you want some?"

"Tony, what the hell are you thinking of? We're going out for a meal. Of course I don't want any bloody chocolate cake."

She twisted round in her seat and appeared to be less than impressed with the sight that greeted her. I had been as careful as I could while dividing the chocolate cake. But it's not easy without a plate or a knife. And obviously a few bits had come adrift. Natasha had a fairly large portion smeared into her dress. Simon had dropped his bit and had sat on it while looking for it.

I felt a crumb of chocolate on my bottom lip and hastily licked it off, hoping Sam wouldn't notice.

Her look pierced through me, and I felt all of my earlier good humour being drained like the blood from a vampire's victim. This was going to be real hard work trying to inject some fun into this evening. I wasn't sure if I was up to the task.

But I was willing to give it a go.

Chapter 3

We parked on a set of double yellow lines right outside
of the Indian restaurant. I tried pointing this out to Grahame.

"Oh! I shouldn't worry about that," he said and switched
on his hazard warning lights.

Grahame was one of these people who thinks he can
park wherever he likes as long as he leaves his hazard lights
going. He probably reasoned that the intermittent flashing
was designed to frighten away Traffic Wardens.

Sam, being the logical one, voiced her concern that this
might result in a flat battery.

"No! Don't worry your pretty little head on that one,
pet," Grahame said. "You could run a small African town
from the battery in this thing." He patted the steering wheel.

The look on Sam's face made me genuinely fear for
Grahame's safety. A sudden image of Grahame with a fork
stuck in his forehead flashed across my mind.

I gathered my possessions together into the brown paper
bag that I'd been given in the store and jumped down from
the back of the Porsche. Sam was on the ball tonight.

"What have you got there?"

"Just my things." I could see she wanted to take my
things away from me. Well, she wasn't going to have them.
They were my chocolates. But she was too quick for me.
Her hand snapped out like a lizard's tongue and snatched the
bag out of my hand. I hadn't seen that coming. She opened
the bag and peered inside. She was very still and didn't say
anything. I know that look. It's a look that says I need to be
three miles away at this moment. If Mount St Helens had
had an expression just before the eruption, this is what it
would've looked like.

"It's only a little snack," I said, trying to get my defence
in first.

"Tony, I don't know what's the matter with you tonight. There's more chocolate in here than I have ever seen together in one place before. And what do you want all of these cans of Coke for?"

"I was thirsty."

"Put it back in the car, Tony"

Grahame looked at the offending bag, and then he looked at me. "Are you mad? You can't take a fucking picnic into an Indian restaurant!"

"Grahame!" Sam scolded. "Please, not in front of the children."

"Uncle Grahame said, 'fucking', mummy," said Natasha.

"Yes, I know he did, dear. But I don't think..."

"Why did uncle Grahame say, 'fucking', mum?" Simon asked. "You always say we shouldn't say 'fucking'. Why can Uncle Grahame say 'fucking' and I can't say 'fucking'?"

"Simon!" Sam shouted. "Now look what you've started, Grahame."

I used this distraction to surreptitiously sneak one of the bars of chocolate into my pocket before returning the bag to the back seat of the vehicle.

Once inside, we were shown to a table by a very helpful Indian waiter that Grahame insisted on calling Ramesh. We had been reserved a large circular table by the window.

I had come over slightly chilly and with relief, I noticed that one of the seats was next to a radiator. I sat down at it before anyone else could. Grahame looked annoyed. Well, all the wheeler dealing in the world doesn't guarantee a radiator seat.

A different waiter brought the menus; huge plastic covered beasts in the shape of the Taj Mahal. Grahame ordered a bottle of champagne and called this waiter Ramesh as well. So I guess that wasn't their names and that Ramesh was just a term of affection he uses.

I heard a loud pop come from the kitchen and briefly wondered if they had a cuckoo clock. It certainly didn't bode well that they had opened the champagne in the kitchen and not at the table. But Grahame didn't seem to notice.

The sound of laughter erupted from one of the other the tables and I looked over. I felt a little electric shock jolt through me when I noticed that it was Astrid and the hippies that I'd met earlier in the coffee bar. For some reason, she chose that very moment to look up.

Our eyes locked.

She gave a huge smile.

I gave my impersonation of a goldfish. Mouth opening and closing slightly in a little 'O' shape. She tipped her head to one side in a gesture of curiosity. I wanted to smile, to give a devil-may-care toss of the head. But all that happened was that I felt my cheeks start to flush and turn red. I was blushing. Of all the idiotic things to do, I was blushing like some pre-pubescent school kid. Astrid nudged the hippy sitting next to her and then pointed in my direction. They both looked at me, huge grins smeared across their faces.

I tried a smile and at that moment I felt a sharp pain in my left ankle.

"Ow!" I looked round to see what had happened. Sam's eyes were like a pair of bayonets that skewered me to the wall.

"What are you staring at that girl for?" she hissed.

"I wasn't! I was... I was just looking for the waiter. I wanted to order some poppadoms."

"We'll discuss this later." Her tone of voice made it quite clear that this wasn't going to be a discussion at all.

The waiter came to collect the order. I tried very hard to look at him as he was speaking. But for some reason, my eyes kept wandering back to the far corner table where Astrid sat. I felt like one of those ventriloquist dummies where just the eyes move and the head stays motionless. I tried to stare at the waiter, to give my eyes something to do. Grahame was discussing with him the relative strengths of the various curry dishes and settled on a prawn Madras. The waiter looked at me.

I was feeling competitive

"What have you got with a bit more punch than a Madras? I asked. Grahame's head jerked upwards.

"We have Vindaloo, sir." The waiter suggested.

"No! Something with a real kick, a man's curry!" I smiled at Grahame; he was looking slightly perturbed.

"Well, we can do you a Phall, sir. But it is extremely hot." the waiter looked worried.

"That will do," I announced. "I'll have a chicken Phall" I looked at Grahame. I knew what was coming.

"On second thoughts," he said, "make mine a prawn Phall."

The waiter raised one eyebrow; he was obviously used to this kind of bravado. Sam ordered a Shish Kebab for herself and Chicken Tandoori for the children. The waiter disappeared back into the kitchen.

A young waitress appeared carrying a tray with five glasses and the already open bottle of champagne. She held the label towards Grahame. He smiled at her.

"That will do, poppet," he said.

From where I sat, the bottle looked suitably aged and expensive. But I was willing to take on any bet that it wasn't the bottle in which this particular blend had started its days.

My dry throat received the champagne gratefully and I downed it in one. Grahame promptly refilled my glass. The waitress returned a few minutes later and deposited a pile of popadoms on the table. This time Grahame called her 'His love'. It's amazing how expressive the human face can be. The waitress's eyes smiled, as did her mouth. She even nodded politely, but somehow, the adding together of all these elements, produced an expression which said 'I hope you choke on it'. I had never socialised with Grahame before, and I hadn't realised quite how obnoxious he could be.

I had an idea, but I needed to extricate myself from the table to carry it out.

"Grahame," I started, "Sam was interested to know how the introduction of the Euro impacted on the world exchange rate mechanisms."

"What?" Sam queried.

"Ah, yes! Very interesting that. We saw the effect first on the Yen... " He was off.

Sam glared at me, but she was trapped, Grahame was in full flow. I excused myself saying I needed to go to the toilet. I headed in that general direction and when I was sure that neither Sam nor Grahame was watching, I slipped into the kitchen.

The kitchen was a cacophony of clattering pans and chattering voices. I stood just inside the door for a moment while I located our waiter. As he came over to me, he appeared to be staring at my groin. I wondered if I'd left my flies open, but I wasn't going to check while he watched. I braved it out. A quick bit of negotiation and I was ten pounds the poorer but Grahame's curry was going to be significantly hotter.

I slid back to the table, hoping they hadn't noticed my absence. Sam gave me a despairing look as I sat down. Grahame was still waxing lyrical about the follies of the single market economy.

The food arrived. I tentatively dipped my spoon into the curry sauce and risked a taste. It was hot. I like my curries hot, but this was close to the limits of endurance of even my taste buds. I dreaded to think what Grahame's was like. He raised a spoonful to his mouth, oblivious as to what was about to happen. Almost before he had closed his lips around the spoon his eyes started to water. By the time he'd returned the spoon to the plate, there were droplets of sweat forming across his brow. It looked like I'd got my ten quid's worth. He had a funny smile on his face as he reached for a glass of water. Oh dear! Big mistake! Worse thing you can do, drink water. It has a similar effect as throwing water onto a petrol fire. As Grahame was about to find out. His watering eyes turned into a downpour and he started coughing. He drank the best part of two glasses of water straight down.

"Quite nice isn't it, Grahame?"

"Yes," he said. "They certainly do a hot one here, don't they?"

I almost felt sorry for him as I saw him trying to smother the taste of the curry sauce with rice. Almost, but not quite. My enjoyment of his suffering was further heightened by the thought that this was going to be hotter coming out than it was going in. As I was rejoicing in the cleverness of my plan, I remembered the waiter who had been staring at my groin. I put my hand down to check if my flies were open. Instead of finding an open zipper, I found a sticky mess. I retrieved my hand to examine it. It was covered in chocolate. It took a moment to sink in as to how this had happened. I remembered now putting the bar of chocolate in my pocket. Being seated next to the radiator had done the rest.

I glanced at Sam. She was engaged in a joint project with Natasha to try and remove the chicken from the bone on Natasha's plate. Good, she wouldn't notice me. I risked a look down. The devastation was total. I didn't know one bar of chocolate could go so far. It was all over my groin and half way down the inside of my right leg. No wonder the waiter had been fascinated. What must he have thought? Oh, no! I know what he must have thought! I looked across the table to see if anybody had noticed my frantic fumbling. Sam and Natasha were still pushing pieces of chicken around the plate. Simon was busy crumbling up several large popadoms over his plate of rice, and I don't think Grahame could see anything anyway. His face was the colour of a London bus and there was a waterfall running down from his forehead.

Time to do something before anybody noticed. I stood, with the serviette held against my front.

"I'm just off to the… err..." I whispered to Sam.

"What, again?"

I darted off in a peculiar sideways fashion, trying to keep my front towards the wall.

There was only one cloakroom, which served both male and female customers. There was no lock on the door and I had to jam my foot against it while I set to work. I soaked the serviette and kept sponging. To start with, I just seemed to make things worse. I was spreading the chocolate over an even wider area. But gradually, I managed to remove the worst of it.

I was also starting to feel like shit. The effects of the grass were wearing off and the alcohol was aggravating the let down. My head was hurting and felt like it was full of water. That champagne must be stronger than I thought.

There was a knock on the door

"I won't be a minute," I called.

I scrubbed harder. The knock came again. Damnit! At least I had got rid of most of the chocolate, but my trousers were soaking.

Another knock, more insistent. That would have to do for the moment. I opened the door and slid past an annoyed looking middle-aged woman.

I managed to resume my seat without anybody noticing the state of my trousers. I continued my meal. Grahame had carefully eaten most of the rice and left the curry sauce in the centre of his plate. He pushed the plate to one side.

"Oomph! I'm full now!" he said.

Full of bullshit more like. He was starting to annoy me. He had taken to calling the waiter Abdul. A move guaranteed to secure the worst possible service from the staff. My stomach felt slightly queasy, but I still managed to finish the curry. I had to; it was a matter of honour.

My trousers were a sodden mess around my groin. I realised that I would have to do something about this before we left the restaurant, or I was going to be even more unpopular with Sam. I remembered that there was an electric hand dryer in the cloakroom. It might just be powerful enough to do the job. I pushed my plate to one side.

"I'm just going for a... to the... You know…"

"Again?"

I repeated my earlier sideways manoeuvre, and darted into the cloakroom jamming the door shut behind me. I tried to get the hand dryer to work. But it was one of these that only work when your hands are directly underneath it. The trouble was, the very act of putting my hands underneath, prevented the airflow reaching my trousers. There was only one thing for it. I was going to have to remove my trousers and hold them up to the drier.

It was a complicated manoeuvre, keeping my foot jammed against the door while divesting myself of my trousers. But I managed it. The hand dryer was highly effective. I moved the cloth around underneath the airflow, drying each area a piece at a time. That was how I came to get the belt loop caught up on a piece of protruding bracket. I pulled and twisted. There was a rattle, and change fell from my pocket and clattered across the floor. Every muscle in my body tensed in frustration. The situation was deteriorating. My whole mind was focused on the stupid belt clip, and I was consumed with anger towards the person who'd left that bracket protruding. I braced myself to give a good hard tug, and at that moment, the door swung open. In my confusion and temper, I'd forgotten to push my foot against it.

Astrid stepped in just at the moment the trousers tore their way free from the clip. The sudden jolt scattered the last of my small change across the floor at her feet. She didn't look at all fazed by the scene in front of her.

"You seem to be having some difficulties," she said.

"Umm," was all I could think of to say.

"Did you find the grass to your liking?" Her eyes sparkled with mischief and warmth.

"Oh! Yes! I think I ate it."

"That would do it!" Her gaze wandered downwards, past my naked legs and to the floor.

"Here, let me help you." She knelt down on the floor to start collecting the change.

That was when the door swung open for the second time.

In retrospect, I could quite see how Sam could take this the wrong way. My frequent disappearances from the table, and now finding me here without any trousers, and the pretty girl that I had been eyeing up all evening kneeling in front of me.

But even then, I think her reaction was a little bit over the top. That lightning-fast hand that I had witnessed earlier connected with the side of Astrid's face sending her sprawling into the puddle of water that I had created earlier.

Sam turned her laser eyes towards me. I felt myself cowering. I held the trousers up in front of me as some sort of protection.

"No! Sam, you've got this all wrong. You're making a dreadful mistake." Clichés! I was talking in clichés. But she had me flustered. I had never seen her looking so pissed-off before. I usually rely on her to be the calm one in situations like this. For a moment, she seemed to have lost the power of speech.

But that moment wasn't long enough.

"Get your fucking trousers onto your fucking backside and get you're fucking self over to the fucking table and sit fucking down. And I don't want to hear another fucking peep out of you all fucking night."

The last time I'd heard Sam use the F word was when Natasha was being born. So this outburst told me that I was probably in a little bit of trouble here.

Astrid slid out through the door, rubbing her cheek. I followed Sam's directions precisely and resumed my seat at the table. Sam followed me and as she sat down, I'm sure I heard a little growl.

Grahame looked up, cheerful as ever. "Everything all right, old girl?"

Sam didn't answer. She just continued to stare at the tablecloth. Her whole body seemed alive and vibrating. It was almost as if every cell in her body was giving off sparks. The electrical field surrounding her was tangible.

Grahame returned his attention to the big ice-cream sundae in front of him. I appear to have missed out on dessert. Not that I fancied it. My stomach was going through a series of knots that would have challenged a Boy Scout's ingenuity. If this carried on, the reappearance of my Chicken Phall was a distinct possibility. My head thrummed, and I realised with horror that my bladder was full to bursting point. I tried to visualise how Sam would react if I suggested a return visit to the bathroom. I followed the image through to the point where she was holding my genitals in one hand and a kebab skewer in the other and decided another accident with my trousers was probably preferable.

The waitress came over and brushed down our table with a serviette. As she leaned forward, Grahame patted her buttocks. "You can brush my bits off any day, love!"

He was really starting to hack me off. I reached across the table, grabbed hold of his stupid tie, and pulled his stupid face towards me. His eyes bulged as his head jerked forwards. My fist connected with his nose with a reassuring squelching noise. I had never hit anybody before, and I didn't realise how much it hurts. But the feel of nose cartilage compressing against skull-bone more than compensated for the pain.

I stood up and walked out of the restaurant. The cold air hit me and my head started spinning. I was losing the battle to stay friends with my dinner. Sam bustled out of the door, children in tow. She stopped square on in front of me. For a moment she didn't speak, and then all she said was, "You disgust me!" She spun on her heels and a marched off, presumably in search of a taxi.

My mouth felt very dry, A sure-fire precursor to a Technicolor yawn. My vision came over blurred for a moment, and when it cleared, Grahame was standing in front of me. He held a bloodstained handkerchief to his nose.

"Tony, I always rated you as one of the best money men in the City. But lately, you've become a liability. I want your resignation on my desk by Monday morning and I want you out of the cottage by the weekend."

I suppose it could have looked like I'd done it on purpose. But I didn't. It was just timing. With one huge contraction of my stomach muscles, my half-digested curry deposited itself onto Grahame's patent leather shoes.

I staggered back into the restaurant and made for the bathroom to clean myself up. And to relieve my aching bladder. By the time I emerged from the restaurant for the second time, I saw that Grahame was engaged in a heated argument with a Wheel Clamper. The source of the disagreement appeared to be a big yellow clamp on the nearside front wheel of the Porsche.

I eventually found a taxi and made my way back to the cottage. It was in darkness. I let myself in and settled down on the couch. I figured I was probably Persona non-Gratis in the bedroom. For tonight at least.

Chapter 4

I awoke the following morning with a head full of broken china and a mouthful of sawdust. My spine felt frozen into the shape demanded by the couch.

Sam made a great point of not talking to me. I realised how much dedication that took as she probably had an awful lot to say.

I sat down expectantly at the breakfast table. Maybe if I just behaved normally, this would all blow over in a few minutes. She passed me my breakfast. It was a loaf of bread and a tin of baked beans. No… maybe this was going to take a bit longer after all. My stomach was still feeling rebellious after last night's onslaught so I decided to pass on her kind offer and made my way to the bathroom to freshen up.

I splashed water across my face then stared at my reflection. Not too bad, little bits of grey around the edges I hadn't noticed before. It made me look distinguished though.

I ran my hands across the morning stubble then reached for my electric razor. I stopped. No, I'll grow a beard. I've always wanted to grow a beard. Now that I don't have to look like a clone of Michael Douglas in 'Wall Street' I can grow a beard if I want! I slipped the razor back in its case just as I heard the door swing open behind me.

"So!" Sam started, "What have you got to say for yourself then?"

I recognised this gambit. This was dangerous. Whatever I said at this point was going to be used against me.

"Sorry," I suggested.

"Sorry is it? You think you can assault Grahame, cavort with half-naked women—"

"Err, actually it was me that was half-naked, and there was only one woman." I'm not too sure that helped.

"Even worse! And then you have the gall just to say 'Sorry' as if somehow that magically makes everything better." She sat down on the edge of the bath.

"It's not—"

"I should have listened to mother. She told me I should never have married you. Did you know that?"

"Yes. I did, you—"

"She wanted me to marry Martin Braithwaite, you know. He's doing very well for himself now."

"Yes. You mentioned it once—"

"He's got his own clinic in Harley Street. He's..."

This was likely to be a long one. I was well and truly trapped here. She sat with her feet spread out across the doorway. My ears shut themselves down, and my conscious went into standby mode, just selecting the odd word in order to keep track. Martin Braithwaite featured heavily.

A beard, yes, definitely, I'll grow a beard. And a pony tail! Grahame hated ponytails. 'Didn't matter where the ponytail was,' he always used to say, 'it's still attached to a horse's arse.'

"...gave up my career to look after your children..."

And jeans! When had I stopped wearing jeans? Isn't it funny how you don't notice these things? Changes slide up on you. At one time, all I'd ever worn was jeans. Now I didn't think I even owned a pair.

"...if you hadn't dropped out of university, you would..."

That was it! Beard, ponytail and jeans, and screw the world.

"... I said, are you listening to me?"

Whoops! To answer that question with any sort of honesty would be like asking Dracula to give you a neck rub. Quick calculation. Where was she? About five or six minutes in, that must put it approximately at her brother, 'Something-in-the-City-Selwyn'.

"Of course!" I said. "You know I'll always be grateful to Selwyn for getting me the job with Grahame." I paused. My insides tensed as I waited to find out if I'd got my timing right.

"And so you should. He pulled a lot of strings to get you there. What do you do? You throw it back in his face. He always…"

That was a close one. How had I ever got myself into this? I probably just happened to be in the wrong place at the wrong time. I think it was at a point in Sam's life when she wanted to stick two fingers up at her parents. I just happened to be there.

I returned my attention to Sam. She was winding down now, her spleen well and truly vented. I held both of her hands and looked into her eyes, putting on my best puppy-dog expression that I kept for extreme emergencies.

"All I can say, Sam, is that I am very, very sorry. You see… I think…"

She was giving me that look that says 'You've got one chance only, pal. Or there's going to be blood'

My mind froze.

I had never been what you might call a quick thinker. My thread was lost. I groped for some profound words.

"You see, I was feeling insecure. I thought you might not love me any more." That was good! Where'd I got that from? Oh shit! I remember! But maybe she wouldn't.

The look on her face told me, no. No such luck.

She jumped to her feet. "Are you taking the piss? Here I am pouring my heart out, and you're reciting John Lennon at me!"

She spun round and marched out of the room with such violence that it left a little tornado in her wake. The toilet roll fluttered in the breeze.

I was definitely losing my touch. I'd handled these situations much better before.

I waited about five minutes before venturing downstairs. I dipped my toe on each step in turn as if testing the temperature. Way below zero. In fact, if absolute zero is the simple absence of all heat then this was the other side. The actual presence of cold.

I slid out of the front door without a word and caught a bus into town. I wandered aimlessly for a while, pausing at the occasional shop window. I wasn't really seeing. I was still carrying in my mind the image of my reflection this morning in the mirror. The grey around the temples and the fine lines gathering around the eyes and across the forehead.

Sometimes I think there's a force at work, where if you just give way and let it take you then things have a way of working out.

The force took control and deposited me in front of a chemist's shop. A loud and prominent window display proclaimed the virtues of a very discreet hair colorant. My feet took me inside. It was an Aladdin's Cave for the insecure forty-something. That's not what I counted myself as of course. I just thought the products looked rather fun and amusing to try out. Only curious really, wondering if they'd work.

So, in the interests of research, I purchased the subtle hair colorant, some Retinal 'A' – just to test their outrageous claims at fine line eradication – some Royal Jelly, Ginseng and a tub of 'Instant Weight Loss Mega-Slim'.

I wasn't happy about the prospect of returning to the cottage just yet, so I continued to wander the streets. A remarkable coincidence took me to the Cafe Oceanic. I might as well have a coffee while I'm here, I thought. I noticed that somebody else was sitting at my table and felt vaguely irritated. I sat down at a corner table. It wobbled as I dumped my bag on it. I looked around for a waitress, any waitress, it didn't matter which one. There was not one in sight, only a blonde-haired youth. He wore a white apron the size of a handkerchief. I've never understood why they do that. I thought aprons were supposed to be for protection, the only conceivable purpose for this piece of cloth would be to highlight the area of his anatomy that it covered. I ordered a Mocha, whatever that was.

I dipped my hand into the plastic bag, feeling like a child at a lucky dip and pulled out the first of my prizes. It was the tub of Retinal 'A'. I squinted at the label. I'm sure there's a conspiracy going on between label printers and the manufacturers of spectacles. In fact I think the whole spectacle manufacturing industry is a conspiracy. How did we ever get to the situation where being short sighted is a fashion statement? And why doesn't Gucci manufacture gold rimmed hearing aids? Now there's a market!

I turned the package around in my hand, trying to find something legible. "Guaranteed to reduce the signs of ageing..."

"Hello! Planning on zapping your wrinkles then?"

I looked up to see Astrid standing above me, a cup of Mocha in her hand. I don't know which was more embarrassing, being caught without my trousers, or in possession of my anti-ageing kit.

"Oh! Hi! No, I haven't got any wrinkles. Just a few laughter lines."

"It must have been one hell of a joke, " Astrid replied. There was that smile again. "You'll have to tell it to me some time."

I felt like a clumsy child under her gaze as I hurriedly stuffed my chemistry-set back in the bag.

"It's not for me anyway. It's… err... For my wife."

"Oh," she said. Her raised eyebrows and a slight tip of her head indicating she didn't believe a word of it

For the first time, I noticed a slight sign of bruising on her left cheek. A dreadful feeling of guilt crept over me. "Look, I'm really sorry about last night."

"Don't be. It was probably as much my fault anyway. We set you up."

"What?"

"The grass, it was skunk weed. Home-grown, very strong. " She rubbed her cheek. "I probably got what I deserved."

No, she didn't deserve that.

I nodded at the coffee. "Is that for me? "

She smiled and placed the cup on the table. "I see you're being a little bit more adventurous today"

"I felt it was about time I broke free of the shackles of establishment."

"Quite the rebel!"

She had this familiar way of talking to me as if she had known me for years, which I found at once disconcerting and alluring.

A family of five at a nearby table clicked fingers and waved hands to attract her attention

"I've got to go," she said. "We're getting busy."

I finished my coffee and left. I felt it was about time I ventured back to the cottage. I would have to one day, so I may as well get it over with now.

An empty cottage granted me a reprieve. I found a note on the kitchen table it read, "Taken the kids to the beach for the day. Your lunch is in the supermarket."

I took my bag of chemicals upstairs to the bathroom to begin my experiments. I started with the easy projects first. I swallowed twice the recommended dose of both the ginseng and the royal jelly. The Mega-Slim recommended drinking three large glasses of water and swallowing five of the tablets. I took eight. The tablets were huge. I had to break them into quarters before I could swallow them. They looked like little bales of hay. Within a few minutes, a satisfying fullness had settled on my stomach.

I now felt brave enough to tackle the more complex of the projects. The instructions on the hair colorant suggested mixing the two enclosed bottles together in a small bowl. A search of the kitchen cupboards turned up negative. I settled on a large mug instead. There was only just enough room in the mug to take the mixture, with a little bit slopping over the side. I mixed thoroughly as suggested and then read on in the instructions. The recommendation was to wear gloves. Another search of the kitchen cupboards, another fruitless task. The best alternative I could find was two plastic bags secured with rubber bands around my wrists. I congratulated myself on my inventiveness.

With the products thoroughly mixed, I smeared the resulting goo over my hair. This was not an easy task and made all the more difficult by the plastic bags. A big dollop landed on my right eyebrow, and an attempt to wipe it off simply smeared it across my forehead. I decided to forgo the plastic bags. As long as I washed the stuff off my hands, it shouldn't have any effect. This was much easier. I left the mixture on for twice the required amount of time and then rinsed it thoroughly. By this time my stomach had started to feel uncomfortably bloated. If the idea of this stuff had been to curb my appetite, then it was certainly working. The thought of eating anything made me feel positively nauseous.

I dried my hair with Sam's hair dryer and then examined the result in the mirror. The grey was gone. The effect was startling. I looked a good ten years younger, albeit slightly less distinguished. I tipped my head to all angles, admiring my handiwork. This was wonderful! And then I noticed my eyebrow. My left eyebrow was its normal soft brown, but my right, this was jet-black. It took me a moment to realise what had happened. I remembered the dollop of mixture falling on my right eyebrow. Well, I couldn't go around like this, only one thing for it, I would have to dye the other one. Damnit! I'd rinsed the rest away and washed up the mug. I couldn't go out like this, I looked ridiculous.

The distended feeling I was experiencing in my stomach was now moving down to my bowels. This was decidedly uncomfortable.

I had an idea. A quick rummage through Sam's make-up bag produced a black mascara. With great care, I applied this to the brown eyebrow. I paused to examine the result. Not a perfect match, but it would have to do. The colouring made my eyebrows look unnaturally heavy. I thought I resembled a Russian Prime Minister.

I would have to go back to the shop and buy some more of the colorant in order to finish the job properly on this eyebrow. A spasm in my lower bowel alerted me to the need to release little bit of pressure. I broke wind, and the room at once filled with the most noxious fumes I had ever experienced. This Super Mega-Slim may well curb the appetite, but I was certainly not going to be socially acceptable while using it.

A light rain began falling outside, and I reached for my coat. That was when I noticed my fingernails. They were black. Perfectly black. Just as if I had carefully painted them. What sort of dye is it that can leave your hands natural and turn your fingernails black?

I hung my coat back on the hook and headed for the kitchen sink once more. The dye resisted all attempts to remove it. I felt the need to release a little more gas, and then had to evacuate the kitchen.

The gods were certainly not on my side today. I had one black eyebrow, ten black fingernails, the worst case of gas since Chernobyl, and I wasn't happy about having to venture out again in order to purchase some more chemicals with which to repair the damage.

I checked myself in the mirror. The mascara was doing a fair job, and I would just have to make sure I kept my hands out of view.

The rain seemed to intensify at the very moment I stepped out of the door. By the time I had got to the bus stop, it was driving through my light, summer mac as if it wasn't there.

I had to wait twenty minutes for the next bus/ When it finally arrived I was drenched. It was a small, shuttle type bus; only enough room for around ten or so passengers. I had the bus to myself. This was just as well, as the Mega-Slim was continuing to make its presence known in a most unfriendly manner.

After about half a mile, the bus pulled over to allow an elderly couple on board. The woman's husband helped her up the steps. She stood by the driver and searched through her purse for the correct change. She was just counting out the money onto the small counter when she turned to look in my direction. She screwed up her face in an exaggerated manner and shook her head slightly. She swept the change back into her purse and turned to walk back down the steps again. I saw the driver glaring at me in the mirror. We drove on leaving the old couple standing in the rain. I felt guilty.

We reached my stop, and I left the bus. The driver seemed glad to see me go. As I walked away, I turned to look back. The bus was still there and the driver was inside opening all of the windows.

I set off back for the chemist's shop. I picked up another packet of hair colour and took it to the counter. The young girl behind the counter was very understanding when I explained what had happened to my fingernails. She suggested I try surgical spirit.

Clutching my white paper bag containing my latest acquisitions I headed back towards the bus stop. I was just passing a newsagent when I spotted Astrid coming the other way. This was a meeting I hadn't intended. I pulled my coat collar up and turned to face the newsagent's window pretending to stare into it. I felt like a spy in a bad 'B' movie.

"Oh hi!" I heard Astrid's voice.

Chapter 5

"Oh, hi, Astrid" I said, turning to face her.

"What are you doing? "

My eyes returned to the newsagent's window, desperately searching for something I could possibly find there of interest

"I was just... looking at this... It caught my attention as I was passing. "

I scanned every inch of the window, eventually settling on a poster that advertised this week's local paper. "That!"

Astrid came closer to peer in. She seemed to be unnecessarily close; I could feel her warmth. She looked at the poster. It read, "Flower show rained off."

She looked up at me. "Fascinating, isn't it?"

I could see she didn't find it fascinating at all. Was she being sarcastic, or just kind? I turned to look at her, trying to read her face. The Mega-slim was still working as efficiently as ever. I fought hard to retain the purity of the air around us. But I feared I was losing the battle.

A look of concern pinched her face. "What have you done to your eye?"

"What?" I raised my hand to my face instinctively

"Still kicking at the establishment I see."

"What?"

"The black fingernails. Is this your Goth phase now?"

"No... No! It's..."

She pulled a tissue from her pocket. "Here, let me." She reached forward and held my head steady with her left hand while her right dabbed the tissue around my eye. Her fingers connected with my soul and her breath smelled sweet. She tipped her head back to have another look at my face, and then at the tissue paper. It was black. I could think of lots of places I would rather be right now. She examined the tissue more closely. "Looks like mascara!"

Of course! The rain must have made the mascara run. Just when things seem to be going downhill nicely, along comes fate to knee you in the groin.

"I'm tempted to ask", she said." But then, what the hell! We're all here to find our own way, aren't we?"

"No! It's not like that..." I gave up. Sometimes I wish life had an 'Undo' button. Let's just try that bit again.

At that moment, the latest offering of the fermenting Mega-Slim escaped without my consent.

I froze.

How bad was this going to be? I didn't have to wait long for the answer. I looked around for something to blame.

"Damned Council really should do something about these drains!"

"Hmm!"

She pursed her lips together into a straight-line smile. "I think you need help."

Did I ever.

"What gave you that idea?"

"Come with me."

Just like that. No please. No idea what she had in mind. Just, "Come with me. "

Without a word, she led me a few doors up the road. Astrid went into a health food shop, where, after a brief chat with the assistant, she emerged carrying a brown paper bag.

As we continued walking, Astrid said, "You'd better come back to my place. I'll sort you out there."

That could be taken the wrong way.

I hoped.

She led me on a tortuous route through some of the narrowest streets that St Ives had to offer. For some reason, I felt quite safe. If I'd accepted this offer on the streets of London, I'd probably be minus my wallet by now and maybe even my clothes.

Astrid lived in a flat above a carpet shop. It was accessed via an iron staircase behind the shop. She let herself in, I followed.

"Mind the rabbit."

"Rabbit?"

"Yeah, don't leave the door open too long, or he'll escape."

"You've got a pet rabbit then?" I could enter for Mastermind. My specialist subject, re-stating the bloody obvious.

I pulled the door shut behind me.

"Yes! His name's Harvey," she said.

"Like Harvey Goldsmith?"

"Who?"

"The millionaire entrepreneur."

"No! Like Harvey the rabbit! The Jimmy Stewart film. With the six foot rabbit? Whimsy. Remember whimsy?"

"Oh, yes. Of course. I see." I didn't.

I ran my eyes across the carpet in search of any small furry objects. The carpet was a patchwork of different colours and styles. Obviously one of the advantages of living above a carpet shop. There appeared to be no furniture in the room apart from heaps of cushions and what appeared to be a slice of tree balanced on four house-bricks. Drapes hung across walls and windows alike, making it difficult to see where one ended and the other began.

Astrid slid through some bead curtains, hardly disturbing them, and into an adjoining room.

"Take a seat," she called.

The only thing that in any way resembled a seat was the lump of timber. I perched uncomfortably on the edge of it.

"I'll just mix this stuff up," I heard her call from what I assumed was the kitchen. "Be with you in a minute."

She came back through the curtains, holding a mug in each hand. Her eyes widened slightly when she saw me.

"Why are you sitting on my table?

"I thought... "

"I'm sure you'd be much more comfortable on a cushion."

I transferred my rear end as suggested. She was right. It was more comfortable.

She deposited the mugs on the dead tree. "There you go."

"Which one's mine?"

"They both are. One's for your bowels, the other's for your fingers. I'll leave you to work out which is which." She smiled.

I leaned forward to examine the offerings. One of them was murky brown in colour and smelled sweet and sickly. The other was a clear liquid, and the vapours it was giving off left me in no doubt that it was alcohol based. It brought tears to my eyes.

There was still room for error here. If I got this one wrong there was likely to be a repeat of last night's performance. I pointed to the sweet smelling brew.

"This is the one I drink, right?"

"Your choice. Live dangerously."

I took the cowards way out and dipped my fingers into the clear liquid. I left them there for a moment then withdrew them. The dye was already running from my fingernails. It was a good job I hadn't drunk that one. I dried them on a pink tissue she had provided.

Time to venture deeper into the unknown with the second offering.

As I lifted the cup to my lips Astrid picked up a box of matches from the window ledge and slipped behind one of the curtains. I assumed there was a door there somewhere. I sipped cautiously. I knew now how the old food-tasters must have felt while testing their master's dishes. After the battering my system had taken over the last twenty-four hours, I decided things must improve some time and I drank it down.

The taste was quite pleasant, a sort of nutty taste. Astrid appeared from behind the curtains again, like a magician's assistant. She sat cross-legged on one of the larger cushions. "Well?" she asked.

"Not bad."

"Essence of acorn."

The drink was having a warming effect on my stomach. It felt comforting, and I relaxed.

"I like the hair, "she said.

"What?"

"Looks good! Pity about the eyebrows."

So she had noticed then. I had never known anybody this forthright before. My life with Sam had been a continuous dance of etiquette and half-truths.

"I think I splashed some." I wanted the cushion to suck me in and hide me.

"We'll sort that out for you in a minute."

She exuded an air of confidence. I felt like a child being picked up by its mother after a fall.

"Oh, right. Thank you, that would be a help."

Astrid appeared to be watching me, a look of anticipation on her face. Was she expecting me to perform again? Perhaps she had decided I was a good source of entertainment. Maybe she had put something in the drink after all. Maybe there was some really powerful hallucinogen in there, and she was waiting for me to give an impersonation of a chicken. Perhaps I was going to have delusions of being able to fly! Was she waiting for me to jump out of the window shouting, "Look at me, I'm an albatross!"?

"Do you know, I don't even know your name?" she said.

"Tony. Tony Ryan." I looked around the room waiting for the wallpaper to start melting. The curtains looked brighter than when I had arrived.

My fingers were feeling strange.

Yes, definitely. They were feeling... sort of... fluffy! Fluffy fingers! What sort of drug causes fluffy fingers? I felt my heart racing. That must be another sign. Why had I trusted her a second time?

I ran my fingers across my cheek. No, that felt normal.

"What are you doing, Tony?"

Oh, no! I must look like an idiot playing with my hands like this.

"My fingers are sort of..." I couldn't admit to 'fluffy', "Tingly." I said.

"That'll be the wood-alcohol."

"Huh?"

"The stuff you've just cleaned your hands with. It has that effect."

"Oh." A sense of relief settled over me.

"That's not what I meant, anyway. I was referring to life."

"I'm a stockbroker. Or I was, until yesterday. I don't know what I am today." There was a thought. What am I? I had always been measured by what I did, where I worked or with whom I socialised. But those things seemed to have changed now.

She leaned her elbows against her knees and rocked forward slightly. She had a slight elfish look about her.

"No! I mean life! Not the stuff you're forced to do. What do you choose to do? You know, this thing that happens between when you're born and when you die. That's life. I am not interested in what society makes you do. Who is Tony?"

"I am a... a... I'm... I am a stockbroker." No. That was what I was and I couldn't see what else she meant, I had been a stockbroker for too long. I continued to think about her question for a while. Maybe she was being esoteric? Yes that must be it. Well I could do esoteric. "As well as being a stockbroker, I am also a father. And a member of the golf club." I was sure that would impress her.

Astrid rocked forward again. The top three buttons on her white cotton shirt were undone.

It gaped open inviting me to peep. I didn't, of course. I didn't see the gentle curves that nestled within, the lacy—

"So that makes me a waitress then, does it?"

That sounded like a challenge, but I couldn't for the life of me think why. I felt the question was some sort of trap, but I couldn't see it.

"Err, yes. But I'm sure you're a very good waitress." When in doubt, compliment.

"When was the last time you climbed a tree, Tony?" That was a sideways question if ever there was one.

I tried to rearrange myself on the cushion. It was difficult to sit on this infernal thing without looking like a complete slob.

"About six months ago, I think. Yes, I had to get Simon's kite down out of a tree."

I noticed a trace of incense in the air. I glanced around, but I couldn't see where it was coming from. It was a heavy, musky smell. The aroma somehow made the room feel more welcoming. The warming glow the drink had left in my stomach had turned to a slightly heavy, bloated sensation. She was still studying me with that anticipatory look.

I tried once more to rearrange myself on the cushion. I found that by stretching out and lying back it was actually quite comfortable.

"So, what do you do in your spare time?" I asked. This was a strange conversation, and I wanted to gain control of it again.

"I waitress."

"No, I meant in your spare time."

"Yes, that's what I meant as well. I wait tables in my spare time. "

"Well, what do you do with the rest of your time, then?" This conversation was still getting away from me.

"Whatever I please." She tipped her head to one side as if she couldn't understand why I was asking such stupid questions.

The warming, bloated feeling was making its presence felt further down. I was going to have to excuse myself sometime soon. Correction. Now! I was going to have to excuse myself now.

"I need... I have to... Where is there…?"

"I know. I thought you might. It's waiting through there for you." She indicated the curtains through which she had done her earlier disappearing tricks.

I regained control of my untidy legs and groped my way through the curtains. There was a small hallway with a door on each side and another straight ahead. The one in front of me was open and showed the soft glow of candlelight. A strong smell of incense drifted out. I stepped inside. It was the room that I was looking for. I shut the door behind me. The smell of the incense was almost overpowering, even with the window open. She had anticipated well.

A few minutes later I rejoined her. She gave me a big smile. "Feeling better?"

"Yes, much better. Thanks." And I was. The earlier gassy feeling had left me completely, and I felt alive inside. I also felt totally relaxed. More relaxed than I had felt in many months.

I collapsed back onto the cushions and immediately adopted a recumbent position. It was surprising how comfortable this cushion could be. Why hadn't I realised that before? I let my gaze wander round the room.

I noticed the bottom of one of the curtains bobbing about. For a moment I thought it was the wind, and then a little white shape broke free and dashed across the room. Harvey's fur was of the purest white. As he hopped across a particularly blue patch of carpet he looked like a summer cloud drifting across an azure sky.

"What about your hair?" she asked. "Shall we have a go at that?

She led me into the bathroom. It was an unusually large room, with a claw foot, free-standing bath in the middle. She turned abruptly to face me. We were standing not three inches apart. There was a tangible aura around her, a zone of sensuousness, and I was breaking the surface. She reached forward and began unbuttoning my shirt.

"You'd better take this off." She pushed it across my shoulders, her hands just brushing my skin as she did so.

My shirt fell to the floor. I felt blood rush to places that it hadn't been for a long time.

Was I being seduced? I'd never been seduced before. Sam had never seduced me. She had swept in like a vulture after a mouse and snatched me away in her claws. There had been nothing subtle or seductive about that.

Astrid motioned me to kneel on the floor in front of the bath. I placed my head across the rim, feeling like a potential victim of the guillotine. She lifted the shower handset and soaked my hair. I marvelled at the skill with which she mixed the dye without spilling a drop. She worked it into my hair, her fingers probing and pressing. Each touch electrified my nerve endings. I didn't know that hair could feel. With great care, she applied the last of the dye to my errant eyebrow.

Later, after she had rinsed and dried my hair, I surveyed the results in the mirror. I was impressed. She had made a much better job of it than I had.

I looked at my watch. Hell! It was late!

"Look, I am going to have to go. I have got to get back. Thanks for your help."

"My pleasure." She said it as if she meant it.

"I'll... I expect... I might bump into you again?" I was behaving like an adolescent school kid.

"Have you seen the fairies dance?"

"No, where do they do that?"

"I'll take you there tomorrow."

It sounded like an order.

"When?"

"When the tide turns."

And that was that. End of conversation. I was still mulling over the obscurity of this last exchange as she saw me to the door.

Chapter 6

I spent another uncomfortable night on the sofa and slid out of the cottage before anybody was up.

The bus dropped me off in the centre of town. I looked around the immediate area. There was a pet shop, a bookstore, and a shop dedicated to ornamental teapots. Just over the road, was a bakery and next to that, a clothes boutique called, 'Wear on Earth'. I thought it warranted a look. I'd decided I was going to experiment with denim again, so it could be worth seeing what they had to offer.

A curtain of hot air washed over me as I stepped inside. My ears were assaulted by an incessant thump, thump with an irritating three-note riff over the top of it. It sounded more like the engine room of a ship rather than music.

I was just beginning to think that I'd made a dreadful mistake when a young woman intercepted me. She appeared to be wearing nothing more than a white T-shirt.

"Can I help you, Sir?"

I responded in the time-honoured fashion, "No thanks, I'm just looking."

"For yourself?" In a tone of voice that said, what are you doing in here?

"Yes. I was looking for some jeans." And why shouldn't I be in here?

"They're just through there. She led me towards the rear of the shop. The shelves were piled high with blue denim. She scanned me up and down.

"Thirty-six?"

I was very flattered, but why would she be trying to guess my age?

"What?"

"Your waist size? Thirty-six inch?"

So that's what she meant. It had been a long time since I had bought my own clothes. I usually relied on Sam for that particular chore. As far as I could remember I had always been a thirty-two waist. I felt somewhat affronted.

"Thirty-two, actually."

"Of course." She pulled a pair of Levi's out from the stack and held them up to me. "The changing room's just through there, if you'd like to try them on." She nodded at a row of cubicles.

I noticed most of them were in use. I could see both male and female legs below the three-quarter length curtains. The legs danced and contorted as their owners tried on various items of clothing. Did I really want to show my white, hairy calves to a shop full of teenagers? Oh what the hell!

I entered the first available cubicle and pulled the curtain closed behind me. Well, as far closed as it would go. It left a one-inch gap down the middle. I struggled out of my clothes, trying to keep my naked bits away from the gap. It was no easy task. I hung my clothes on the hook and stepped into the Levi's. They pulled up as far as the tops of my thighs, and stopped there. I slipped them off again and checked the label to see if she'd made a mistake. No, thirty-two it said. It must be a slim-cut then.

I peeped over the top of the curtain. She was waiting expectantly.

"I think I'm used to a slightly looser cut," I said.

"Try these." She already had another pair in her hands, and she passed them in to me. I checked the label. Thirty-four.

"But these are thirty-four?"

"Yes I know but the fashion today is for slim-line thirty-two's. I thought you'd be more comfortable in the these."

"But I'm not really a thirty-four."

"Yes, I know."

I slipped them on. I could get these on, but they wouldn't do up over my waist.

"These are the right size," I said. "But they're just a bit tight round the waist band. Do have any other thirty-four's I could try?"

"No, but I'll tell you what I do have. We had a batch of wrongly labelled thirty-two's come in. We're supposed to be sending them back."

"Wrongly labelled?"

"Yes. They were labelled wrongly as thirty-six, but they're really thirty-two's. You could try a pair of those if you like. Although, I'm not really supposed to separate them."

"Separate them? From what?"

"They are jeans and shirt sets. You want to try one?"

"You're sure they're thirty-two's?"

"Yes. Just wrongly labelled."

She disappeared and returned after a few moments with a pair of jeans and a white cotton shirt. She passed them over the curtain. I checked the label. She was right, they said thirty-six.

"And you sure these are thirty-two's?"

"Oh, yes."

I tried them on. They fit perfectly.

"And you're saying I can't buy these without the shirt?"

"No, I'm afraid not. We're supposed to be sending them back, you see. They are in sets.

I put on the shirt on and stepped through the curtains to check myself in the full-length mirror. I was pleased with the result. I looked at the assistant expectantly.

"Well?"

"Hmm, I suppose you'll look better when you've got your proper shoes on."

"What do you mean, proper shoes?" I couldn't see what was wrong with my suede Hush Puppies.

"When you wear your trainers."

"Oh, yes of course."

"We've got some special offers on trainers at the moment. If you're interested?"

And so it went on. I emerged from the shop an hour later with two huge carrier bags stuffed full of bargains and special offers and sets that couldn't be separated. I was going to have to be a bit more careful in the future. Until I secured another source of income, I would not be able to continue bashing the American Express card like this.

I stopped off for a pub lunch then headed back to face Vlad the Impaler.

The lights were on in the cottage when I returned. I braced myself as I slid the key into the lock.

"Oh! You're home then?" Sam called. This translates as; do you want a fight now or later?

"Yes, did you have a nice day at the beach yesterday?" That's the code for I don't want to fight at all, thank you.

"It was all right." Okay then, I'm going to sulk until we do fight.

I shut the door behind me.

"What have you got there?"

Her highly tuned shopper's ear could detect the rustling of a carrier bag at twenty meters.

"Clothes, I just bought a few clothes."

"What're you buying clothes for? It's not like you to buy clothes." She twisted round to look at me across the back of the sofa.

"They were a bargain. They were in the sale."

"Oh, that's alright then." She returned her attention to Columbo on the television.

The best way of diverting Sam from the real nature of my expenditure was to say that I had bought something in the sale. It didn't matter what it was or how much it cost. I could've arrived home in a shiny new Ferrari if I'd told her I'd got twenty quid off it in the sale.

I headed upstairs to try on my new outfit. I put on one of the pairs of wrongly labelled jeans and the not-to-be-separated white cotton shirt. The jeans didn't want to let me bend down, and I had trouble tying up the laces on my new Nike trainers. The girl in the shop had assured me that I needed a leather thong around my neck to set off the ensemble. I was beginning to think that it wasn't a leather thong I needed, more a sign on my back saying, "Sucker". But I clipped it around my neck anyway.

Just then, Sam came in.

"What do think you think you look like?"

She has this way of knowing exactly what to say at the right moment to make you feel great. Couldn't she for once return the years of favours I had bestowed upon her every time she asked me if her bum looked big in this?

"Thought I'd try a new look."

"Tony, I think we need to talk."

I hate those words. They don't mean, 'We need to talk' at all. They mean, I have to listen.

"I know we have enough money put aside to see us through for a while," she continued. "But what are you planning on doing with your career? We don't want you turning into a layabout like your father do we?"

No, we don't, I thought, do you.

"Yes, I've been thinking about that. I think a change of direction is in order. You know, Sam."

"Okay," she said, hesitantly. "You know Selwyn's got some contacts in the insurance world. Perhaps we can get you in there."

I didn't want them to get me into anywhere.

"No, I mean a complete change. Maybe run a lobster boat or something."

"A lobster boat! Are you out of your mind?" She sat down on the edge of the bed.

I always thought you weren't supposed to say things like that to somebody recovering from a breakdown.

"No, do you know what? I think I'm just beginning to find it." Something Astrid said had just started to come into focus. "I don't want to be what I do, I want to do what I do and be what I want. I mean what I am… Who."

"Have you been drinking?"

"Of course not! Can't you see it's all quite easy? I am a stockbroker, that's a 'what', it's not a 'who'. I want to be a 'who'; I only want to do the 'what'. And when I want, not when I have to. And I want a pet rabbit."

Sam's incredulous look told me I probably hadn't explained myself very well.

"Perhaps I ought to book another appointment for you to see Dr Massey again."

"There! He's a 'what'! Everybody calls him Doctor. Who is he? What's his first name? What does he like on his toast? Has he ever seen the fairies dance?"

Silence hung in the air like fog on a spring morning.

Why had it taken me all these years to see this? I turned back to the mirror. Yes! That was different! I undid the third button on the shirt. It showed off the leather thong better.

Something strange was happening. The room was quiet. I turned back to face Sam.

She was silent.

There's a first. She actually seemed at a loss for words. Her eyes had lost focus, and her mouth was open, but no sound came from it. I was slightly worried. I had never seen this before.

"Are you okay?" I asked.

"Hmm? Oh, yes. I think we'll discuss this when you're sober."

"Right you are, then." I kissed her on the forehead and left the room, leaving her sitting on the bed staring at the wall.

As I opened the front door, I noticed a slight chill in the otherwise sunny afternoon. I picked up my grey cardigan from the hook and slipped it on.

A light breeze drifted in from the sea as Astrid and I walked along the promenade. The sun had put in its first appearance for many days and sparkled on the water like fairy lights on a Christmas tree.

As we left the eastern end of the town, the paved walkways gave way to rocky under-cliff trails. By necessity, we were forced to walk close together. I felt an overwhelming desire to reach out and hold her hand. I resisted it

My feet felt strange in the trainers as I picked my way across the ragged terrain. They gave good grip, but I was not about to take any chances.

Astrid moved easily across the rocks. She had probably been a cat in a previous existence. She stopped on a large rock to wait for me to catch up.

"I like the outfit, by the way."

"What?" I puffed.

"The clothes and trainers, good move. Shame about the cardigan."

"It was chilly when I left." I sat down on a rock next to hers. I think I managed it in a nonchalant enough manner. I stared out across the sea to accentuate the point that I wasn't sitting down because my legs were about to give way and I couldn't breathe; I just wanted to admire the view. Oh, so, casually, I turned my head round to look at what lay ahead of us. Even bigger rocks. And even less beach. In my best, casual, controlled, and curious voice, I asked, "Much further?" Well maybe just a hint of pleading crept in there.

"Just around the headland there." She pointed out a rocky promontory at least thirty miles away.

"Oh." I still hadn't got a clue where we were going, or why, for that matter.

"Come on then! Best to turn to or we'll miss them."

It wouldn't do to miss the fairies. Once more she bounded across the increasingly ragged surface with the grace and confidence of a mountain lion. I stumbled behind with all the confidence of a three-legged tortoise. After five minutes, I had to stop to remove my cardigan. I tied it in a jaunty manner around my shoulders. Another five minutes, I was still overheating, so I removed it from its jaunty position and tied it around my waist.

My legs were hurting, I was sure that I had shin splints. I wasn't quite sure what shin splints were, but I knew that runners complained of them so they must be brought on by excessive exercise. Undoubtedly of the type that I had been experiencing now.

We continued on our way, pressing forward against the almost impossible terrain. The cliffs loomed overhead on our left for maybe some two hundred metres, and the sea on our right lapped against the base of the cliffs. We stumbled from rock to rock, picking our way between sea and cliff. In contrast to its earlier benign appearance on the beach at St Ives, the sea had now turned into a predatory, white crested monster snapping at my ankles waiting for me to make the tiniest slip. Watching for the slightest lack of concentration, when it would snatch me off my precarious perch and drag me into the waiting depths below.

"Come on! Hurry up, nearly there!"

"How deep is this water here?"

"Here? Now, at low tide? Only about a foot."

"Oh."

After another five minutes of heroic persistence, we reached a small sandy area. The sea appeared to be much calmer here. I looked around, I wasn't quite sure what I was expecting to see. I'd come here in search of dancing fairies. I could see none. Dancing or otherwise.

"Well, where now?" I couldn't quite bring myself to say, 'Where are the dancing fairies?' Perhaps I had misunderstood her. I didn't want to make a complete idiot of myself if we were here to see the fishing seafarers or something that sounded similar.

"Just in here." She indicated a crevice in the rock face that I hadn't noticed. It was about half a metre wide and a metre high. It had a rocky floor that just touched the tiny sandy beach on which we stood.

"In there?"

"Yes. It opens out inside. It's hollow at the top. Light comes down. Come on, follow me"

She turned sideways on and slid into the entrance like a coin in a slot machine. And all of a sudden I was alone on a metre wide beach with two hundred metres of cliff above my head, and the prospect of inserting myself into a hole in the side of Cornwall no bigger than a letterbox. My heart was thumping. I had never realised before that I was probably claustrophobic. The thought of the cramped space and thousands of tons of rock above my head made fingers of fear clutch at my throat.

Perhaps I should just call it a day and head back. Leave Astrid sitting in her hole watching the fairies. But I couldn't. The same force that had propelled me into buying the tobacco tin and then filling it, was now exerting its pressure. And I knew I would have to go through with this. I was not quite as slim as Astrid, and I had a mental picture of being wedged half in, half out of this hole. I drew in my size thirty-two waist and forced myself into the crevice. It was tight, but only momentarily. Once through, I saw that Astrid was right. It opened up into a space about the size of the average living room and the shape of a bell. Light streamed through a circular hole in the roof. In the centre of the floor, directly underneath the hole, was a small rocky pool of, about two metres diameter. The water level in the pool rose and fell rhythmically.

Astrid sat cross-legged on the sandy floor of the cave, a huge smile on her face.

"Cool, isn't it?"

Could she see my chest thumping? Even if she couldn't see it, I'm sure she could hear it.

I looked at the pool. The water looked inviting. It resembled a hot tub.

"What now?" I asked.

"Now we wait for the fairies to start dancing. But before that, we have to make sure we're wearing the right heads." She undid the clip on the belt pouch that she was wearing and extracted an exquisitely rolled spliff.

Oh no, I thought, not again.

Chapter 7

Astrid handed me the spliff and a box of matches.

"You going to do the honours?"

I don't think I should, really. This got me into a lot of trouble last time you know."

"I did notice. Why don't you try smoking it this time? You might find it suits you better."

I sat down and leaned back against the wall, the spliff in one hand and the matches in the other. I felt I was being drawn along a road that was leading some place I really wanted to be. I just didn't know where it was, or what the journey would be like.

I lit the joint and drew deeply. The effects were instantaneous. Whether it was the cannabis, or the tobacco I don't know. A wave rolled through my head and sparkled along every blood vessel and every nerve in my body. It lifted the heaviness I had felt inside me for so long and replaced it with a warm breeze. I took another deep draw and handed it over to Astrid.

"Good?" she asked.

I smiled and nodded, holding the breath down in my lungs. My head flew, and my skin prickled. I watched the red, glowing end run down along the white joint as she drew deeply several times.

"Okay?" she asked.

She seemed very concerned for my well-being.

"Yes, fine." I wasn't sure though. My heart was still racing, and my mind was definitely not happy with being in this tiny hole and under all that rock. I felt a strange combination of soporific haziness and panic.

Astrid noticed my discomfort. "Relax, Tony. Let it take you. "

I wasn't quite sure I wanted to be taken. Not yet. I wasn't ready.

"How much longer?"

"Not long. Tell you what, let's have a dip."

"A dip?"

"A swim. In the fairies pool."

"I haven't brought... I mean... I didn't bring..."

"You forgot to pack a cozzy?" She lifted one eyebrow and smiled.

"Yes, I didn't think..."

"Doesn't matter. We'll swim as nature intended. Not embarrassed are you?"

Yes I was, deeply embarrassed. "No! Of course not!"

She flipped her T-shirt over her head with casual ease. As she unzipped her jeans, I felt my insides tingle, partly in expectation and partly in embarrassment. I didn't know whether to look, or to purposefully not look. Either way seemed wrong.

She wore nothing underneath the jeans and T-shirt, and within seconds, she was standing naked by the pool.

"Come on then!"

Her body was slim and evenly tanned. She had small breasts and narrow hips, and had shaved her bikini line to allow the wearing of the tiniest bikini thong.

"Right... I'll just take my clothes off then."

She sat down and dangled her feet in the water. "Ooh! That's fresh." She wasn't looking in my direction, either by intent or simply because she found the pool more interesting than what lay underneath my clothes.

As I undressed, I couldn't help thinking that perhaps I should have invested in some snazzy boxer shorts rather than the tired Y-fronts that I was currently wearing. She smiled at me as I folded my clothes neatly and piled them on the floor.

For some reason, I felt more at ease than I thought I would. Somehow this felt natural. With Sam there was always a degree of self-consciousness, and most of our dwindling sexual activity consisted of The Saturday Night Fumble with the lights off.

Astrid slid into the water, and I heard her involuntary gasp as the cold closed around her. I slid into the pool on the opposite side. My lungs spasmed with the sudden cold. The pool was surprisingly deep and reached my chest. I lifted my feet from the bottom and bobbed with the natural rhythm of the water. I guessed there must be an underground link to the sea. The rising and falling of the pool water was reflecting the movement of the sea outside.

Astrid still held the spliff. She passed it to me. Our legs touched. Electricity ran. I took another deep pull. The flow of euphoria inside my body coincided perfectly with the rising and falling of the water level.

A sudden, irrational thought showed me a picture of Sam bursting in here and finding us both like this. Involuntarily, I drew my legs in, adopting an almost foetal position.

Astrid watched me. "You look very tense. Relax." She pressed my legs down with her hand.

I smiled, and deliberately extended my legs as if to show how relaxed I really was. "I'm fine," I said.

She maintained the contact on my leg. Our eyes connected and I felt her presence run into my soul. Strange things were happening in my chest. She slid her hand up along my side and around my shoulder. We moved closer together. Her breath fluttered across my lips. I wanted to close in on those lips. I wanted to so badly. She seemed to catch herself and then pulled away, as if someone had just called her. I felt a hollowness in my chest like something had just been taken away me, something that belonged.

Astrid's long hair floated on the surface of the water around her. It reminded me of a lily pad. Her breasts kept breaking the surface of the water, and below, her body drifted in and out of focus as the ripples distorted her otherwise perfect image.

I noticed she was watching me again.

"Is that for me?" she asked.

"What's that?"

She nodded towards my groin area. I suddenly realised I had an erection.

"I am... I... I didn't... Oh dear..."

"I am very flattered. But we're not going to have sex, Tony."

"Oh, why?" That was a stupid question. It was obvious why. I was a middle-aged, overweight burn out. And she was Aphrodite incarnate.

"Look, I'm sorry if I... If you thought we were going to... You see… I don't do that, Tony."

"I see."

"Nothing personal. You're not free."

"I'm trying!"

"That's not what I mean. You made a promise to another human. I can't interfere with that. I don't take what isn't mine. But I'll tell you what, let me deal with that for you." She moved alongside me. "Let's see if we can't relieve some of your tension."

I felt her fingers closing around me. The warmth of her hand quickly dispelled the cold of the water. The gentle pressure. She was right alongside me, her skin touching mine. Her hand moved slowly, rhythmically. Her face was close to mine; she was watching my eyes.

"Relax, shh, relax, Tony."

Although her fingers were only in contact with one part of me, I felt as though she were caressing every square inch of my flesh. She increased the speed and length of her stroke. All the while, she maintained a soft, cooing sound. I had never felt so alive, and so relaxed at the same time. An intense warmth overwhelmed the centre of my body and with a final convulsive shiver, release came. I lay back in the water; it felt like a warm bath now. My eyes closed, and my breathing settled.

"Better?" she queried.

Speech escaped me. I felt a peculiar mix of relief and disappointment.

The water level in the pool had increased dramatically, and the surface was chopping violently.

"It's just about time," she said.

We pulled ourselves out of the water and sat back against the rock face. Astrid lit another spliff. My head was just beginning to drift again when a geyser of water erupted from the centre of the pool. It reached upwards towards the light.

"Hell! What on earth was that?"

"Dancing fairies. Watch."

A few minutes later, the same thing happened again. There was a loud hissing, whooshing noise. The sound of a hundred beer cans being opened filled the cavern. A jet of water climbed skywards. The column of water reached nearly two metres before disintegrating and raining down in tiny droplets that sparkled in the sunlight.

"What's causing it?" I asked.

"It's the waves. When the tide turns and the waves are about the right height, they force their way through the underground passage and push the water upwards like this. Don't analyse, watch."

The water jets became more frequent, and my eyes attuned to the water droplets as they danced in the sunlight.

It wasn't long before I saw the fairies dancing. Whether it was the cannabis, a trick of the light or a combination of the two, I didn't know. But as each jet of water reached its zenith and then disintegrated, little, luminous figures danced in the air.

I lay back in the sand, rested my head against a small rock and watched this incredible sight. An intense feeling of well-being flooded my body. I had never felt so at peace before. The warm sunlight streamed down onto my naked body, and my ears were filled with the hissing sounds of each new wave as it forced its way into the cavern. I felt my eyes becoming heavy, keeping them open was a strain.

I decided to just listen.

I awoke with a start. Cold water was lapping around my lower half. For a moment, I thought I must have fallen back into the pool. I sat up. No, the floor of the cave was awash. I glanced over to where Astrid was lying. She was on a slightly higher part of the cave floor, still in the dry.

"Astrid! Astrid!"

She wasn't stirring. I crawled over to her and gently rocked her shoulder. Reluctantly, she broke free of the folds of sleep.

"What's happening?"

"Look!" I pointed at the floor of the cave.

"Oh shit! We've got to get out of here."

I looked round the cave.

"Where's our clothes?"

They were gone.

"They must have been sucked out in the outflow," she said.

"Oh great."

"Come on, we might find them outside." She stood up and forced her way through the crevice. I followed. My skin was scratched in several places by the time I emerged.

We came out into the bright, afternoon sunlight. We were knee deep in water, and each crashing wave seemed to take the water level higher. I looked around desperately for our clothes. But the only item I could find was the grey cardigan, clinging bravely to a small rock half in the water.

"What are we going to do now?" I was close to panic. "We can't walk back to town like this!"

"We can't walk back to town anyway, look." She pointed the way we had come. Rough seas crashed against the base of the cliff. The path we had earlier negotiated was gone.

"What about the other way?" I asked.

"Not a chance," she said. "That's even worse. Sheer cliffs all the way, ten or twelve miles."

"Oh this just keeps getting better. What do you suggest then?" I snapped. "Do we swim for it?"

"Only if you want to die."

"What?"

"Well, either you're going to get sucked out to sea, or you're going to get smashed against the rocks."

"So, what then? Wait here for the tide to go out again?"

"I don't think we can do that, either."

"Why?"

"Well, in the next couple of hours, it's going to be twelve feet deep here."

I turned to look at the rock face above our heads, hoping beyond reason to see a nice set of steps cut into it. It looked about as welcoming as the north face of the Eiger, and I wasn't about to attempt it without a ladder. I turned back to face Astrid.

"This is another one of your set-ups, right? Any minute now, some of your mates are going to come round the corner in a boat, yes?"

"No. I'm afraid not, Tony."

I pulled the cardigan out of the water and wrung it out. That would never be the same again. Sam's mother had knitted that for me as an anniversary present. Sam would be furious. If we ever got out of here, that was.

I turned back for another look at the cliff face. There was a ledge about two metres up. It was small, but maybe just reachable.

"Look," I said. "If we can get up there, it will give us more time."

"Okay," she said.

"You go first. I'll push you up."

She braced her foot in my hands, and I gently pushed her up. The rock scraped along her flesh leaving red traces. She continued to climb. I held my hands outstretched and raised upwards, as if I could levitate her by the force of my will. In other circumstances this would have been a very nice view.

She reached the ledge and twisted round into a sort of crouching position.

"Okay," she said. "Now you."

I stretched my foot up into a tiny fissure in the rock face and braced my toes into it. My hands grabbed two small outcroppings, and I pulled myself up. The toes of my right foot bore the main part of my weight. I scrambled on up. The rock tore at my skin. Eventually, I made it to the ledge. I twisted round and adopted a similar squatting position next to Astrid. We sat there like a couple of gargoyles watching the waves crashing beneath us.

"Tony," Astrid looked at me, her eyes were wide. "I'm frightened." Her voice was weak and trembling.

"It will be all right," I said. "Here." I bundled the cardigan over her shoulders. It was more of a gesture than anything sensible to do. I wasn't frightened. I was absolutely petrified. It was probably a good job there was nowhere to walk to, as my legs wouldn't have carried me anyway. My insides felt cold and there was a pain in my chest as the adrenaline rushed around the heart muscles.

"Astrid,"

"Yes?"

"Why did you invite me here?"

"I'm sorry," she was crying. "I just thought..."

"No! I didn't mean it as a criticism. I was just curious."

"I thought you looked lost. You looked so sad when I first saw you with your little bag of bits and pieces. You reminded me of a small boy with some new toys and nobody to play with. You looked like you could use some fun. I'm sorry, Tony. I'm really sorry I got you into this." The tears flowed freely down her cheeks.

I put my arm around her, and pulled her close. Just then I heard voices overhead. "Are you all right down there?"

"No!" I shouted. "Can you get help?"

They shouted something back, but I couldn't hear what it was. I craned my neck upwards, but all I could see above was unforgiving rock. I called again several times more. But there was no reply.

"Do you think they heard us?" she asked.

"I am sure they did." I wasn't sure at all.

We waited for what seemed like another half an hour, and in that time, the water started lapping at our feet. I had just about given up hope and was contemplating making a swim for it whatever the consequences when I heard the sound of the helicopter.

And that's how we came to be on the evening news.

At first, I thought it was going to be an Air-Sea rescue helicopter. I strained my eyes against the reflected sunlight as the machine came around the headland. We both stood up and started waving. Me as naked as the day I was born, and Astrid wearing nothing but my grey cardigan.

We waved and shouted. We whooped and laughed.

Then I saw the cameras pointing out of the open door, and a moment later, I saw the words 'Carlton Television' along the fuselage. My first thought was to try to cover myself. I dropped my hands to my groin. Then I thought about Astrid and tried to stand in front of her to protect her from the cameras. But the ledge was tiny, and the only way I could interpose myself was to hold on tight to her.

In retrospect, I could quite see how the press would get hold of the wrong end of this.

The helicopter continued to swoop and circle as the rescue boat came into view. The rubber Surf Rescue craft pulled up alongside us, and still the cameras pointed and probed.

We were bundled on board and wrapped in blankets. Within a few moments we were bouncing across the waves on our way back to St Ives.

And the Press
And Sam.

Chapter 8

A police car waited for us at the beachfront car park, along with, what seemed like half of the world's press.

I was beginning to see problems in keeping this away from Sam.

We were bundled into the back of the police car. My blanket fell open just as I was sliding into the seat, much to the delight of the waiting photographers. Three hundred flash bulbs went off simultaneously and I couldn't see for several minutes.

By the time we reached the police station, my vision had almost cleared, apart from a couple of orange dots in the centre of my field of view. This made it impossible for me to look at anything directly, and I had to sort of look obliquely in order to see things.

We were led into separate cells although they didn't lock the doors, so I assumed I wasn't under arrest. On the way in, I was handed a set of white cover-alls made out of some sort of paper. I wondered briefly why they had separated us. But then it dawned on me. They probably figured we were a couple of sex-maniacs judging by the position we had been found in, therefore they couldn't leave us alone together in case we were at it again like rabbits the moment their backs were turned.

I had just finished zipping up the front of my cover-alls when a young policewoman came in. She carried a mug on a small tray. Her face held a badly concealed smile. Not quite the professional detachment I had come to expect from Her Majesty's Finest. "Coffee? There's sugar there, if you want it. Although I'm sure you're sweet enough!" She handed me the tray. "The F.M.E. will be along in a minute to check your over. He's with your girlfriend now."

"No! She's not my girlfriend. She's... Well, she's..."

The policewoman waited expectantly.

"She's just a sort of acquaintance, really."

"Oh, I see." She eyed me up and down as if trying to work out what Astrid saw in me. What was it that made me so irresistible to a young girl like Astrid that she should throw herself at me in public like that?

Shortly afterwards, I was prodded and poked by the police surgeon who pronounced me fit and healthy and mentally competent enough to be interviewed. The policewoman returned to escort me along a green-painted corridor to the interview room. She remained with me, and we were soon joined by a uniformed officer who introduced himself as police sergeant Treluggen. He was about six foot six and his broad shoulders strained at the seams of his uniform. He wore thick lensed, gold-rimmed glasses that he had to keep pushing back up his nose with his forefinger. We sat opposite each other across a wooden table.

"Now then, young man," he said. His broad Cornish accent was almost musical. I warmed to him straight away. I was ready to warm to anybody that called me 'Young man'. "Name?"

"Tony Ryan." I couldn't see his face properly as the orange dots were dancing across his nose. I focused on the top of his head, that way I could see his face out of the bottom of my vision.

He looked up at me. His eyebrows wrinkled, and he touched his hand to the top of his head. He patted his hair as if trying to find something there.

"What have you got to say for yourself, then?" he continued.

I proceeded to give him a reasonably censored version of the events that led up to my rescue. He made copious notes in spite of the fact there was a tape recorder whirring away in the background. When I had finished, he very deliberately clicked his pen shut, placed it inside his notebook, and returned it to his pocket. He looked up at me.

"Well, I don't see any reason to be holding on to you, young man. But if you want my advice, you'll stay away from that Stryker girl."

"Who?"

"Astrid Stryker. Surely to goodness you haven't forgotten her already? You remember, the young woman on the cliff?"

"Oh, no! It's just that I didn't know her surname."

"Well, she's a wrong'un all right. We tend to keep our eye on her, we do. I'm sure you don't want to be seeing any more of the inside of this place now, do you? I suggest you stay away from her."

I most certainly did not want to be seeing any more of the inside of this place.

"Mary will drop you back home," sergeant Treluggen said. He nodded at the policewoman.

The police car dropped me at the end of the drive outside the cottage. I glanced across at it, the curtains were open, and there were no lights on. Straight away I knew it was empty. I also realised with horror that I didn't have a key. At this present time, it was somewhere at the bottom of the North Sea.

I thanked the policewoman, and gave an exaggerated wave of my hand, as if to say, 'on your way then'. She took the hint and drove off.

I made my way round to the rear of the cottage. I picked up a stone and tapped at a small pane of glass in the back door until it broke then reached through and undid the catch. I made my way into the kitchen to put the kettle on. The note was waiting on the table, propped up against a milk bottle.

"Tony, we watched you on the television. I hope you're pleased with yourself, and that you and that strumpet of yours will be very happy together. Mother has offered me the use of her London flat, and I will be staying there until we have sold the house and sorted out the divorce. Have your solicitor contact me when you want to arrange collection of your things. Goodbye."

My legs decided that they didn't want to play the standing game any more. I collapsed onto the sofa. This was turning out to be quite an eventful week. I reached behind the sofa in search of the drinks table. I could just about reach a glass and the bottle of gin, but not the tonic. That must be a sign, I decided. I poured a large glass and drank it straight down. It left a trail of fire down my gullet that was quite pleasing in a sort of masochistic way. I refilled the glass.

The television remote control lay on the coffee table just in front of me. I reached for it and clicked the set on. It was the local early-evening news. I should have turned it off really, but a morbid fascination kept me watching. Mine was the bit of whimsy at the end. The "And finally..." bit.

At the time, the helicopter had seemed like a long way away. But these close-up shots were really quite remarkable. They showed in glorious detail how I had turned my back on their film crew to wrap my arms around the almost naked Astrid. My Day-Glo white buttocks were blanked out by an amusing smiley face. No doubt to preserve the innocence of the six o'clock news. The commentator was explaining that despite the presence of their helicopter and the rescue boat, the still unnamed couple seemed oblivious of their surroundings, and only had eyes for each other.

My eyes remained glued to the television while my hand reached for the bottle of gin. By the time I had swallowed the third glass, there was no trace of fire, it was going down as smoothly as milk.

Time to take stock of my assets, I decided. Except that I didn't seem to have many left. I no longer had a job, anywhere to live, or a wife and family. I had a fair bit of money stashed way in the bank for a rainy day. But that was it. Something told me that I should really be feeling terrified at this point. Or wracked with grief and shame. But I wasn't. The only thing that I was feeling, was something akin to euphoria. Of course, it may well have been just the gin. But I didn't think it was.

I was free.

I was my own boss, and my life was my own. I could do anything I wanted. I could eat bacon and eggs for breakfast

instead of muesli. I could watch Benny Hill on the
television without being called chauvinist. I could listen to
music at a sensible volume. Damn it, I could even leave the
toilet seat up if I wanted to! I would never have to endure
another cheese and wine party. I could eat pizza straight out
of the box with my fingers, and I would never have to wear
another tie. Ever again. The only sort of work I would
accept from now on would be tie-less. Even if Tony Blair
rang me up tomorrow and asked me to run the Bank of
England for him, if he was going to make me wear a tie, I
would say forget it!

As I refilled my glass, some of the liquid slopped over
the side, it felt cool on my fingers as it evaporated.

In fact, as a symbolic gesture of my new-found freedom,
and tie-less beginnings, I was going to burn all of my ties.
Like those women in the sixties who burned their bras. That
had always impressed me as being a powerful symbol of
liberation. Well I was going to do the same. I hadn't brought
more than half a dozen ties with me, but they'd do.

I rose unsteadily to my feet, and even more unsteadily,
climbed the stairs. I went through the wardrobe, carefully
draped each tie around my neck, and then started back down
the stairs. Each step seemed a little bit more hazardous on
the way down than it had on the way up. I had to
synchronise the placing of my foot with the exact moment
that the step passed in front of me. It wasn't easy. A couple
of times I had to stop and wait while a step came around
again.

I made my way to the back door, picking up a box of
barbecue fire-lighters on the way. It was raining. I stood in
the open doorway with the rain beating on my face, my
grand gesture battered into submission by the English
summer. No! I wasn't going to be beaten that easily. I went
back into the kitchen and picked up the biggest saucepan I
could find and took it into the lounge. I placed the saucepan
on the coffee table and the fire-lighters in the bottom of it.
Then I carefully arranged all of my ties inside the pan. For

good measure, I screwed up a newspaper and bundled it on top.

I sat back to survey my handiwork and poured myself another drink. I couldn't find any matches, so I lit a roll of newspaper from the gas cooker and brought it back into the lounge. I dropped it into the saucepan. The fire-lighters caught instantly. The flames reached surprisingly high. It was then that I noticed the Bart Simpson tie. Well maybe I'd just hang on to that one, I thought. After all, you never know, do you? And that had been a favourite of mine. Simon had bought it for me.

I dipped my fingers into the burning saucepan and picked the tie out. It wasn't until I'd extracted it fully that I realised the end of it was on fire. Once exposed to the air, the flames climbed up the tie like a monkey up a tree. There was a little hiss as the hairs on the back of my hand frizzled, and I dropped the tie with a small yelp. The tie landed half in the pot and half across the leg of my police-issue overalls. Although the overalls were probably fire retardant, they were certainly not heat retardant. The heat of the burning tie passed straight through to my leg, and the sudden pain made me jump up. In doing so, I knocked over the table, complete with burning pot. Within seconds there was a nice little bonfire under way in the centre of Grahame's lounge.

I ran into the kitchen and filled a bowl with water. By the time I had returned I realised the futility of my efforts. The inferno was growing by the second. I threw the water into the fire. It hissed at me ineffectually. I ran back into the kitchen. There must be a fire extinguisher around here somewhere. I crashed through each cupboard in turn, but with no luck. I looked back towards the lounge; the whole room was glowing now. I figured that it was probably about time I handed this little project over to the professionals and I ran out of the back door in search of a phone box.

The fire brigade did their best. But it was a timber-framed building, and by the time they'd arrived, the fire was already well out of control. I stood by and watched, with a sort of bewildered detachment as the flames crackled away in front of me.

I heard somebody move up alongside me and guessed it was a fireman. In an attempt to bring a little bit of levity to the situation, I said, "I don't suppose you remembered to bring the marshmallows, did you?"

"I think we need to have another little chat, don't we, young man?"

A horrible, tingly, icy feeling flickered across my insides. I turned to face police sergeant Treluggen.

Chapter 9

Sergeant Treluggen sat down at the table. He gave a heavy sigh that coincided with the settling of his bulk into the too-small seat. The vinyl covering on the seat gave a raspberry sound. At least, I assumed it was the seat. Either that, or he'd been at the Mega-Slim.

"Right then, young man. Let's just see if I've got this right. You claim you were setting fire to your tie collection. Is that right?"

"Yes"

"And then you decided that you wanted to rescue Bert Simpson?"

"Not Bert, Bart. It was his tie... Well not his exactly... It was my tie... It had Bart Simpson on it... I couldn't very well rescue Bert... I mean Bart. He's a cartoon… Isn't he?"

"Well, leaving that to one side for the moment then, Sir," This was a bad sign. He had taken to calling me 'Sir' Instead of 'Young man'. I wondered if they trained them how to do this in Police College. How to infuse the word 'Sir' with so much contempt and disbelief. He continued, "The fire investigation officer tells me that the back door has been broken into. Would you care to explain?" He pushed his glasses back up his nose.

"I lost my key, you see. When my clothes got washed out of the fairies' cave." I wondered if that sounded quite as ludicrous as I thought it did. Sergeant Treluggen remained silent as he looked at each piece of paper in turn on his desk. I glanced around the room. It was the same room I'd been interviewed in earlier that day. I hadn't really paid much attention to it then. The walls were covered in an assortment of posters that suggested we 'Turn in a dealer' or 'Be on the lookout for smugglers'.

"So, you claim this is your property and that you simply lost the key?"

"No, it's not my place. It belongs to my boss. My ex-boss."

"Would that be the gentleman that you had a fight with in the Indian restaurant?"

"Yes." Wow! This guy was good!

"And after which little contretemps, he dismissed you from his employ?"

"Err, yes." I didn't like the way this was heading.

"Now, you see how this could look, don't you, Sir? In a drunken rage after being dismissed, you break into his cottage and burn it down. You have been drinking, haven't you, Sir?"

The questioning went on for another twenty minutes, after which time I was left alone in the cell. This time the door was locked. I stayed there for another two hours. It was nearly ten-o-clock by the time I was released on bail. My sole possession was a brand new set of white paper overalls to replace the scorched ones. I had no money, credit card or proof of identity. So a hotel was out of the question. The only thing I could think of was to throw myself onto Astrid's mercy. I hoped that she was in as I headed for her place.

I clattered up the iron steps and tapped on the door. She swung it open and seemed genuinely pleased to see me.

"Oh, hi Tony! Nice outfit! I've hung mine up. I'm only going to wear it on special occasions. Come on in."

"Thanks." I shuffled into the room. The air was thick with the smell of cannabis. The only light in the room was provided by several candles that seemed to pulsate in time with the music. One of the more untidy cushions moved, and I realised there was somebody sprawled across it.

"This is Pete," Astrid said.

He sat up, and I recognised him from the Cafe as being one of the hippies that had sold me the original skunk weed.

He waved his arm in my direction, "Hey, man. Cool."

"Sit down, Tony. Fancy some wine?"

"Thanks," I settled onto a vacant cushion.

Astrid picked up a box of supermarket white and held it over a McDonald's cup. She didn't stop pouring until the liquid was level with the rim. No room to smell the bouquet there. I thanked her and took a long sip. It wasn't too bad.

"I'm out on bail," I mumbled.

"Really! They didn't keep me in."

"No, it's not for that. I burnt the cottage down."

"Oh. That would do it!"

"I've got nowhere to stay." I was still talking to the floor. "I was wondering... If you could..."

"Of course! I suppose in some way I'm partly responsible for this mess."

The experience at the police station had sobered me up, but it didn't take long for the wine to re-stimulate the gin, and a warming, relaxed feeling spread throughout my body. I raised my arms above my head to give a big stretch. At which point I heard two tearing noises, one from under my arm and the other from my groin area.

"Hey, man! I can see your balls!" Pete said.

Astrid laughed. I reached between my legs and realised there was a big, gaping hole.

"Let's see if I can find you something more comfortable," Astrid said. She disappeared momentarily and returned with a blue caftan.

"Try this," she said.

I drew it over my head and then shrugged myself out of the remains of my overalls. The caftan stopped at my knees and was a bit tight around my waist. Apart from that, it was quite comfortable.

I relaxed back into the cushion again. The music pulsed and flowed around the room in a most hypnotic manner. It seemed to run through my very body and intertwine with my natural rhythms. I was on the verge of drifting off to sleep when I had a sudden thought.

"Astrid?"

"Yes?"

"Do you think I could use your phone?"

"I haven't got one. But there's a phone box just across the road."

"I can't go out like this!"

"Why not? Nobody will see you. It's dark."

She was probably right.

"I hate to ask... But I haven't got any money."

"Here," Pete said. "Have this one on me." He pulled a plastic bag from his jacket pocket. It was full to bulging with ten-pence pieces. He shook a handful out and passed them to me.

"Thanks," I said. "I'll repay you."

"Hey, don't sweat it! It'll come round again."

I wasn't quite sure what he meant by that, but I thanked him again.

I ran across the road as quickly as I could. The wind was cold around my bare legs and seemed to blow upwards in a most unfriendly manner. I shivered as I pulled the door shut behind me. I deposited two coins in the slot and piled the rest onto the small ledge. I wracked my brains to try to remember the number of Sam's mother's flat. I punched in what I thought it was. A man's voice answered the phone. "Yes?"

I was taken aback slightly. I had been expecting Sam to answer.

"Is that Mayfair three seven six five two one nine?"

"No!"

I was positive that's what I'd dialled.

"Are you sure?"

"Look, pal. Have I ever lied to you before?"

"No," I admitted. The line went dead. Damn it!

I dialled the number again, more carefully this time. A continuous, high-pitched tone told me the number was unobtainable. I replaced the receiver and put my hand down to the coin tray to retrieve my money. There was nothing there. Hell, this was supposed to return coins in case of non-connection. I banged the side of the telephone.

Nothing.

I leaned back as far as I could and gave it a good hard kick with my bare foot.

Still nothing.

Even the bloody phone box was against me. With growing frustration, I grabbed hold of both sides of the coin box and tried to shake it. Of course, it wouldn't move. It had been designed to withstand an assault by sledgehammer, so my puny efforts were hardly likely to put it under any sort of strain.

I poked my finger up inside the coin return slot. I could feel something there. Something sticky. I poked and prodded. It wouldn't move. I managed to get two fingers inside and after some uncomfortable wriggling, I grabbed hold of the corner of what felt like a piece of paper and gave it a good tug. It came away followed by a shower of coins that fell to the floor. Oh well, perhaps things were beginning to look up after all! There must be three pounds there. I bent down and started gathering up the money.

I felt, rather than heard the phone box door open.

"Well, well. What have we got here then, Sir? Your own private money box, is it?" The voice of sergeant Treluggen boomed inside the narrow confines.

I straightened up clutching two handfuls of coins. He eyed me up and down.

"Nice frock, Sir."

"It's a caftan," I protested.

"Looks like your lucky day!" He nodded at my cupped hands that were over-flowing with coins. "Win the jackpot, did we, Sir?"

"No, I was just trying to make a phone call."

"And at what point during this phone call, did you feel the need to physically assault the telephone?"

"What?"

"These things have silent alarms, you see, Sir. We've been watching the phone boxes in this area for sometime now. It seems that somebody has been stuffing up the return coin chutes in order to rob poor innocent members of the public of their 'hard earned'."

"Well, it's not me! I just found it like this!"

"Of course you did, Sir. I think you'd better come along with me now. Time we had another little chat."

He pulled a plastic bag from his pocket and dropped inside it the chewing gum and paper that I'd extracted from the coin chute. He then gathered the money into a separate bag and ushered me into the police car.

This time, I was kept in for the rest of the night. The following morning, I was once more released on bail pending further investigations. The custody sergeant had decided that I couldn't very well be thrown out of the police station in just my caftan and had arranged a lift to the Salvation Army hostel. I was greeted by a very pleasant lady who found me a bacon sandwich and a huge mug of coffee. I thanked her profusely and took my breakfast into the day-lounge.

There was only one other occupant in the lounge. He looked to be in his late sixties. He wore a threadbare green jumper and a blue peaked cap. I would have believed that he was asleep except for the fact that every few minutes he sat up with a start and shouted, "Fucking chickens!"

When I had finished my breakfast, the nice lady returned with a pile of clothes.

"Try these. They look to be about your size."

"Thanks!"

I took the pile and found a quiet corner in which to change. A couple of minutes later, I was wearing green cord trousers, brown leather sandals, and a sweatshirt that advertised the Iron Maiden tour of 1984.

I was allowed to use the phone. American Express subjected me to several minutes of bizarre questioning involving maiden names of various relatives. Eventually they agreed to send me an emergency card.

My bank wouldn't deal with me over the phone, and so necessitated a visit into town. It was a long walk, but the sun was out, and the day was quite pleasant. I had to stop a couple of times on the way to catch my breath though. I decided I really had to do something about my fitness level.

The assistant manager was understandably suspicious about my appearance. I was dressed like a beatnik, and I hadn't shaved for twenty-four hours. They phoned a description of me through to my own branch and faxed my signature back and forth several times before they were satisfied. The whole process took nearly two hours, but by the end of it, I was solvent once more. As I still had no plastic, I had to draw out a large sum of money in cash. I headed for the nearest clothes shop. It was not quite as fashionable as 'Wear On Earth', but I was still determined in my pursuit of denim and this seemed a likely place.

No sooner had I entered the shop, than a security guard slid alongside me.

"Come along then, sunshine," he said. "We don't need your sort in here."

"Wait, I've come here to buy some clothes."

"I'm sure you have. Why don't you try the Red Cross shop? I hear they do a good range in sacking. Bit more to your liking I'm sure."

"I have got money. Look!" I pulled the envelope full of twenty-pound notes from my pocket and riffled them under his nose.

"Oh, I see. And just where did you get that?"

Oh Lord, spare me from make-believe policemen. I was having enough trouble with the real ones; I didn't need this one giving me a hard time as well.

"I've just got it from the bank, and I was intending to spend it in your shop. If you don't believe me, you can ring the bank yourself."

"Well, maybe you were all right then."

He finally let me in.

As I browsed through the racks of denim, it dawned on me that I'd handled that situation particularly well. I felt quite pleased with myself. The new assertive Tony was no longer going to be pushed around or manipulated by anybody. This was still my new beginning, albeit a couple of false starts later.

I pulled a pair of jeans from the rack and held them up. They looked all right.

"We've got those on special offer at the moment."

I turned to see a middle-aged woman standing alongside me. She wore a sensible skirt and sweatshirt bearing the shop's logo. Oh well. At least it's not some commission-hungry young assistant like last time!

Twenty minutes later, the new, assertive Tony emerged from the shop with three bags full of clothes and no money. If I was going to survive very long in this world on my own, I was going to have to get the hang of this shopping business. I couldn't keep doing this. I would be potless in a fortnight.

I headed back to the bank in order to refill my envelope. The assistant manager with whom I had spoken earlier had now gone to lunch, and as there was nobody there who had witnessed my earlier identification, I had to go through the whole performance again with a different junior manager.

My next port of call was a small hotel on the seafront, The Fisherman's Steps. I was wearing some of my new clothes, but I was still in need of a shave and lacking any real luggage. The hotel insisted on a deposit, and they were somewhat taken aback when I paid in cash.

It was a family sized room, but as it was the only one they had left, I had little choice. There were three beds, a fridge and a television. I collapsed onto the nearest bed, exhausted. Within a few minutes, I had dozed off.

It was late afternoon by the time I stirred again. I was feeling decidedly hungry. I had a quick shower and headed for the hotel snack bar. I hadn't remembered that the words 'Family Hotel' really mean 'Children's Hotel', and I found myself in a queue at the snack bar behind eight little darlings all clutching their pocket money and unsure of which flavour ice cream to go for this time. I wondered what Simon and Natasha were doing at this moment. I would have to try phoning again.

As each child was served at the counter, they turned and walked back past the queue. I watched the assortment of brightly coloured ice creams with bits of biscuit and chocolate sticking out of them troop past me. I thought about how bad that must be for them. The colourings, the high fat content and the inevitable tooth decay.

My turn came eventually. The selection consisted of pizza and chips, burger and chips or chips. I was beginning to realise that I was in the wrong hotel, but I was starving, so I ordered pizza, burger and chips. And for good measure, an ice-cream sundae with chocolate chips and grated nuts.

With my appetite sated, I felt more human, and I set off into town to buy washing essentials. While I was out, I thought I would drop by Astrid's place. I wanted to meet Pete again and have a little chat with him about ten-pence pieces. But there was nobody home.

I stocked up on my essentials and went back to the hotel. I propped myself up on the bed and surveyed the room. It was a large room with the double bed I was lying on and two single beds towards the window. Beyond that, the furniture was sparse. There was a framed print of Van Gogh's sunflowers hanging on the wall behind the beds. I gazed across at the other two beds.

They looked very empty.

I reached for the telephone. Who to call? Sam had changed the number of the flat. Sam's mother must know, but would she tell me? Probably not. I dialled the number anyway.

Sam's mother answered on the third ring, "Hello?"

"Hello, Mrs Fortescue?"

"Yes, who is that?"

Why hadn't I thought this through better? "It's… err… Selwyn!" I offered. "You know, your son!" That didn't seem to be quite as convincing as I'd hoped.

"Anthony? Is that you? Why are you trying to confuse me?"

"I'm sorry, Mrs Fortescue." Twenty years of marriage and I still had to call her Mrs Fortescue. "I thought you might not talk to me."

"Well, you thought right! You're a cad and a scoundrel! I knew this was going to happen from the day Samantha brought you home. But did she listen to me? That nice Martin Braithwaite was courting her, you know."

"Do you have her new number?" I knew I was pushing my luck.

"She doesn't want to talk to you. I've sent her away to Chapney's Health Farm to recover."

"What about the children? Can I talk to them?"

"Don't be ridiculous! They're in a state of shock!" The line went dead.

This was not the way I would have chosen to do things, but neither was I heart-broken at the way things had turned out. I missed the kids, but I had surprised myself by how little I was missing Sam. It was as if a smothering blanket had been lifted. I felt as determined as ever to press forward with my 'Brave New Beginning'.

I clicked the television set on. The local news was doing a piece on a suspected arson case at a holiday cottage. I quickly changed the channel.

Chapter 10

Channel Four were showing the 'Great Escape' again. It had always been one of my favourite films, but today it seemed to take on special significance.

When the film had finished, I headed off into town once more. I was feeling peckish, and I'd decided that I might as well eat in the Cafe Oceanic as anywhere else. I certainly wasn't going to brave the children's tea party again.

I saw Astrid the moment I stepped inside the Cafe. She was busy gathering up crockery. She saw me come in and motioned me towards a corner table. I looked and saw Pete and another youth sat there. It was where I'd seen these two at on the first day I'd visited this place. I wandered over and joined them.

"Hey man!" Pete said, as I sat down. "That was a long phone call!"

"Yes, I've been wanting to talk to you about that."

"Hey, chill, the money's yours."

"Well it certainly wasn't yours!"

Astrid slid into the seat next to mine. "Have you met Woody?" she asked nodding at the other man.

Woody gave me a big grin. The gaps in his teeth made his mouth look like castle battlements. He had shoulder length straggly blonde hair and a weathered face that made it almost impossible to guess at his age. But he was certainly not as young as I had first thought. He held his hand flat in the air. There was an uncomfortable pause until I'd figured out that he was waiting for a high-five. I obliged.

"Yow!" He said then returned his attention to his plate of chips.

I looked back at Pete. "Those ten pence pieces you lent me, just where did they come from?"

"Hey what is this? I lend you some money, and you want to know its history?"

"No, just curious. I got picked up by the police."

"Way to go, man! Who was that? Old Tree Lugger I suppose? You'll have to watch out for him. Always there to stop you turning a penny, he is."

"It all depends on whose pennies you're turning I suppose."

"Tony's a stockbroker," Astrid interrupted in a blatant attempt to change the subject.

"Parasites," Pete announced.

Woody looked up from his chips, "Where?"

"Not on you, Woody," Astrid said. "Don't worry, no need for the Borax again just yet."

"Whoa, that was close," Woody said, without looking up. He had a sort of mid-Atlantic accent.

"What do you mean, parasites?" I asked. Although I was intending to leave that life behind, I still felt somewhat affronted.

"I've got to get back to work," Astrid said. "Tony, do want anything to eat or drink?"

"Yes, what do you have?"

"Baked potatoes?"

"Of course. Any cheese?"

"If you like!"

"And a coffee, please?"

She picked up her pad and disappeared into the kitchen.

"What do you mean, parasites?" I asked Pete.

"Well, what does a stockbroker actually do? He doesn't make anything, does he? Just moves money from one place to another and takes some of it on the way across. The money never needed to be moved in the first place."

"But if people want to own shares in a company, that's the only way to do it."

"These people don't want to own shares in a company. They're not interested in what the company does, or makes, they just want to make money off the back of it. Stockbrokers, insurance companies, bankers, parasites the lot of them. None of them make anything. None of them create anything. They all just move a bit of money from one place to another then stand there with their hands out."

I felt there should be a simple counter to this challenge, but it was eluding me at the moment.

Woody swivelled round in his chair and leant against the wall, "I had parasites once."

"Yes, we know, Woody," Pete said.

"Ugly mothers. Too many legs."

"Yes, we do know that. You gave them to half the town."

"But without stockbrokers," I'd thought of my counter. "Companies wouldn't be able to expand. They wouldn't be able to find the money.

"Of course they would," Pete said. "It would be a little bit harder for the investors, that's all. They'd actively have to seek out a company to invest in. But that would mean they'd do some homework. They'd end up investing in a company they had an interest in. Not just somewhere that looked like turning in a fast profit and then bailing out again."

"Yes, but look. If say I want to invest in, I don't know, say Microsoft—"

"Hey, why would you want to invest in Microsoft? Do you know how to programme computers?"

"No, but that's not the point—"

"Of course it's the point. If you don't know anything about computers, why do want to own part of a company that makes a living out of programming them?"

I was stumbling for an answer that didn't include the word 'profit'. Astrid saved the day by returning with my potato and coffee.

"Do you know, man?" Woody said. "They've got computers that can watch you every minute of the day? Even do your shopping for you! It really blows me away!"

I was beginning to think that Woody was one sandwich short of a picnic.

"Who got him started on computers?" Astrid asked.

"Our banker friend here." Pete smiled.

"I am not a banker! Banking's different.

"Woody's got a thing about computers," Astrid said. "Best avoid the subject if you can."

I started into the potato. It was quite delicious. Astrid disappeared again to attend to two business types sitting at a nearby table.

"So," I said to Pete. "What do you do, then?"

"Me? I am an entrepreneur. Bit of this, bit of that. But always ethical."

"What's ethical about stuffing up the coin return slot in phone boxes?"

"Hey, look, British Telecom was stolen from the people originally. Now they exploit their monopoly position on the land-lines to make over a million pounds profit every minute."

"Yes, but you're not stealing from British Telecom are you? You're taking the money from the people that lose it in the telephone box."

"Only temporarily."

I had to manipulate hot cheese around my mouth before I said, "What?"

"Well, what do people do when they lose money in a phone box? They ring up the operator and complain! And what does British Telecom do? They send them a voucher, usually for more than the amount of money they actually lost as a sign of good will. So who loses? The person who put their money in made a profit, British Telecom gained some good PR and I get ten pence! I fact, I come out the worst-off out of all!"

I had to marvel at his logic. That was the second time in the last few minutes he'd managed to tie me up like this.

Woody slowly drew himself to his feet. He was surprisingly tall.

"Whoa, man! I have got to go. The angel will be dry."

The angel? I thought. Does everybody talk in riddles around here?

Pete noticed my puzzled expression. "He paints. He's got a little studio just back from the sea front."

"What sort of things does he paint?"

"Dragons, unicorns, angels, he does a nice line in tobacco tins as well." He gave a big smile. I realised now why Astrid had started talking to me that day. She had recognised one of Woody's tins.

Pete stood up. "I've got to go and do my rounds. Catch you later." And off he went.

I finished my potato and sat back enjoying the feeling of not having to do very much or be anywhere. I suppose eventually I was going to have to find myself some work and a flat. But for the moment, there was no hurry. Astrid made frequent visits to my table when her duties allowed. We chatted in short snatches and made arrangements to meet later.

I made my way back to the hotel intending to have a quiet drink in the bar. But I quickly abandoned that idea the moment I set foot in the place. The hotel lounge bar was awash with children. There was a noise reminiscent of a jumbo-jet taking off as the children thrilled to the delights of Uncle Tom and his 'Amazing Punch and Judy show'. I was definitely going to have to find a different hotel.

Astrid finished work at ten p.m. and we had arranged to meet at the 'Slipway', a small seafront pub. The lights from across the bay twinkled on the water. We sat at a wooden table outside and watched the fishing boats coming in.

I had begun to wonder where I was with Astrid. Was this a relationship? I certainly wasn't going to ask because I was as sure as hell I wouldn't understand the answer. She didn't seem to be involved with anybody else. It was clear that neither Pete nor Woody figured on that level. I was used to putting things into nice tidy boxes. This box has relationships in it, that box doesn't. But nothing about Astrid or her friends seemed to want to fit into any of the boxes in my mental filing system. I should probably just go with the flow and see where I ended up.

"So," Astrid said. "What are you going to do now then, Tony?"

"Well, I suppose at some stage I'm going to have to find myself a flat and a job. It might as well be around here as anywhere." In truth, I was growing rather attached to St Ives. It had a sort of leisurely, laid-back feel about it and seemed good for my soul.

"Not much call for stockbrokers around St Ives. Have you given this any thought?"

"I told Sam that I wanted to run a lobster boat. I don't know where that idea came from, but it's been growing on me ever since."

"I expect the idea has been there for a long time. You've just been suppressing it. If it's what your spirit is telling you to do, then you must do it."

This looked like it was turning into one of those weird conversations again so I tried to head it off.

"What's with Woody? Is he American?"

"We think so."

I should have known that there would be no simple answer to even that question.

"Huh?"

"Well, as far as we know, he arrived in this country just in time for the 1970 Isle of Wight Rock Festival. He had been to Woodstock the year before. That was how he got the name Woody, it was all he ever talked about. After the festival finished, he just stayed. He seemed to have left most of his brain at Woodstock, probably took the brown acid! Then he cemented in the damage at the Isle of Wight. So even he's not quite sure where he comes from any more."

I was doing some quick mental calculations. That must put his age close to mine! Quite a thought.

"So, what's his real name?"

"We don't know. Not even sure he does any more. He's been Woody for so long."

"How long have you lived in St Ives?"

"About twenty years. As soon as I left school I came down here on holiday with my friends. My first taste of freedom. I liked it, and I stayed."

My mental calculator was working again. This would put her in her mid thirties! At least ten years older than I thought she was! What was going on here? Was the spring of eternal youth located around here somewhere? If so, lead me to it. I noticed that she was watching me. She had a mischievous grin on her face.

"I'm twenty-five."

"But... You said..."

"Yes, I know. I decided to stop getting older at twenty-five. I liked that age, and I stayed there. Come on," she said. "We'd better get you back to the hotel, or you'll miss the bedtime story."

Chapter 11

The following morning I was called by reception, who informed me there was a courier waiting for me in the lobby. It was my replacement American Express card. I was human again. Once more I was a person with an identity.

I headed into town; Woody intrigued me and I wanted to visit his studio. It took me a while to find it, tucked away as it was in a shopping arcade that appeared to have once been a warehouse. Woody sat at the back of the shop reading a comic.

"Hi, Woody!" I said.

"Whoa! Hey, Johnny. Cool."

"Tony," I corrected.

"Yeah, right. Well, you know these things."

"Thought I'd drop by to see some of your work."

"Where?"

"Here. Your work." I pointed to his paintings.

"Oh, hey, I did those!" He looked pleased with himself.

I looked around the shop. His paintings were quite spectacular. Warriors on horseback riding through the clouds, maidens rising up from misty lakes and an ethereal goddess in amongst the stars gazing wistfully at Atlas shouldering the globe. The colours were vibrant and seemed to reach towards me in an almost tangible manner. In other corners of the shop was a selection of painted natural slate, incredibly detailed bead necklaces and various painted tobacco tins.

"They're fantastic, Woody."

"What are?"

"The paintings. Do you sell many?"

"Too many."

"What?"

"I don't like selling them. But Astrid says I must."

I thought about that for a moment. But I couldn't quite see the connection, so I decided not to pursue it.

"Where do you get your ideas from?"

"Out there!" He pointed through the shop doorway. "It's what I see. It's all there, man."

I should have seen that one coming.

Woody returned to his comic. I was leaving the shop when I noticed an interesting display in the next door window. There was a white porcelain figure about two feet high, it was covered in a series of lines with Chinese symbols at each intersection. Candles of various colours and an assortment of bottles containing different coloured liquids surrounded it.

I ventured inside. The smell of burning incense was almost overpowering. Bamboo wind chimes tinkled as I passed. I held them gently in my hand to stop the noise. Another one of life's little mysteries. People move to the countryside to escape the noise and then they hang up wind chimes all over the place.

A youngish, oriental looking man stepped round from behind the counter to greet me.

"Ah! Come, come." He wore a brightly coloured, wide sleeved robe. His waist length black hair was tied back in a loose ponytail. "So, you come at last."

"Huh?"

"I thought you must come yesterday."

"I think you've got me confused with somebody else."

"No! No! Not wrong. You!" He stood in front of me, bowed his head slightly, and made a circular gesture with his arms indicating that I should follow. "I feel big disturbance. No good you not come yesterday. Make work harder. The disturbance you feel, make big waves."

This was strange. Perhaps he... No... He couldn't...

"You feel your spirit becomes weak. Not worthy of battle you face."

This was uncanny.

"Look, how do you... Are you sure you haven't..."

"No time questions. Your chi has big disruption. Too many choices. You must rebalance. Yin yang. Why you not make choice? Why you put off? Bad for spirit."

This was quite unnerving. He led me to the back of the shop and sat me down at a small wooden table. He sat opposite and took hold of my right hand. He studied it carefully, probing around the wrist.

"Your warmer meridian is blocked. Your spirit wants one thing, your head challenges. Is causing dis-balance. You must release flow. When flow released, way become clear."

"How do I release the flow?" I was astounded. It was like he could reach straight into my head. He seemed to know exactly what I was feeling.

"You must take the juice of the crushed juniper berry, then soak it in fermented spirits of the grain."

"Do you have any of that?"

"Wait. I look see."

He stood up, and rummaged through an assortment of bottles that filled several shelves at the back of the shop. He was muttering to himself as he searched.

"Very rare, very rare. Not often get this."

I was so engrossed in what he was doing I hadn't heard the shop door open.

"That will do, Charlie," Astrid said.

I turned to see her standing in the shop doorway.

"Put him down," she continued. "He's a friend, not a punter."

I looked back towards Charlie. His serene inscrutable expression had gone and had been replaced by an annoyed frown.

"Oh, hi Astrid," he said. All trace of his heavy, almost impenetrable oriental accent was gone and had been replaced by a distinctly London tone. "Oh sod it, Astrid! I haven't had a decent punter all day. I thought I was in here."

I turned to Astrid.

"What?"

"Hi, Tony. What was he going to sell you?"

"I need my chi unblocking. Juniper berries soaked in grain alcohol."

She looked at Charlie. "Oh really, Charlie. That's taking the piss. Juniper berries in alcohol?" She looked at me. "Think about it, Tony."

I thought. But I couldn't see what she was driving at.

"Gin," she said. "Gin, you cloth-head. He was going to sell you a tiny bottle of gin. And probably at an outrageous price."

"What? But he knew about my decisions. It was like he could see inside of me."

"Oh yes, he's good. Aren't you, Charlie?" Astrid gave Charlie a big smile.

Charlie put on his best inscrutable expression again. "Just poor humble China-man."

"Woody told me you'd been in, so I thought you might fall into Charlie's clutches."

I looked back at Charlie. I didn't want to let this go, just yet.

"But you do know things? You can do this stuff? Can't you? That yin and yang thing?"

"Sorry, mate," he said and shrugged his shoulders. "All guesswork."

"You should consider yourself lucky, Tony."

"Why?"

"Well, you were going to get gin. Usually all his punters get is a little plastic bag of dried twigs and a couple of stones."

"Hey, I was feeling generous. He looked like he could use a drink."

I felt like one to. I couldn't believe I'd been taken in so easily.

"What about all this stuff in here?" I looked round the shop of. Books, candles and incense jammed every corner of the place. "Any of this real?"

"I don't know. I get it wholesale."

"He does a nice line in Feng Shui as well. Don't you, Charlie?"

"Just one of my many talents." He smiled

"For two hundred and fifty quid a he'll come round your house, plant a tree in your lounge and rearrange all of your furniture."

"Hey, don't knock it. Got to keep those channels clear!"

"The only clearing that interests you, is how quickly their cheques clear."

Charlie feigned an expression of deep hurt. "Oh, Astrid you do me wrong."

"I have to go," Astrid said. "I only popped out to get some bread rolls from the bakery."

"I'll give you a hand," I volunteered.

As soon as we were clear of the shop, I asked Astrid, "Is he at least Chinese?"

"He's as English as you are. He's got some Chinese ancestry, and a Chinese name, but that's about it."

"Charlie?"

"No, his real name is Chou Li. Woody took to calling him Charlie and it sort of stuck."

"Is anything he does genuine?"

"Not as far as I know."

"But that's outrageous!"

"Why?"

Astrid was setting a fast pace, and my breathing was ragged.

"Well he's ripping people off." I panted.

"Only if you believe what he's doing is a fake."

"Yes, but it is!"

"That's because you know. If you don't know, then you're not being ripped off. You're buying a genuine product."

"What?"

"Let me explain." She stopped and turned to face me. "You buy a Rolex watch from a jewellers, it was reduced from a thousand pounds to five hundred. What have you got?"

"I've got a Rolex watch."

"Are you happy with it?"

"Very happy!"

"Twenty years later, the watch is still going strong and never lost a minute. Still happy with it?"

"Yes! But I don't see—"

"Hang on. Let's say you buy that same watch, same amount of money, but the next day a friend of yours tells you that the jeweller is a rogue. He tells you that the works inside the watch are just Taiwanese crap. What have you got now?"

"I've got a fake."

"Are you happy with it?"

"No! Of course not!"

"Why?"

"Well, because it's not the real thing."

"But it's the same watch you had in the last example. The one you were happy with. It's only your attitude that has changed not the watch. So where is the value? Is the value in the watch, or in your attitude?"

"You're as bad as Pete. Of course it doesn't work like that."

"Let me try it another way." She stared walking again; I had to do a little skip to catch up. "You recommend a share to somebody because you think it's going to go up. Your client buys it. Lots of other people buy, and up goes the value of the share. Is your client happy?"

"Yes, of course he is."

"And does he have value for money?"

"Yes," I couldn't quite see where this was going.

"What if the share had gone down? What is the value of your advice worth then?"

"The same! The value of my advice doesn't change."

"But you just ripped him off!"

"Of course I didn't."

"So once somebody has purchased your advice for a perceived value, you wash your hands of the results, and if their attitude shifts that doesn't matter to you?"

"No! It's not like that. It's... No... I don't know. You lot are doing my head in."

"Here's the bakery. You can give me a hand to carry them."

I'd very kindly offered to carry the whole lot before I realised how many there were and that the journey to the Cafe was uphill all the way.

"At least Woody's got some genuine talent." I said. I needed to score at least one point here.

"Has he?" Astrid challenged.

"What do you mean?"

"Again, it's just your perception. His talent has value because you like what you see. If you didn't like it, would it still have value? And if it didn't have this value, would he then be conning you."

The combination of the sack of bread-rolls and the steep climb forestalled any further conversation. But I thought about what she'd said; these guys were living on their wits. They had no job security, no pensions. But on the other hand they were never going to be bounced out of work on the whim of one individual who had taken a dislike to them. I'd started wondering about my own situation again. I really didn't want to go back to an office. But the lobster boat just seemed like a pipe dream. Somewhere inside me something panicked and told me I should really go and throw myself on Grahame's mercy to plead for my job back. Or ring up Sam and beg her to ask for Selwyn's help.

I squashed that little part of me with my mental size ten.

I left Astrid at the Cafe, and headed back to the hotel. I tried to ring Sam again, but the number was still unobtainable. Directory enquiries informed me that the number had been changed and that it was now unlisted. It was probably just as well, as I really hadn't got a clue what I would have said to her.

I was feeling slightly peckish so I decided to go down to the hotel restaurant to see what was on offer. I chose chicken dinosaurs with clown-shaped potatoes, and jelly and ice cream to follow.

As I was leaving the hotel that afternoon, I noticed my legs were aching quite badly from all the walking. It was time I either got fit or got some sort of transport. I settled for transport.

A nice little run-about, that's what I needed. Something economical to run, and easy to park.

Two hours later I was the proud owner of a slightly used camper van. I think I'd always secretly hankered after one of these ever since I'd first seen Alice's Restaurant. Of course, they've come on a lot since then. My new possession boasted three foldaway beds, a cooker, fridge, television, and even a satellite dish.

There was something romantic about the idea of being able to just up and go whenever the fancy took you. I could travel the world in this, or so the man at the showroom had told me. It had a heating system that would keep me warm in the Arctic and an air conditioner that could bring icicles to my hair in the Sahara. He'd been very helpful and even thrown in a full tank of petrol. Now all I needed was somewhere to park it.

I found a Camper Park at the northern end of town that claimed to offer 'Plentiful facilities'. I chose a site under some trees and hooked up to the electricity. I tested the cooker, the TV and all of the other bits and pieces. Everything seemed to work fine. Then I unhooked and went back to the hotel to check out and collect my things. I settled the bill with my shiny new American Express card then drove off into the sunset. Well, late afternoon smog anyway.

That evening, in the Camper Park bar, I met Maurice and Ivy. They told me they'd been coming here for twenty-three years. I asked them why, and they explained to me that it was the most wonderful place in the Southwest of England. I took up their kind offer to show me the highlights of the site. We looked at the outdoor swimming pool complete with floating deck chair. We looked at the children's climbing frame, and they showed me the 'Well equipped' recreation lounge complete with a pinball machine, space invaders and a foosball table.

We went back into the bar in time for the evening's bingo session. They were wearing matching jumpers, and I felt somewhat out of place, although I don't think they minded. They were too busy trying to win the big one. Tonight's jackpot, eighteen pounds and a bottle of sherry.

I made my excuses and retired to my camper.

An island of sanity in an insane world.

Chapter 12

The following morning, I went into town and bought every imaginable gadget. I bought a compass, an indoor/outdoor thermometer, a police radar detector, a gimballed drinks holder so that I wouldn't spill my cup of tea when taking corners at sixty mph, and a gadget that could tell me where I was on the planet to within three feet. I think when I bought that last item, I may have been being a bit optimistic in my roaming potential. But it had lots of flashing lights and made an interesting beeping noise when it locked onto a satellite. I was a sucker for flashing lights and beeping noises.

I stopped off at the café on the way back. Only Pete was there. He waved a tired hand when he saw me.

"Yo, Tony!"

"Hi Pete," I said and sat down at the same table.

"Been shopping again?" He nodded towards my bag. "Hope you've got some money left, I've been looking for you."

"Oh, really?" I was suspicious. I had the measure of Pete by now, and I wasn't about to fall for one of his scams.

"I kept one of these back for you." He pulled a cellular phone from his rucksack. He took it from the box and passed it to me.

"What makes you think I need one of these?"

"Well, if you're going to travel around now you can't very well get Telecom to hook you up, can you?"

He had a point there.

"Where did you get this from?" I was still suspicious.

"I had a batch of them. They've been re-chipped."

"Huh?"

"They're last year's models but with an updated chip inside. Teenagers don't want something that looks like last year, so the firms dump them cheap. I just got lucky, and I wanted to share my good fortune with you!"

Sam had always been dead-set against these. She always insisted that mobile phones gave you brain cancer or turned the user into a gibbering idiot.

I parted with another twenty quid.

All I needed now was somebody to telephone.

It was lunchtime before I returned to the campsite. I settled down in my deckchair to fiddle with my new toys. I had just started to enter the numbers into my phone when it started playing Mozart 40 at me. I answered it, and a man's voice spoke.

"Hello, is Cindy there?"

"No," I said. "I think you have—"

"Will she be free in about half an hour?"

"I don't know. I think you might—"

"Tell her Bob will be round anyway."

The line went dead.

Great, I thought. First time my new toy gets used, and it's for a wrong number.

I sat back once more to read the instruction book. It explained how I could customise the menu and move the items around in the order I wanted them. I tried to follow the instructions and instantly the whole display turned into German, a language that I don't speak with any more fluency than eighteenth century Mandarin. As it was no longer possible to read where I was in the endless maze of menus and sub-menus, I couldn't find out how to turn it back into English. I decided that on my next visit into town, I would have to buy an English/German dictionary. I put the phone to one side.

I relaxed back and closed my eyes. The sun beat down on my face warming me through. It was then that I noticed the enticing aroma of barbecuing sausages. I sat up and looked around. It seemed that outside of every camper-van there was a barbecue going. They ranged from fairly sophisticated gas affairs to little single ring burners. Here was something I'd neglected! How had I overlooked that?

Another journey into town.

I was beginning to realise the disadvantage of having a camper van. The fact that even if I wanted to pop down to the shops for even a packet of sugar I had to take my home with me. I would have to give that some thought.

I found a camping supplies shop where a very helpful salesmen introduced me to a state-of-the-art gas barbecue. I had never realised that these things could be so sophisticated. This had four burners that could combine to roast a pig if necessary. It had an electric rotisserie, a built-in drinks dispenser, and a remote control so that I could ignite it from the comfort of my deckchair. And of course it had lots of flashing lights and made a pleasant beeping noise when you switched it on.

I had just handed over my American Express card when my phone started playing Mozart again.

"Hello," I said.

"Hello, can I a book a session with Cindy please?"

"No you've got—"

"Does she still do B.S.M.?"

"B.S.M.?" I queried.

"Bondage. Does she still do bondage?"

"No! There's nobody here does bondage or S.M," I said. "I think you've got—"

"Sorry." The line went dead.

I puzzled over this for a moment then looked up to see the salesman staring at me, his jaw hanging loose and eyes open wide.

"Wrong number," I explained.

"Of course," he said and nodded in a knowing fashion.

I stopped off at the Cafe for something to eat. Pete and Woody were at their usual table. As I sat down I had an idea.

"I am having a barbecue tonight," I announced.

"Hey, cool," said Pete.

"I thought it would be nice if we all got together. Something to eat and a drink or two."

"What are you cooking, man?" Woody asked.

I hadn't thought about that. Sausages seemed a bit mean. Then a thought struck me.

"I'm going to roast a pig!"

Finding a pig was not quite as easy as I had thought it would be. The local supermarket stocked nothing larger than a family size pack of pork chops. There was a fair sized leg of lamb in a nearby compartment, and I was just toying with the idea of going for that when my phone rang again. Someone wanted to know would Cindy punish him if he brought his schoolboy uniform along.

A rather prim looking lady standing nearby gave me a scornful look as I tried to explain to the caller that schoolboy uniform or no, Cindy would not be punishing him today. As I switched off the phone, she gave an audible tut. I gave her a big smile in return.

I had another prod at the leg of lamb and decided it wasn't quite the thing and went in search of a more traditional butcher.

I found one nearby and explained that I was looking for a pig to barbecue. He took me through to the cold room and told me I could choose. I had never seen a whole dead pig before and hadn't realised quite how big it would be. Even given the size of my new barbecue, there was no way one of these things was going to fit onto it. I was beginning to think that the man in the camping supplies shop had been a bit prone to exaggeration.

"Do you have any smaller pigs?"

"No, that's the size they come. I can do you a suckling if you like?"

"What's a suckling?"

"A baby pig, of course!"

That seemed unfair. The thought of roasting a baby pig was somehow uncivilised.

"No thanks."

"I could do you a quarter?"

That would be more like it. I tried to visualise a quarter of a pig. That should fit.

"Okay," I said.

He asked me to wait outside in the shop as he went to work with his cleaver.

While I was waiting, my phone gave a little squelching noise. I looked at the display. Very helpfully, it informed me that, Aufladen jetzt'. I hadn't the faintest idea what that meant.

The butcher reappeared with a polythene sack with my quarter of a pig inside it. I paid him, lugged the thing over to my camper van and set off back to the site.

I quickly discovered that my pig wouldn't fit inside the small camper fridge. The only thing I could think of doing was to slide it underneath the vehicle in its plastic bag. That was the coolest place available. I set up the barbecue as best as I could, following the Pidgin English instructions. By the time I'd finished putting it together, I had three pieces left over that didn't seem to fit anywhere.

Keen to try out my new acquisition I placed three sausages on the rack and pressed the remote control button. The flames leapt up from underneath with a big whumph. Within three seconds, the sausages had turned into little black twigs. I was going to have to learn to control this a bit better if I was to successfully barbecue my pig

My phone repeated its little squelching noise. The screen reminded me it was still Aufladen jetzt'.

I checked the instruction book for the barbecue in order to find out how to regulate the flames. The closest I could get to it, was the section that said, "The gyration of spigot 'A' in the order of the clock will give augmentation of hotness and degradation when inverted." I couldn't quite figure out what spigot 'A' was, but it looked suspiciously similar to one of the pieces that I had left over.

Try as I might I couldn't find a home for spigot 'A'. Oh well, not too much harm done. I guess the pig will just cook a bit faster that's all.

I went across to the campsite shop to buy some bread, potatoes and wine. The bread and potatoes were fine, but the shop assistant informed me they were not licensed to sell alcohol, though there was an off-licence about a mile up the road.

Damn it! I was running out of time. I wanted to get the barbecue well under way before they arrived. I would have to rush to the off-licence. I jumped in the camper van and started the engine. I had just begun to roll forward when I felt a large bump. I stopped and thought for a moment, and then remembered the pig. I'd just run over the bloody pig.

I jumped out of the vehicle ran round to the back to survey the damage. The polythene sack had split open. One end of the pig was squashed flat and had been driven into the ground. Bits of blood and polythene dangled from the wheel arch. It looked like something out of a John Carpenter movie.

I checked my watch. It was 6.00 PM. There was no way I was going to be able to replace this tonight, I'd just have to make the best of a bad job. I'd deal with it later. I dumped the remains of the mangled pig into the back of the camper and set off once more for the off licence.

By the time I came out of the off licence, a group of dogs had collected around the camper. They were showing great interest in the rear offside wheel. The leader appeared to be a big black Doberman. He growled as I approached. I quickly ran round to the passenger side and jumped in, slamming the door shut behind me. As I set off down the road, the dogs started following, and I had to get up to 30 mph before I finally lost them.

I was about half way back to the campsite when Mozart started playing from my jacket pocket. I nearly ended up in the ditch as I struggled to answer the phone. Driving with my knees, I stabbed at the answer button.

"Yes!" I shouted.

"Err... Hello... Erm... Is Cindy there?"

"No, Cindy is bloody well not here! I don't know any Cindy, and I have no desire to ever meet Cindy. Cindy has gone. She doesn't want to tie you up any more, and she doesn't want to play schoolboys."

I jabbed the 'off' button. The phone squelched at me, informed me 'Energie niedriges Abschalten', and then promptly switched itself off. I wound down the window, and threw it out.

By the time I'd returned I had precisely half an hour to get the meat cooked. As I lifted the remains of the pig out of the back of the camper van another piece fell off onto the floor with a loud thud. I looked at it despairingly. I only had one spit and now two pieces of meat. I decided to leave it there, we'd just have to have smaller portions.

I set the spit at the highest possible level to give the pig a fighting chance of being roasted instead of incinerated, in the absence of spigot 'A'. I stood back and hit the remote control button. The barbecue burst into life and the flames leapt skywards engulfing the ever-dwindling piece of meat. There was a loud sizzling sound, and I jumped back. I tried to reach forward to turn it off, but I was driven back by the heat. My piece of pork was beyond saving now. All I could do was sit and watch helplessly as the once magnificent side of pork turned into something resembling a piece of coal

"Hello, old man! Having a spot of bother?"

I turned to see Maurice with a fire extinguisher in his hands.

"Erm, yes."

He pointed the nozzle at my barbecue and pulled the lever. Within an instant, the flames were out. He reached forward to turn the valve off.

"Aha! I see you've gone for the Thunderer 5,000. Great machine! I had one of these, but I've moved up to the 6,000 now. It's got an integral plate warmer, you know."

"Good," I said.

"Here's your trouble." He peered at the machine. "You haven't got spigot 'A' on. No wonder you were having trouble controlling it. Here, let me do this."

He removed spigot 'A' from the little plastic bag full of excess parts and instantly clicked it into place on the front of the barbecue. "There you go! That will do it, now!"

He re-lit the barbecue and demonstrated that by the judicious gyration of spigot 'A' in the order of the clock he could give augmentation of hotness and degradation when inverted.

"Thanks, Maurice. Can I offer you a drink?"

"No thanks, must get back. A group of us are playing twister. Come and join us if you like!"

"Er, no thanks. I've got some people coming shortly." The thought of playing twister with Maurice and Ivy was too horrible to contemplate.

Maurice wandered off with his fire extinguisher, and I headed for the door of my camper van to retrieve the last piece of meat that I'd remembered dropping earlier. As I stepped inside, I heard a loud growl.

I froze.

The Doberman from the off-licence sat in the middle of the floor with the piece of meat between his paws. He looked up at me, his eyes narrowed, and he gave another grumble. He pulled his lips so far back that I could count every one of his teeth. Had I so desired.

"Good boy," I said. "Good boy." I backed slowly out of the door and slammed it shut behind me.

I ran across to the camp shop and bought two packets of sausages. Mean or not, it was the only option left. I hurriedly threw them onto the wire griddle, pressed the button on the remote control and turned spigot 'A'. The flames spluttered and popped a few times and then died.

The gas cylinder was empty.

Chapter 13

The pizza deliveryman arrived at the same time as Astrid, Pete and Woody. Woody looked at the pile of Domino's pizza boxes.

"Hey, flat pig! Cool!"

"What happened to the spit-roast, Tony?" Astrid asked.

"I had a little bit of trouble with the barbecue."

"Hey, man," Pete said. "I've got some wine here. Fridge inside, is it?"

"Oh, yes." I suddenly remembered Cerberus. "No!"

"Okay, where do you keep your fridge then?"

"Yes, the fridge is in there. But there's a wild dog in there as well."

"Oh, Tony!" said Astrid. "You've got a dog. How lovely! Let me have a look?"

"No. It's a stray. It's wild. It tried to kill me earlier."

Astrid had started towards the camper door, but hesitated at my warning.

"What sort of dog is it?"

"It's a Doberman or a Rottweiler. Not sure, one of those killer dogs anyway."

"Why did you lock a savage dog in your camper?"

"I think it was hunting for food. It sneaked up on me and tried to attack me. I managed to lock it in there. It might even be rabid."

Astrid moved tentatively towards the door. She raised herself on her toes so she could look through the window.

"I'd be careful," I warned. "He's probably strong enough to burst through.

The face of Cerberus leapt up at the window just as Astrid was peering in. She jumped back with a little, "Oh!"

The wolfhound-from-hell barked fiercely.

Astrid once more ventured towards the door. "Oh, Tony! He's cute. It's a Labrador I think."

Before I could move to stop her, she'd opened the door. The dog leapt up at her, and she knelt down to greet it. It licked her face furiously between excited barks.

"Oh, isn't he cute?"

"Whoa, man. I had a dog once," said Woody.

"What happened to it?" Pete asked.

"They took it away from me. The queen wanted it back."

There was silence for a moment as all three of us stared at Woody. Each of us tried in our own way to come to terms with his latest revelation. It appeared that we all came to a similar conclusion.

"Got a corkscrew?" Pete asked as he waved the bottle of wine in my direction.

Oh dear, that was another one of life's little essentials I'd forgotten. I explained that we appeared to be one corkscrew short at the moment. Along with plates or anything to sit on. But I did have a choice of 108 different television channels to choose from and a gadget that would see me across the Amazon jungle without any trouble at all.

Pete gave me a demonstration of how to remove the cork from a bottle by using a piece of string. I was genuinely impressed; I had never seen anything like that before.

We sat down on the grass and set about the pizzas and wine. The dog lay snuggled up alongside Astrid. She stroked it and fed it pieces of pizza. I felt a pang of jealousy. We finished the pizza, and it wasn't long before the inevitable joint was being passed around again. The more I smoked and drank the more comfortable the ground became.

Night settled over the site, and one by one the stars took up their positions. All around us were the sounds of social chatter permeated the warm evening. Barbecues burned in front of every camper.

"So," said Pete. "How are you enjoying your new-found freedom?"

"I have to say, I'm happier than I have been for a long time. Further back than I can remember, in fact. It's just a shame that I'm going to have to give some of my freedom up to find a job."

"Why?"

"Well, I'm going to need some sort of income."

"Yeah, sure. We all need money, but why a job?"

Oh no, it was going to be one of those conversations again. There was obviously a clever answer to this that I was missing.

"Well, how am I supposed to get an income? I'm sure those phone boxes of yours don't keep you going completely. You must have another source of money?"

"Yeah, I have got several."

"Well, there you go."

"But none of them involves a job." He propped himself up on one elbow. "The tools to money are all out there. You just have to know which buttons to press."

"For instance?" I sat up and took another sip from the bottle as Astrid passed it to me.

"Take car parks," Pete said. "They can be a nice little earner if you use them properly."

In my mind, car parks had always been someplace where I paid out money. It was only the local councils that seemed to make any profit. Unless of course, you set up a hotdog stand in the corner of one of them. But that still looked like a job.

"Go on then," I challenged. "How do you make money out of a car park?"

"Right, but this is mine, right? I mean, I don't want you taking over my car parks or anything. If you want to run this, you move somewhere else, okay?"

"Agreed."

"I cruise the car parks two or three times a day. I have these things printed up by the hundred." He passed me a scrap of paper that looked as if it had been torn from a larger sheet. It was about two inches square and contained what appeared to be a hand-written note that said, "I noticed your time was out and the inspector was getting close so I booked 25p into the machine for you. If you feel like reimbursing me, my address is..."

"So, you put a twenty five pence ticket on a car. All I see is that so far you are down twenty-five pence with a remote chance of getting it back again. Doesn't seem like much of an income to me."

"But don't you see, Tony," Pete said. "It's perceived value. The fine in these car parks is fifty pounds. That's what I've just saved them. And nobody's going to write a cheque for twenty-five pence, are they? So, they either do nothing, which is extremely rare, or the more usual amount they send is ten pounds. And I do this some twenty times a day."

"You get much from this?"

"On a good week, I can collect two or three hundred quid"

"What!" I thought back to Astrid's conversation earlier. She was right it was all about perceived value. The drivers were saving forty pounds even if they paid Pete a tenner. The only people losing were the car parks. I realised now what he had meant the other day when he'd said he was off to 'do his rounds'.

"So, you have any other scams?"

"Of course, but I don't call them scams. Income opportunities." He laughed.

Astrid sat forward and pulled her legs up underneath her. "You've got to be thinking seriously about doing something though, Tony. Make this world work for you, instead of against you all the time. Why don't you make a list of the things that you can do well? Then we'll help you find a way of making money at it."

That should be a short list.

"I can do fire walking," offered Woody. "The Lamas in Tibet showed me how to do it." He paused for so long that Astrid looked just about to say something when he continued. "All to do with making yourself lighter." He stopped again, and we waited for a bit longer this time just to make sure he'd finished.

"I know a bit about the money markets, but that's about all," I said. "I don't see how I can make any money out of that without winding up back in a stockbroker's office again."

"Okay," said Pete. "Let's explore that avenue a minute." He sat forward. His eyes gleamed. It seemed I had sparked his entrepreneurial instincts. "The key to a good income, is lots of little bits of money from lots of people. Rather than one big bit from one place. Agreed?"

"Yes, I suppose that makes sense."

"Right, so what does Joe Punter want from the stock market?"

"He wants to make a profit by buying shares and then having them increase in value."

"Okay, so what makes shares go up in value?"

"When the company does well, or they land a big potential order, change of management, the government—"

"Bullshit!"

"What!"

"Bullshit! Share prices do well because people talk the prices up. Or down, because people talk the prices down. Nothing to do with company profits at all. It's all perceptions. If the public thinks a company will do well, they buy the shares, which in turn forces up the price! Everything else is just window dressing. Agreed?"

"Well, I don't know... That's not quite... Well you might have a point. But that's a bit simplistic."

"This world is a lot simpler than most people realise. So is making money out of it." Pete took another long pull of the joint as it passed his way.

The sound of raucous laughter drifted across the campsite. I guessed that Maurice and Ivy's game of twister was well under way.

"How about this for an idea?" Pete said. "I give you a tip on a share on the understanding if it goes up you pay me, let's say, ten quid. But if it goes down, you owe me nothing. Sound like a deal?"

"That sounds fair. But I'm hardly likely to make much of a living at that."

"You're still missing the point, Tony," Astrid said. "Don't you see what Pete's driving at? Little bits from lots of people."

"Yes, but I can't very well stand in a car park and sell share tips, can I?"

"What about the Net?" Pete suggested.

"Huh?"

"The Net. The Internet. Sell share tips on the Internet. The stock markets are international."

"But I don't know anything about the Internet."

"You don't have to worry about that side of it. I've got a pal would look after that for you. All you have to do, is come up with some suitably impressive sounding gobbledegook to justify your 'Pick of the day'."

I thought this through for a moment. I was sure this must be full of holes.

"But it's dishonest! If I don't believe the shares going to go up, how can I sell advice?"

"Of course it's not dishonest. You're only taking money from people if the share goes up and your advice is validated. What's dishonest about that?"

"But my advice should at least be genuine."

"It will be genuine. If enough people listen to you and buy, then the price will go up, yes?"

"Yes."

"Therefore, your advice is genuine."

"How do I keep track of who's taken my advice and who owes me the money?"

"You don't. You trust in human nature. Like me with the car parks. Yes, some people will take your advice and not pay you. But there are enough honest people around who will send you the money after they've seen their shares go up. And anyway, you can always put a warning on saying they'll be refused further advice if they don't pay."

The dog gave a little snuffle and nuzzled its head more deeply onto Astrid's lap. She tickled it behind its ear. I felt jealous.

"Come on, Tony!" a voice said behind me.

Terror seized my insides and gave them a little wriggle. It was Ivy. "Why don't you bring your young friends over for a game of twister with us?"

I turned round to face her. I'm sure she must have noticed my horror. I was trapped by her gaze. The mouse hypnotised by the cobra's dance.

"Err... Umm..." was all I could think of to say even though my insides were screaming, "RUN!"

I looked around quickly at the others. I saw they were all trapped in the same force field that held me. I turned back. Maurice approached her from behind. Was he going to save us?

"You'll have to excuse my little munchkin," he said. "I'm afraid she's been on the Liebfraumilch. Come along, Ivy. I'm sure these young people don't want to be playing games with the likes of us."

"Oh, but we'd love to!"

My head span round like something out of the Exorcist to stare at Astrid. 'Traitor', I thought. I screwed up my face at her to try to convey a message of extreme distaste. I shook my head slightly and hoped that Maurice and Ivy wouldn't notice. I prayed Astrid would get the message.

"Oh lovely, that's settled then," said Ivy.

My head did another hundred and eighty-degree turn. Ivy's hand reached towards mine like some long necked monster. I wanted to cower. Suddenly, Astrid was beside me and pulling my other hand up. "Come on, Tony. It will be fun. I haven't played twister for years."

We followed them over to their camper. I felt like a child being dragged along by its mother on the way to school. By the time we had reached their camper, we had lost Woody and Pete.

There was another couple there. They appeared to be in their late fifties and wore matching shell-suits. Maurice introduced them as Cyril and Gloria. Maurice led me over to his Thunderer 6,000 and picked a perfectly cooked sausage from the griddle. He placed it with great precision into a bread roll of just the right size then handed it to me on a pre-warmed plate.

Although I'd only just finished a pizza an hour before, I was feeling hungry again. So I tore into it with enthusiasm. It was delicious. But then I'd known it would be. I made an attempt at small-talk to forestall the onset of twister, but Ivy was not going to be put off, and the inevitable moment came.

The game had its moments. At one point I found myself entwined with Astrid and my head in a very similar position to where the dog's had been earlier.

That was wonderful.

A few minutes later, I was in a similar position with Ivy. That wasn't.

Maurice was the epitome of the good host. He made sure our plates and glasses remained topped up. The more wine I drank, the more fun twister seemed to take on. Then Ivy suggested we play charades. That seemed like a wonderful idea, even though I knew I would be deeply embarrassed about all of this in the morning. I launched myself into the game with great excitement. I wasn't even fazed when I was given 'Moon over Paradour' to act out. Although I'm sure Ivy and her friends will probably still be talking about my interpretation of that one for many months to come.

I was almost disappointed when the evening wound up, and I headed back towards my camper with Astrid. Cerberus bounded up, to her as we approached. She knelt down to cuddle him.

"What are you going to do with this little fellow then?" she asked.

"I suppose I'll have to hand him into the police or something."

"Oh, can't you keep him?"

"No, he must belong to somebody."

She dipped her head and pouted. "Oh, come on. Look at him. He's got no collar, and he's got less fat on him than my little finger."

She held up her little finger for me to see. It was a lovely little finger and entirely fat-less.

"Look, I'll take him down to the police station tomorrow. If they can't find out who owns him then I'll hang onto him. Okay?"

She took hold of both of my hands, pinned them to my sides, and pressed her body against mine. Her face was only an inch away from mine. I could feel her breath. Her eyes danced across my face. Silence lay in the air and the smells of dying barbecues wafted across the site.

"You're a wonderful person, Tony."

Gradually, she brought her face closer; all the time her eyes watched mine. She was looking deep into my soul. I felt she was touching me on some hidden level. Her spirit connecting with my spirit. The contact was there; I could feel it, but I couldn't understand it. Each time I tried to bring it into focus, it disappeared. What was happening? She was bringing a part of me to life that I'd never been aware of before.

As if... As if... It was as if she had found the key to a hitherto undiscovered section of my being. An area that I'd been unaware of, but now the door was open, this other part was escaping and spreading through me. Flowing through every part of my id and bringing something to life.

Still, she watched. Still her spirit probed mine. Bringing to life new energies. Creating unknown feelings and making new connections.

She moved her face closer.

Our lips touched.

With the delicacy of a shadow, her lips moved across mine then moved on over my left cheek, leaving in their wake a little trail of fire. Her nose touched my ear. I'd never realised how sensitive ears could be before. In a whisper so quiet I wondered for a moment if I'd imagined it, she said, "This was never meant to happen."

I wasn't quite sure what she meant, and I certainly wasn't going to question her. Even if I had been capable of speech. I pressed my face against hers. Another connection completed. I was being drawn into her, a piece at a time

I broke my hands free from hers and encircled her waist, pulling her closer. Her lips came back seeking mine. They were firmer this time, more urgent. More demanding. Our mouths were open, our tongues flickered together, dancing like fireflies, giving off sparks when they touched. My body was alive with strange sensations as Astrid touched me on every level, from the deepest part of my being to the tiniest cell on my hyper-sensitised skin.

She pushed me back gently and looked at me as if seeing me for the first time.

"What happened?" she asked.

"I don't know." Whether we were talking about the same thing, I had no way of knowing.

Her hands reached about the back of my head and pulled me towards her. I let mine move down across her back and gently onto those perfect, denim clad spheres that had first drawn my attention to her. She pressed forward with her groin, and I responded by pulling tighter.

Her hands left my head and slid down to rest on my hips. She pulled them towards her then relaxed before pulling again. Rhythmically, pulling and releasing. I slid my hands underneath her T-shirt and across her back. Her flesh was hot and slightly moist. I moved up to her shoulder blades. There was no bra-strap to impede my progress. Her hands left my hips, and I felt her tugging at my belt. I breathed in slightly to make it easier for her. The tightness around my waist suddenly disappeared as the tops of my trousers came undone. I ran my right fingers down her spine, and my forefinger found the groove in the top of her buttocks. I stroked gently. The movement of her hips matched my stroking. I felt the night air on my legs as my jeans dropped away, and I realised we were still outside. Although it didn't seem to matter any more. There was probably nobody about anyway.

116

I ran my hands up her sides and continued on to her shoulders, forcing her T-shirt up. She raised her arms for me, and her T-shirt lifted over the top of her head, breaking for a moment that precious contact between our mouths.

I felt her fingers popping the buttons on my shirt. One by one. Then she stroked her hands across my shoulders, and my shirt fell free. Kicking off my shoes, I wriggled my feet free of the jeans. Once more, I was naked before her. But this time there was meaning. Not just lust.

My hands came round to the front of her waist and found the clip on her jeans. A quick flick, and I slipped my hands inside them and across her hips, forcing the jeans down. Both naked now, we entwined like the double helix of life itself.

My erection pressed against the flat of her stomach. She forced herself against it with little rolling movements. Each movement brought new fire to my groin. Her hands reached for me and closed tightly. Gone were the ever so gentle movements of the last time she had held me. Her hands were firm and demanding. Long forcing strokes. My fingers found the top of her thighs and ran lightly between them. My hands felt hard and callused against her soft skin. She widened her legs slightly to allow me access. Before I had even found my target, she was moving her hips back and forth. Her neatly shaved hair ran against the palm of my hand as my fingertips probed her warm moistness. My middle finger slid easily inside, exploring for a moment the gentle pressure before withdrawing.

She moved her pelvis gently, showing me the movement she wanted. I responded, increasing the pressure. Her lips broke from mine, and she buried her face in my neck. She was saying things I couldn't quite make out.

Our hands moved in harmony. My fingers moved lightly and easily aided by her thrusting body. She continued making little noises just below the level of comprehension. Then her voice died to a barely audible whimper. I felt her shivering, and she leaned against me, using me for support. Her hands had stopped moving, and she just held me tight.

Her weight increased, and I felt her leaning backwards. I lowered her gently to the ground. She pulled me down with her, guiding me as I dropped. By the time my elbows touched the grass, I was already deep inside her.

It felt like the most natural place in the world to be. She held my face just away from hers and watched me as we moved together. Astrid locked my gaze for a while, and I noticed a hint of something approaching sadness in her eyes. She seemed to recognise that I had spotted something and pulled me down again, wrapping her arms around my back. She nibbled at my neck.

We became one on every level.

Astrid controlled the movement, the pace. Pushing her hips up from the ground encouraging me to go deeper. Softly she spoke again, too softly for me to hear. Her teeth bit into my neck. Just hard enough to be painful, just painful enough to be pleasurable. My movements became harder and firmer. Taking control, I pressed myself against her with each thrust. I moved harder and firmer as if by increasing the depth of my penetration I could bind our souls even more strongly together.

Astrid reached between my legs, and her fingernail traced a line firmly along the underside of my scrotum. I lost control at that point. I thrust faster and longer. I couldn't hold back. For too many years I had wanted to experience this without even realising that it was possible. She shivered again. Her warmth spasmed and gripped me tightly. It was too much. I lunged forward one final time. Then my orgasm spread outwards, and every cell in my body signalled its pleasure simultaneously. She gasped, and her fingernails dug into my back. I collapsed onto my elbows. I pushed her damp hair away from her forehead and kissed her gently on each eye.

"Astrid," I said. "I think—"

"Don't say anything. Shush. Please don't say it." She pressed two fingers against my lips. "Just be."

We lay there for a while letting the cool night breeze caress our bodies. Gradually, the chill became noticeable, and we gathered our clothes and went inside the camper. Cerberus followed and jumped up at Astrid.

The double bed was a narrow one, but we didn't care. It just brought us closer together. We lay in each other's arms until passion took us again. And then, more slowly this time, we made love again.

Chapter 14

I was propelled into wakefulness by a herd of seagulls taking tap-dancing lessons on the roof of my camper. The leader was forcing his students into greater and greater activity by the use of loud squawking noises.

My arm stretched out looking for Astrid, hand patting the vacant pillow. The bed was empty. Struggling into a sitting position, I cursed as my eyelids refused to co-operate. I had to use my fingers to help them. The bedroom was empty, and as this space also served as my lounge, kitchen, and dining room, it was safe to assume that Astrid had gone. She must have gone in to work for an early shift.

On my way to the bathroom I tripped over the dog at the foot of the bed. He growled at me.

My reflection stared back at me from the mirror as I drained my bladder. I hadn't shaved for a few days, and the beard was progressing nicely. My still dark hair was a touch on the long side, and ordinarily, I would have cut it by now. But this was the new me.

I stood underneath a cold shower to wake myself up. It didn't work.

The search for breakfast yielded a bag of potatoes, one onion and last night's sausages. I half-filled a frying pan with oil then chopped up the potatoes and onions and threw them into the pan along with the sausages. Ten minutes later, I was tucking into my breakfast of overdone sausages and raw potatoes. But it didn't seem to matter a great deal, as the whole mess tasted of burnt onions anyway.

After eating what I could, I put the remainder down for Cerberus. He decided that he wasn't quite that hungry. He looked up at me as if to say, "Is that it?"

I went to the cupboard expecting to find some clean jeans and a shirt. They weren't there. A quick search revealed that Cerberus had fished them out of the cupboard to make a bed out of them. They were crumpled and hairy but otherwise clean. I put, 'Visit the laundry' on the top of my mental 'to-do' list.

I stepped out of the camper to find a group of children pointing at the roof and giggling. I shooed them away.

As Cerberus had been an unbidden visitor, I didn't have a leash for him. I had to scavenge around the site and eventually came up with a piece of string. It was a nice morning, and I figured the walk would do me good. So I locked up the camper and set off with Cerberus towards the police station.

By the time I reached town I severely regretted my over optimism. I really was going to have to get fit. I'd never owned a dog before, and I didn't realise what a large part of their life was devoted to sniffing. Walls, lampposts, even car tyres. It seemed that everything that wasn't actually in motion needed to be sniffed at and explored. And it didn't matter how persuasive I tried to get with my end of the piece of string, he was going to go at his own pace and that was it and all about it.

It was when we reached the Post Office that things really took a turn for the worse. I guess to a dog, the Post Office must represent a sort of bulletin board. So many of the creatures had been parked outside while their owners went in to do their business that there must be hundreds of little olfactory messages scattered around outside. Cerberus wasn't going to move on until he had carefully examined each of these messages. He sniffed at walls and letterboxes, pavement and doorframes. He snuffled back and forth making happy little snorting noises. My legs had had enough by this time. I hadn't the strength to either move him, or to stand there and wait while he checked his mail. I gave up and sat down on the pavement, my back against the Post Office wall.

I'd only been there a few minutes when an elderly lady emerged from the Post Office, looked at us both and said, "Oh, you poor dear."

I was about to protest that he wasn't "A poor dear" when she fumbled in her purse and dropped a one pound coin at my feet. My jaw dropped as I watched her walk away. She was just disappearing around the corner when I heard another clink, and I turned back to see a fifty-pence piece had just arrived next to the pound and a man in a suit was walking away in the opposite direction.

Before I'd gained enough energy to continue my walk I'd collected nearly five pounds, two French francs and a copy of the Watchtower.

When I reached the police station, Sergeant Treluggen greeted me like a long-lost friend. "Good morning, Mr Ryan, sir. Wanting your old room back?"

"No thanks. I've got this dog, you see..."

"Oh, that's what it is then. And there was me thinking it was a tractor! But I'm just a country copper. What do I know?"

"I've come to hand him in."

"Why? What's he done? Robbed a bank has he?"

"No. He's lost. I expect he's valuable. Looks like a rare breed to me."

"It looks like a moth-eaten fleabag to me. Tell you what, sir, you hang on to it. We'll let you know in due course if anybody turns up for him. I very much doubt it though, as by the looks of him, nobody in their right mind would want that thing back again once they'd got rid of it."

It looked like I was the proud owner of a dog.

I made my way to the Cafe to secure myself some real breakfast. I tied the dog up outside and went in. Pete was at his usual table, and Astrid was nowhere to be seen. My good humour dropped a notch or two. Pete asked me how we'd got on at twister and expressed his great disappointment that he and Woody had become lost on the way there. I told him I didn't particularly want to discuss it, but if he wanted us to arrange a return match, I was sure Ivy would oblige.

I told Pete what had happened to me outside the Post Office. He seemed impressed.

"What have you done with the dog now?" he asked.

"Tied up outside."

"Can I borrow it?"

"You want to borrow my dog?"

"Hey, come on. I told you about my car parks, the least you can do is lend me your dog."

"Okay, but on one condition."

"What?"

"If you lose him, you don't look for him."

Pete smiled, "I'll go down the high street then. I'll let you keep the Post Office."

Before I could argue he was gone, collecting Cerberus on the way.

I ate a hearty breakfast of bacon, sausages, eggs, and fried bread. I idly wondered if they called it hearty because that's where it all settled. But hey, I was free. I could run with scissors now if I wanted to.

I decided to buy myself a bicycle. I couldn't cope with all this walking, and I certainly didn't want to bring my home into town every time I needed a packet of tea-bags.

I resisted the best attempts of the salesman in the cycle shop as he tried to persuade me that what I really needed was a thirty-six gear titanium monster and settled instead for an eighteen gear version with alloy wheels.

I went for a wobbly ride around town. It's not true; you *can* forget how to ride a bike. I managed to annoy both motorists and pedestrians in the process. By the time I'd found my way to the seafront, I was getting the hang of things, and I was able to ride in a reasonably straight line. This was much easier than walking. I spent the rest of the morning cycling around the outskirts of the town then returned to the Cafe. Cerberus was tied up outside. I parked my bike next to him and then went inside.

Woody and Pete were there as usual, but there was still no sign of Astrid.

"Good dog, man," Pete said.

"Oh?"

"Yeah, made fifteen quid in a couple of hours."

"I painted a dog once," said Woody.

"Oh, really! What sort?" I asked.

"Just to the usual sort." He frowned at me as if unable to understand why I'd asked such a stupid question.

"What's the usual sort?" I knew I was going to regret asking.

"On canvas! Square ones with a wooden frame."

"Oh, right. Okay then. What sort of dog was it then?"

"It was a brown dog… With fleas."

Pete stood up and announced that he was late for a meeting with a man about a truckload of flood damaged wet suits, and did I want one at a good price. I remembered the mobile phone and declined. He dashed out of the café.

My coffee and baked cheese potato arrived. The cycle ride had given me a fierce appetite, and breakfast was just a distant memory.

"I'm not good at dogs though," Woody continued. "Can't do their noses. That's how I came to start on the unicorns." He pulled a tobacco tin from his pocket and started building a cigarette.

"Astrid told me that you were at Woodstock and the Isle of Wight? You remember the Isle of Wight very well, Woody?"

"Where?"

"Isle of Wight rock festival, 1970? "

"Yeah, Jimi Hendrix!"His eyes emerged from their usual heavy-lidded appearance as he relived the memories.

We chatted at each other for about half an hour. It would be dishonest to say that we chatted with each other, as very often it seemed that Woody's understanding of the conversation we were having differed wildly from mine. However, there did seem to be plenty of common ground in our earlier experiences. And on the occasions when our conversations did coincide, I realised there were more similarities than differences. We had both dropped out of university and started down the hippy trail. We had both committed ourselves to peace and flowers. But for me, it had been short-lived. I had just started on the path when Sam had 'rescued' me and whisked me away to marital bliss. I hadn't even got to the 'Free Love' bit by then. There had been nobody around to rescue Woody, so he had continued to follow the hippy ideal. I looked at Woody in a new light. Here was the person I would have become, should have become? He was the other me.

As far as he could remember, most of his early days had been spent in the States. So I guessed that made him American, although he didn't seem convinced. He liked to refer to himself as a child of the universe. He told me about some of the rock festivals he had been to and the bands he had watched. He chatted about the time he had travelled across the Sahara on camel. Then he went into great detail about how he had once been rescued from an Iranian prison by the American Special Forces. But he couldn't remember whether that had actually happened to him or if it was a film that he'd once seen.

I finished my lunch and went outside to retrieve Cerberus and my bicycle. I was only fifty percent successful. Somebody had stolen my bike. Now, why couldn't it have been the bloody dog?

I set off back towards the camper site. As I reached the Post Office, I couldn't resist giving it another spin. I sat down on the pavement and this time tried putting on a pitiful expression. Within half an hour I had collected nearly six pounds. It wasn't quite up to my previous hourly rate in my old life, but it wasn't bad.

I was about half way up the hill that led out of town when I saw Pete coming the other way. On my bicycle. He waved at me as he flashed past. I made a mental note to do something very nasty to him with something very pointy then continued on my way home, as I had now come to think of my camper.

The part of me that had been wondering if Astrid would be there waiting was disappointed. I let myself into the camper and collapsed onto the bed. I was exhausted. I was really going to have to do something about getting fit.

After a quick power-nap, I headed across to the site information centre. There was an assortment of leaflets scattered across the counter. I could learn jam making, go potholing, or even take up hang-gliding. The only concession to fitness however, was a leaflet advertising Tai Chi on a Monday evening at the church hall.

The receptionist remembered hearing about a place called Jim's Gym down near the quay and suggested I try there. I picked up the Tai Chi leaflet although that was probably a little bit too tame for me. I needed something a bit more challenging.

I returned to the camper and flopped down on the bed again. Cerberus scrambled up against me. I suppose he wasn't a bad dog after all. I stroked his head the way I'd seen other dog owners do to their canine friends. He rewarded me by licking my face. I wondered where his tongue had been earlier and got up to wash my face.

I was missing somebody. But I wasn't quite sure who it was. Was it Sam or Astrid? Twenty years is a long time, and I supposed that even Reggie Kray would have missed his warders had he been set free after that time. I was certainly missing the kids; I had money in my pocket to prove that. But I knew I would sort that one before too long anyway.

My mind drifted back to last night. Yes, the sex had been good, but there was something else there. A much, much deeper connection. Where was she? It dawned on me that it was Astrid I was missing and I had probably been missing her for many years.

I changed into my last set of clean clothes and headed off into town, locking Cerberus in the camper.

I climbed up the iron steps to Astrid's flat and knocked firmly on the door. There was no answer. I tried to peer through the glass panel on the door, but the inside was in darkness. Maybe she was at work. I set off to find out.

My bike had reappeared outside the Cafe. This time it was neatly shackled to a lamppost with a shiny new chain and padlock. I scanned the Cafe briefly for Astrid. There was no sign of her. Pete waved at me as I walked in. I strode over to the table with what I hoped was a look of thunder in my eyes. I sat down opposite him.

"You stole my fucking bike!"

"Hey, that's no way to greet somebody. How about, hello Pete, nice to see you?"

"You stole my fucking bike!"

"Okay, okay. We'll explore this track then shall we? Which bike is that?"

"The blue one! How many bikes have you stolen then?"

"I don't steal bikes."

My mouth started speaking but neither brain nor larynx co-operated, so no sounds emerged. His outrageous statement had me wrong footed for a moment. He watched me with a slightly curious look on his face as I struggled to put together some sort of sensible counter.

"I saw you riding it. You waved at me."

"Oh, that bike!"

"Yes, that bike!"

"I didn't steal that. I was stopping it being stolen."

"What?"

"Well, it was just out there," he waved towards the door. "If I'd left it there, it would have been stolen."

"What?"

"So I thought to myself, well I can't leave it there. So I did the decent thing and looked after it."

"What?"

"Do you have any other words you want to try out? I think you've worn that one out." He took a long sip from his coffee mug.

"It's my bike. It didn't need looking after. I was doing a perfectly satisfactory job of looking after it myself."

"No you weren't! It wasn't there when you came out was it?"

"Only because you took it."

"Yes, but if I hadn't taken it somebody else would have done."

There was no winning this one.

"How much did it cost you?" Pete asked.

"I don't see what that's got to do with anything!"

"Well, I think I deserve ten percent of the value for having saved the cost of buying a new one. Sort of a finder's fee."

"It wasn't lost! I'm not paying you ten percent for stealing my bike."

"Please yourself." Pete looked hurt.

"Now, if you'll just give me the key..."

"What key?"

"To the chain. You've got it chained up to a lamp post."

"That's my lock and chain. Do you want to buy it?"

"No, I don't want to buy it!"

"You just expect me to give you the key, then? That cost me money."

"You don't have to give it to me, I just want to borrow it."

"I spent that money to protect your bike! What good is the chain to me without a bike?"

"All right! How much was it?"

"Twenty five quid."

"For that?"

"Okay!" He held his arms out in mock surrender. "So I was ripped off! Are you going to punish me for that?"

I gave up and paid him the twenty-five pounds.

On the way out I checked with Billy, the part-time waiter to find out if he'd seen or heard from Astrid. He said not. She hadn't turned in for her shift. I felt a little stab of worry at his words.

Chapter 15

I took my newly recovered cycle for a ride down to the gym. I was shown around by the owner, an extra from an Arnold Schwarzenegger movie. He introduced himself as Colin.

"I thought it was Jim's Gym," I queried.

"It is. But Colin's Gym doesn't have quite the same ring, does it?"

"I suppose," I said.

"What sort of things are you looking to do?" he asked as he led me through into the weights room. The room was filled with all manner of machinery, most of which was occupied by men with the most extraordinary physiology I have ever seen.

"Oh, you know. Just want to tone up a bit. I mean, I'm in pretty good shape really, I like to look after myself. Just need to do the finishing touches that's all."

He eyed me up and down with the expression of somebody who had just bitten his tongue. "Good," he said. "Julian here will be your personal trainer." He nodded towards a particularly large man who was entangled in what appeared to be a combined harvester.

As Julian came over, I saw he was a good six or seven inches taller than I was. He had no neck and his muscles appeared to extend from his ear lobes to the tips of his shoulders. His arms resembled a badly tied sack of watermelons, and his veins were on the outside of his body.

He looked inside out.

He held his hand out to me and spoke in a surprisingly high-pitched voice, "Hi, I'm Julian. So, Tony, you want to shape up a bit huh?" He punched my stomach in a mock boxing fashion. I felt my insides wobble for several seconds afterwards. "We'll do your induction now, shall we?"

"I haven't got any kit with me." That should stall things.

"Come on, we've got a little shop here, they'll have everything you need."

Within five minutes I had already lost fifty pounds. The trouble was, it was from my wallet, not my waistline, but I looked every inch the macho man that this place promised to make me. Julian took me out to a treadmill and strapped an electronic device around my chest. I had never been on one of these before although I'd seen them on TV.

I gripped tight on the handles, and Julian pressed the start button. My feet disappeared from under me. I grabbed the rail as hard as I could, but my nose still collided with the front display panel and slid down it. I was left dangling, stretched by my arms with my feet hanging off the back of the machine. I looked down in a sort of shocked, detached way. Droplets of blood splattered onto the treadmill below me.

"Oh, shit!" Julian said. "Are you all right?" He slapped a big red button on the front of the machine. "You have used one of these before, haven't you?"

"Err, not this particular model. No I haven't." He helped me back into a standing position. When he was satisfied I could stand, he ran to the paper towel dispenser yanked out a handful. I took them and pressed them to my nose.

"You all right?"

"Yes, I think so." I handed him the bloodied tissues, which he took with his fingertips.

"I'll start a bit more slowly for you this time… Until you get used to this particular model that is. When I press the button, you start walking, okay?"

"Okay."

The belt moved more slowly this time and I was able to remain standing. I looked down to see the bloodstain whirl under my feet every few seconds.

Once Julian could see that I'd got the hang of it, he gradually increased the speed. Before long, I had to run to stay in the same position.

"Good," Julian said as I got into my stride. I could see he was impressed with me as he took it all way up to three and a half miles an hour. I guessed that most of the people they had here were fairly unfit to begin with. He must prefer working with people like me who were at least in reasonably good shape.

I noticed him watching a display panel on the front of the machine. A series of red and green flashing dots leapt up and down. He flicked his gaze between the screen and my face and asked me several times if I felt all right.

There was a bit of a cramp in my chest and I was having trouble breathing. "Yes, I feel fine! Great isn't it?"

He watched the red lights as they flashed faster and faster. Obviously some indicator as to how well I was doing. I felt quite proud of myself. I managed to score a full set of red lights and a loud beeping noise.

"I think we'd better leave that for now," Julian said. "We'll try some weights."

He sat me down inside a piece of equipment that seemed to be just a mess of iron bars and pulleys.

"Okay, let's see how many times you can press this bar forwards."

I pressed at the handles, but nothing happened.

"I think it's stuck." I told Julian.

He fiddled with the weights, then said," Try that. "

I pressed at the handles, and they moved slightly. "That's better," I said. The handle moved forwards about three inches.

"How far do you want me to push it out?" I asked.

"All the way!" He fiddled with the weights once more, and this time I was able to move it more easily. In fact, I was able to extend my arms at least five times before they collapsed. The weights crashed onto the stack sending a shudder through the whole machine.

And so we continued around the gym, with a similar pattern being repeated at each piece of equipment. By the time we had reached the door, none of my muscles were working properly. My arms hung limply at my side, and I had to tell each leg to move in turn. He led me back into reception and pointed me towards the locker room.

The room was long and narrow with a bank of green lockers completely covering one wall. There were only two other people in the room and I noticed they were using the lockers either side of mine. How could that be possible? There must be a hundred lockers in here. I wondered what the odds were against us all having adjacent lockers.

The other two men were of similar build to Julian and were both naked. They had obviously just emerged from the showers, judging by the small puddles of water that each of them stood in. Apart from their close-cropped heads, there was not a strand of hair to be shared between them. Their bodies were completely bald.

I nodded and smiled. Not too much, it doesn't do to smile too much in a men's locker room. I tried to slide between them to reach my locker. I did this in a sort of sideways movement to avoid any likelihood of body contact. That was something else best avoided. I pulled out my newly purchased towel and wash-bag then shut the locker and quickly retreated to other side of the room.

They talked in loud voices about one of the girls they'd been observing in the aerobics class. It seemed her bouncing breasts had caused them endless amusement and much speculation as to how she'd managed to avoid giving herself two black eyes during the star jumps.

"Of course, I'd have held them down for her!" one of them said.

Both men laughed loudly.

"Too right!" said the other. He punched his partner playfully on the shoulder.

I needed to get out of there before they started flicking towels at each other. I undressed quickly, pulled my stomach in as far as it would go then headed for the showers.

The showers were located opposite the sauna at the far end of the room. I turned the water on then jumped back with a start. The last person to use this had been into masochism as the water was set to ice cold. I'd just balanced the water and was standing underneath the warming flow, when the two men went into the sauna.

I shook the water from my eyes and observed the sauna. It was the usual timber construction, but with a huge glass door in the middle. The two men sat on a bench on the opposite wall facing me. I wondered what genius had come up with this design. I'd never taken a shower with an audience before. Of course, I'd used communal showers many times, but never where the people were actually seated in front of me. I kept expecting them to hold up cards saying 6.9 or something. I also found it wasn't easy trying to shower while holding in my stomach muscles.

I went to wash my hair then discovered there was something wrong with my arms. I couldn't get them above shoulder level, and I had to soap my head by bending over double with my elbows on my hips.

When I returned to the reception area, Julian had prepared my routine. He showed me that the programme consisted of three of those circuits three times a week. Then a month later, they would review it.

"So, what do you think?" Julian said as he handed me my computerised printout.

I though this is the most awful place I have ever been in. And I'm never going to set foot inside here again. "Yes, I think it's great! I am looking forward to my next session!" Perhaps I'd give the Tai Chi a go. After all, I didn't want to end up looking muscle-bound like these guys. That wouldn't suit me. I was more the middle distance runner type physique.

I left the gym, and a very slow and painful cycle ride took me to Woody's shop.

"Hi Woody!"

"Hi John!"

"Tony," I corrected.

"Right!"

He was sitting in a huge, moth-eaten armchair. He had a canvas on his lap and was putting the finishing touches to a unicorn as it leapt through Saturn's rings. It looked like a peculiar position to be painting in. I had always assumed that artists sat on stools in front of easels.

"Have you seen Astrid?" I asked.

"Gone."

"Gone?" That single word felt like somebody kicking me in the stomach. "Where? Why?"

"Hey, she's a free bird. The original free bird. When she feels a root growing, she switches it off and runs away."

It took a while for my brain to cycle through images of birds switching off roots.

"What roots?" I sat down on a small wooden chair that leaned against the wall.

"I've known Astrid for a long time, man. There's only one thing that she'd run away from."

"What's that?"

"Permanent."

"I don't think I understand."

"You see this unicorn here." He pointed at the painting that he had been working on. "Pegasus has wings like… like a unicorn …with wings... He rises up with the stars breaking through these rings that hold him down."

"How does that relate to Astrid?"

"Astrid? I'm not sure. I think I lost my thread a bit there." He laid the painting carefully on the floor and sat back in his chair. "I think she came too close, like Icarus and the… um… the Minotaur."

Even through the jungle of mixed metaphor and tangled myth I was beginning to understand what Woody was trying to say. She was frightened of being tied down and had run away. Didn't she realise I only wanted to love her?

"Where would she go, Woody?"

"Who?"

"Astrid."

"Where does Pegasus go when he flies off?"

"Does that mean you don't know?"

"I don't know!" He picked up the painting again. "Try asking Pete. He might know."

"Okay, I'll drop by later."

I headed back to the site. The site manager intercepted me as I arrived at the gate. He wanted to tell me that my dog had been barking all the time I'd been away and it had been disturbing the other residents. I assured him it wouldn't happen again. He assured me I'd be out if it did.

I heard Cerberus from a hundred yards away as I approached. His frenzied barking and howling drifted across the campsite like the soundtrack from some second-rate horror movie. As I drew nearer to the camper, the vehicle was actually rocking between each bark.

I opened the door with great trepidation and my worst nightmares were realised. He had absolutely trashed the interior. The seats were torn, the blankets were shredded and what few clothes I had left were in torn mangled heaps around the floor. Yet for all of this, he jumped up and gave me a big kiss. His tail wagged with a ferocity that made it seem in danger of flying off.

That was it. Cerberus was going to have to go. I told him so.

"You're going to have to go!"

I picked my way through the damage and into the driver's seat then set off for the police station.

Sergeant Treluggen was behind the counter. I was beginning to wonder if there was only one policeman in the whole of St Ives.

"Ah, good morning Mr Ryan. I've got some good news for you."

"Oh, really! What's that?"

"The dog! Nobody's been to claim it, so it looks like it's yours. You can keep it."

"Err, well. That's what I'd come to see you about. I don't want him, you see."

"Difficult to live with, is he?"

"Only in the same way that the Kuwaitis found Saddam Hussein difficult to live with."

"Well I don't know why you brought him here, then. Last time I checked, it said police station outside, not Dog's Home."

"I just thought I should leave him here until somebody collected him."

"Leave him here, and I'll do you for littering. By the way, I've got a letter for you. It's from your wife." He said it in a way that made it sound perfectly natural that he should be acting as a messenger for me.

"Why here?"

"Seems she can't find you any other way." He handed me the envelope and I stuffed it into the pocket of my jeans.

Would she be asking me to go back? What if she was begging me to return? What would I do then? I would love to go back and visit. Just to see the kids again would be great. But could I go back? I didn't think so. Not after seeing the direction life could have gone. I needed to find out where this particular road was going.

I returned to the Cafe to settle down with a cup of coffee and read my mail.

Tony,

I hear on the grapevine that since you burned down Grahame's cottage you are living rough. Why would you let this happen? I know that this is all part of your illness, but you must pull yourself together. Whether we have any future together I don't know, but if you come home now we can help. I have spoken to Dr Massey and he knows a clinic for people like you.

Please write to me at my office if you wish to take this matter any further.

Yours,

Samantha J Ryan Ms.

Sam had missed her calling; she should have worked for the Samaritans. Just when some poor soul had reached the very edge, she'd be there with her hand out... to pull him over.

David Luddington

I tore the letter into tiny pieces and sprinkled it into the ashtray, regretting the fact that I didn't have a cigarette lighter on me. But then it was probably just as well, as on my track record I would have burnt the Cafe down.

I gazed out of the window at Cerberus. He had his paws up at the window ledge, and his head tipped to one side. He had a forlorn expression on his face, his tongue lolling out of the side of his mouth. I had lost a wife and gained a dog.

Seemed like a fair swap.

Now, if I could just get rid of the dog as well...

Chapter 16

The seagull's tap dancing display team robbed me of my morning lie in. They seemed louder than ever this morning. I stumbled out of my bed and dragged a coat across my shoulders before stepping outside. A group of children were giggling and pointing up to the roof of my van. One of them had a loaf of bread in his hands. So that was the score. This was their morning entertainment, chucking bread onto the roofs of caravans.

"Go away you little... horrors!" I shouted then climbed back in the van and headed for the shower.

. These kids were obviously having wonderful fun at my expense. I needed to put a stop to this before they drove me out of my mind. What was needed was diversion and attraction. If I could persuade the seagulls to move to some other camper by making it more attractive, whilst at the same time repelling them from mine I might just get my own back on the little monsters. The attraction part was easy. Bread seemed an irresistible delicacy to these birds. It was the repellent that presented more of a problem.

I chained my bike to the lamp post outside the small supermarket and went inside. I bought up the last of their bread supply, nine loaves of Hovis granary and went in search of seagull repellent.

Nothing.

Any number of repellents for insects, moths, rats and even badgers. But nothing for seagulls. Not even here in what surely must be the seagull capital of western Europe. The place where seagulls come on their holidays. The place where a sunny afternoon on the beach can turn into a scene from Hitchcock's Birds at the unwrapping of a packet of crisps. Not one sign of anything resembling seagull repellent.

I decided the closest relative to a seagull for which there were ample stocks of repellent was insects. I know it wasn't an especially close relative, but they both fly. I tried to calculate how many cans I needed to spray my camper, gave up and bought the lot.

I left the supermarket wondering how I was going to balance all the bags on the handlebars of my bike. I needn't have worried. The bike had gone. Neatly attached to the chain that still looped around the lam post was a post it note. 'Have borrowed our bike. Be back in ten minutes. Pete.'

I mentally traced the route back to my camper, feeling the shopping dragging at the joints in my already complaining arms I decided to wait. I knew our bike... MY bike... He'd got me at it now; I knew my bike wouldn't be back in ten minutes. I didn't know what was going to happen, but the safe return of my bike within the allotted time span was not even on the page headed 'Possible Outcomes of this Scenario' But it's like watching a really bad movie, you know you should get up and leave, but you just have to know how it's going to turn out.

I settled down on the pavement, my bags around me and settled down with a sense of anticipative dread. It didn't take long for constable Treluggen to make his first appearance.

"What have we here then, sir?"

I was never quite sure if policeman were trained to ask questions like that at Hendon, or whether it was a sort of natural talent. Maybe it was a calculated ploy designed to fluster suspects. Ask a simple question first then slip the tricky ones in after.

"Shopping", I said.

He knelt down to take a closer look at my shopping, gently opening the top of the first bag with an extended forefinger. I suppose a deranged middle aged hippy with a grudge against St Ives and three carrier bags full of semtex was a possibility and I had to applaud his caution. Even if the concept was about as likely as me ever seeing my bicycle again.

"Insect repellent?" He seemed almost disappointed.

"Yes." No point in arguing. He had me cold.

"But there must be twenty cans of the stuff!"

"Twenty two, actually. It's all they had." As if that explained everything.

"And I estimate ten loaves of bread?"

"Nine."

"I know." he said. "It's all they had."

I nodded agreement.

Treluggen seemed lost in thought for a moment. Perhaps trying to remember from some half forgotten lecture on home made explosives and if 'Insect-a-Gone' and Hovis ever featured among the list of favoured ingredients for international terrorists.

"Expecting a plague of locusts are we, sir?"

I thought about explaining the seagull problem but decided he probably wouldn't be in agreement with my intended solution.

"Just stocking up", I said.

"Well, you'd best be moving along. Can't stay here impeding the flow of pedestrians."

"Just waiting for my bike to come back, then I'll be gone."

A moment's hesitation as he seemed to struggle with the image of my bike returning all on its own, then he headed up the street leaving with a inaudible mutter.

Pete was almost as good as his word. He did indeed return. Not quite within the allotted time span and of course, one bike short.

He struggled up the street under several large and well stuffed black bin liners.

"Here, Tony, don't just stand there, gimme a hand with these will you?"

I took the nearest of the bulging bin bags from him. Lighter than expected, I couldn't resist peeping inside.

Cuddly toys. Teddies, parrots, rabbits and even monkeys dressed as butlers.

"What do we need cuddly toys for?" I asked. Dreading the answer.

"We don't. But a guy who runs an amusement arcade needs them and he has twenty cases of chocolate chip cookies." He passed the next bag out to me.

I thought about asking him the relevance of chocolate chip cookies, but decided it wasn't worth the trouble. I was sure the answer wouldn't enlighten me any.

"Where's my bike?"

"I needed to lend it to a guy in return for top level inside knowledge. People don't just give you top level knowledge without collateral you know!"

I had to bite. "What top level knowledge is this and how does it relate to several hundred teddy bears?"

"This guy knows a hooky crane machine down the arcade. Once you know the trick, you can win every time."

I suppose a part of me always knew that my bike was destined to disappear in the middle of one of Pete's more convoluted deals ever since he first set eyes on it. I'd just hoped to get slightly more use out of it first.

"It didn't occur to you I might not want my bike trading for half a dozen sacks of cuddly toys? And that had I actually wanted cuddly toys, that's what I'd have bought when I was looking for a cheap form of transportation?"

"Why are you so hung up about cuddly toys, Tony? You'll get your bike back soon enough. Anyway, it's chocolate chip cookies we need."

I had to ask. "What is it with chocolate chip cookies?"

"Stoned hippies! Glastonbury's coming up soon. Think about it. Half a million stoned hippies and we'll have the only supply of chocolate chip cookies for twenty miles. We'll clean up.

Pete headed up the high street, leaving me with my seagull kit, six black bags of cuddly toys and rather disturbing image of half a million stoned hippies cramming their faces with chocolate chip cookies.

Inevitably, it didn't take long for the reappearance of constable Treluggen.

"Still here then, sir? I see you're bike hasn't made it back yet."

"No. Shouldn't be long." Trying to stay cool and polite, hoping he wouldn't notice the...

"Cuddly toys is it now then? Need them as bait for the locusts do we?"

"I won them."

"And just how did that happen then, sir? Drive by raffle was it?"

"No. I meant a friend won them. I'm just looking after them for the moment."

"And which friend would this be?" He nudged one of the bags with a well shined boot.

"Have I done something wrong here?" Attack. When in doubt, attack.

"That's just what I am trying to determine." He turned his back on me and spoke into his radio. I couldn't quite make out what he was saying, but the words 'cuddly toys' featured prominently.

"Well?" I asked as soon as he'd finished.

"Seems nobody's missing any fluffy toys. But I've a mind to keep an eye on this. Something's a going on here." He nodded at me in what could be taken as an agreeable manner but I knew was more a 'We're watching you' kind of way.

I watched him turn the corner by the newsagent then decided to examine the cuddly toys more closely. I reached in and pulled out a gorilla dressed as a First World War fighter pilot. Biggles the gorilla. Natasha would have liked that. I wondered how she was getting on.

A white van pulled up alongside the kerb. The side door slid open and Pete appeared in the opening.

"Here, give us a hand with these will you?" And without waiting for my reply, he tossed a large cardboard case in my direction.

"What's all this lot?" I asked

"Chocolate chip cookies. I told you that."

I looked at the box in my hands. Nelsons Chocolate Chip Cookies, the label proclaimed - Mum's Favourite.

We piled the cases on the pavement and then loaded the sacks of cuddly toys into the back of the van. Pete stuck his head through the passenger door window.

"There you go, Dylan, one hundred and fifty assorted cuddlies. Any time you need any more help, just give me a call." He banged the side of the vane as it sped off in a plume of grey smoke.

"Who's Dylan?" I asked.

"He's looking after an amusement arcade for a mate while he's away."

"Not the one you got the toys from?"

"No, different one. Anyway he needed cheap stock, we needed chocolate chip cookies, which he happened to have an excess of, everybody happy!"

"Where's my bike?"

"You know your trouble? You're too hung up with material possessions. You need to chill out more, man. Go with the flow. If your bike comes back, it's yours to keep. If not, it was never yours to start with. Look after this lot for a bit while I try to find some transport."

Once more I was left alone with an increasingly surreal pile of belongings.

Of course it wasn't long before the ever tenacious constable Treluggen made his way back to my location.

He stopped and stared at the cases of cookies. For a moment he seemed lost for words. Then, "I haven't a clue what you're up to, but my copper's nose tells me it's no good. I think you'd better gather up your odd little collection and come along with me to the station. It's about time we had a chat."

I didn't argue. There seemed little point. And he did have the decency to carry some of the boxes.

"You know, Mister Ryan, most people who come to Cornwall stay awhile then go and I never know about it. Most never get to see the inside of a police station unless it's to hand in a bunch of keys they've found on the beach." He threw the last of the boxes in the back of the police Range Rover. "So why do you keep turning up? That's what I want to know."

"Coincidence?" I offered lamely.

"Mind your head, sir." He guided me into the back seat and closed the door.

Just as we were pulling away, Pete came round the corner pushing a supermarket trolley. His idea of 'Transport'. I waved to him as we drove off. He did have a look of genuine concern on his face, whether it was on my account or the loss of his chocolate chip cookies, I had no idea. I relaxed back into the seat and realised I was still clutching Biggles. Oh well, maybe Natasha will get lucky after all.

St Ives's convoluted one way system threads its way through tiny streets and almost loops back on itself before disgorging its victims onto the busy main roads. Pete had obviously taken a short cut and set up a road block at a particularly tangled junction. Although an overturned shopping trolley might not constitute a road block on any normal road, here it was the equivalent to a three lane pile up on the M25.

A white Renault had stopped in front of the trolley, the driver, a man in his seventies, sat patiently waiting for something to happen. We pulled up behind the Renault. Treluggen set his blue lights flashing, jumped out of the Range Rover with a "Don't even think about it." glance at me and went to talk to the Renault driver.

I strained to hear what they were saying.

"Why have you stopped?" Treluggen shouted, assuming that white hair affected hearing I suppose.

"There's summat in road," the old man shouted back.

"Why didn't you just move it?"

"Might be stolen."

"Of course it's stolen! Unless this is an extension of Tesco's car park or this is a sentient trolley making a break for freedom, then it's most definitely stolen."

"Evidence. I watch The Bill. Not supposed to tamper with evidence. Fingerprints you see."

"Fingerprints? You don't really think..."

Treluggen was launching into one of his sarcasm laden speeches. I was glad to see it wasn't just me that seemed to have this affect on him. I was just beginning to feel sorry for the driver when there was a tap on the window and Pete's face popped up into view.

"Move back from the door. I've come to rescue you."

"What? Rescue? I don't need rescuing."

I heard a grating crunch and suddenly there was fresh air where the door used to be. Pete stood just outside empty door with a satisfied grin on his face and a crowbar in his hand.

"That was easier than I thought it would be," he said.

I glanced frantically over to where Treluggen was still lecturing the unfortunate Renault driver.

"Put it back! I don't need rescuing. I haven't done anything wrong," I whispered loudly.

"Innocence doesn't mean anything to a fascist regime. Look at Nelson Mandela."

"Nelson Mandela? I was caught loitering with several cases of chocolate chip cookies, not starting a revolution. Put the fucking door back."

"Can't. It's buggered. Come right off its hinges."

"Oh brilliant!" I glanced over at Treluggen. He had hold of the trolley and was dragging it to the side of the road.

"Come on." Pete's eyes darted side to side. "He's coming back."

"No. I'm not being rescued. Leave me alone."

Pete shrugged his shoulders and disappeared around the corner just before Treluggen returned to the Range Rover. He was grumbling quietly to himself about geriatric drivers. He stopped mid mutter as his eyes connected with the fallen door.

As if doubting the evidence of his own eyes, he turned away, removed his hat then looked back at the door. It was still where he'd last seen it.

"And what the hell is going on here? Planning the Great Escape?"

"No... it err... Fell off."

"Fell off? Doors of Range Rovers don't just fall off. It's a matter of pride with the manufacturers that their doors don't just fall off. Especially Police issue Range Rovers. Doors falling off is a tad inconvenient while transporting prisoners."

I held my hands up in exaggerated innocence. "How do I know? One moment it was there, the next, bang... It's lying on the ground. Must be faulty."

"I don't know what passes for law and order back where you come from, but we have standards around these parts." He picked the door up and dumped it on the passenger seat. "Around these parts it's still illegal to break and enter out of one of Her Majesty's Police Vehicles."

I thought about discussing semantics and whether one could actually break and enter *out* of something but thought better of it. Opting instead for, "Look, if I was really trying to escape, why am I still here with the door gone?"

He thought for a moment then said, "Well, you just sit tight there a while. We'll talk about this back at the station."

The drive back to the police station was short but draughty. After I had helped Treluggen move the cases of chocolate chip cookies into the evidence locker I was left alone in the interview room while he made further enquiries, as he put it. At least it wasn't a cell. The room was sparse. A table that appeared to be attached to the floor and two plastic chairs. The same sickly green linoleum that covered the floor also served as a table covering.

After about twenty minutes Treluggen returned with a mug of tea in his hand. He pushed it across the table. "Here, regulation tea, two sugars. Don't hold with it myself, but the psycho boys say suspects co-operate better if we treat them good."

"Am I a suspect in something then?"

"You're certainly a suspect in *something*. Can't quite determine what yet, but give me time."

146

"Nobody's reported grand theft cookie yet?" I took a sip of my tea. It was revolting.

"The biscuits appear to be on the level. But I can't begin to understand what you want with six cases of the things, and three months past their sell by date at that."

"Can I go now then?"

"Not until we've cleared up another little matter." And with that slightly worrying note, he left me alone again.

So, three months past their sell by. Still, I suppose it wouldn't matter too much. When you've got a head full of Morocco's finest and the sky's a lovely shade of green, what's a little food poisoning going to matter?

Treluggen returned after another twenty minutes. Reluctantly he had to inform me that the police mechanic had inspected the door and it wasn't possible for me to have damaged from the inside. Their best guess was somebody at some time had tried to break in, damaging the hinges. Any slight jolt might have dropped the door out after that. Treluggen looked thoroughly disappointed.

"Don't care what the mechanic says, I know you're behind this somehow."

"Can I go now?"

"No," he said, a grin returning to his face. "Told you. Still investigating that other little matter." The door clicked shut behind him, but like the Cheshire cat, his grin seemed to linger.

It was only ten minute before he returned this time.

"Are you the owner of a blue Montana bicycle with a yellow bell?"

Even if I could feign indifference, my stomach wouldn't. It tightened... then squirled. "Why? Has one been handed in?"

"Not exactly. Seems it was involved as the means of getaway after a particularly unpleasant robbery."

I was going to kill Pete. "What robbery?"

"Old mister Patterson had his lunch bag snatched."

"Lunch bag?"

"He'd just come out of the bank and was on his way back to his jewellery shop when some lunatic cycled by and snatched his lunch bag."

"When was this?" I asked.

"Two thirty five exactly."

I did a quick calculation. "I was in the back of your car at the time." I was almost triumphant.

"With the door gone," Treluggen reminded me.

"Do you really think I had time to slip out of the back of your car, find my bike, relieve mister Patterson of his lunch and make it back all before you realised I'd gone?"

"It wasn't his lunch you... the thief was after. Obviously coming out of a bank clutching a bag, you... the thief thought it was money, not just his cheese and pickle sandwiches."

I almost felt sorry for Treluggen. "Can I go now?"

"This sort of thing is all too common these days you know."

"What is? Cheese sandwich crime? Can I go now?"

"We haven't finished our investigations yet."

"But as you know I'm not the Lunch Bag thief, can I go now?"

"Well as long as you understand we might need further questioning in this matter..." he tailed off.

"Can I have the cookies back?"

"No"

"What about my bike?"

"How about—"

"No! It's all being kept as evidence."

I figured I'd got off fairly light, considering, so I didn't push the issue any further.

Chapter 17

Cerberus was waiting for me when I returned to the camper. As a mark of his disapproval at being left alone, he'd raided the hangers for the last of my clean clothes and scattered them around the floor. I sat for a while wondering if I'd look good in a dog fur jacket. Cerberus looked up at me, his wagging tail flailing my clothes into even more disorder.

Time to go and replace my wardrobe. This clothes shopping business was becoming a habit. I promised myself this would be the last time for a long while.

I tied Cerberus up outside the first clothes shop I came to and went inside. This time, I managed to ignore the sales girls completely and selected three pairs of jeans and several shirts. I took them to the pay counter and dumped them down next to the till. I was feeling quite pleased with my new assertive shopping abilities and decisiveness.

The girl behind the counter gave me a suspicious look as I handed over my American Express card. I supposed I must have looked a sight. My clothes were tatty, my face was in the halfway stage between scruffy and beard and my hair lapped over my collar. I trusted in my American Express card to say nice things about me.

It didn't.

She swiped the card through her terminal then tapped in some numbers and waited.

And waited.

The machine gave a loud bleep, and she ran the card through again. By this time, a small queue had formed behind me. She peered at the screen on her terminal then picked up the telephone. She dialled, and read the numbers from the card to somebody at the other end. I turned to face a middle-aged woman in the queue behind me.

"Computers huh? Don't you just love 'em?" I said in my best shopper's camaraderie voice.

The woman gave me an expression that looked as though somebody was pulling her face in from the inside. I returned my attention to the assistant who was just replacing the handset.

"I'm sorry, sir," she announced in an extremely loud voice. "Your card has been cancelled. I have to retain it." She brought some scissors from under the counter and started cutting my card in two.

"No! Wait!" I said. "There must be some mistake!" I reached out to try to prevent her cutting the card any more.

"Stop!" she shouted. "Security! Security!"

I turned around. The middle-aged woman had backed up against the wall. She was holding her shopping bag up in front of her chest to protect herself from this maniac.

"It's all a mistake," I told her.

"Help!" she screamed.

I couldn't believe what was happening. Sam had cancelled my card! I turned back to face the assistant. She backed away from the counter in an attempt to put distance between us. I reached into my pocket to find my other card. This situation looked in danger of getting out of control, and I needed to resolve it before security arrived.

Mistake.

It was already out of control. As the assistant saw my hand go into my pocket she screamed loudly and threw her arms up in the air. Clearly a bad case of too many cop shows on the telly. Damn it! This was St Ives not Chicago. What did she think I was going to do, pull an Uzi out of my pocket and blow her away over a couple of pairs of jeans?

I looked around quickly, and saw the store security guard heading in my direction from the rear of the shop. That was it! I wasn't going to be a victim any longer! I grabbed the pile of clothes from the counter and ran for the door. I stopped briefly outside to unclip Cerberus then continued running up the street. When I had travelled about a hundred yards, I stopped to catch my breath. I looked back towards the shop. Cerberus was standing outside the shop door. He had the security guard trapped in the entrance. And even from this distance, I could see his teeth and hear his barks. At least somebody was on my side.

I drew in a lung-full of air and continued running for the car park. By the time I had unlocked the camper, Cerberus had caught up. He dived in with a pleased little bark and a wagging tail. I was genuinely happy to see him. I tickled him behind his ear.

"Good boy! Good boy!"

I set off back for the camper site. I figured I was reasonably safe there for the time being at least. Although the shop had my name, the last address the police had on file was the hotel. They knew nothing of the camper.

But I was certainly going to have to avoid Sergeant Treluggen from now on.

Chapter 18

I couldn't risk leaving Cerberus alone in the van again, so I had to take him with me to visit Pete. Cerberus dragged behind me as I walked along the street. Late spring had taken hold and people walked the early evening streets in their shirtsleeves.

I knew where Pete's place was, but I'd never been there before. His was the top floor flat of a converted warehouse. I opened the door and found the stairwell in darkness. My hands searched the wall for the light switch. It was one of those big round affairs that you press in and the light stays on for a set period. I pressed it, and a single fluorescent light bulb flickered reluctantly into life. Cerberus slipped my grasp and ran on up the stairs. I guessed that he had been here before when Pete took him out the other day.

I set off up the steps. When I reached a landing about half way, I had to stop to catch my breath. It wasn't that I was unfit, it's just that I'd worn myself out in the gym. At the recollection of the gym my hand raised unconsciously to my nose. It was still swollen and tender. I took several deep breaths and persuaded my feet to start on upwards again. At that point, the light went out. My allotted time had expired. Whoever had set the timer must have used Lynford Christie as the benchmark. With one hand sliding up the banister and the other hand groping the darkness in front of me, I resumed my climb. At one point, I trod on something soft, and it squeaked. I hoped it was just a child's toy.

I arrived at the top landing and searched for the doorbell. It played the theme from Star Wars, and I heard Woody's voice from inside say, "That'll be the door, man!"

I waited expectantly for the door to open. It didn't. I rang again. This time it played Ode to Joy.

"Cool doorbell, man," said Woody. But still nothing happened. This time I banged on the door with my fist.

"Somebody at the door, man!" said Woody. "I'll get it!"

A few moments later, the door swung back, and Woody's grinning face greeted me. "Hey, Pete! It's John!"

"Tony," I said.

"Yeah. Come on in."

The air was thick with cannabis smoke. A large central light in the shape of the Starship Enterprise illuminated the room. A huge mattress lay in the middle of the floor. Pete lay on it, asleep.

I looked around for somewhere to sit. There were several lumpy objects covered in blankets. I noticed an empty cup by the side of one of them and I guessed the lumpy objects were seats. After my last experience of unorthodox seating though I was feeling slightly apprehensive. I was afraid Woody would tell me I'd just sat on one of his works of art. I settled myself down gently. There were no protestations from Woody. It took me a moment to work out what I was actually sitting on. It appeared to be a car tyre inner tube covered with a blanket.

Pete stirred. "Hey, what's burning?" he said as he sat up.

"Yow! Pete! We've got a visitor. Look it's... It's..."

"Tony," I helped.

"Hi, Tony," said Pete. He returned his attention to Woody. "Woody, what are you burning? I can smell plastic."

I sniffed the air. All I could smell was cannabis. But I guessed that when you're so used to cannabis fumes it becomes easier to separate out any underlying smells.

"Just dinner, man," said Woody. "I'm cooking us a pie."

"You haven't left the plastic on again, have you, Woody?" He stared over at the kitchenette in the corner of the flat where the oven was situated. His forehead had taken on the appearance of a ploughed field.

"No, look, man!" Woody went over to the oven and swung the door open. "See!"

True to his word, a nicely browning pie sat on a baking tray in the centre of the oven. However, alongside it was a large molten blob of white plastic about the size of a large book.

"What the..." Pete crawled off his mattress and scrambled across the floor towards the oven.

Woody looked inside the oven to see what had caught Pete's interest. "Hey, I was wondering where that had gone!"

"What's..." said Pete."That's my fucking alarm clock. You've baked my fucking alarm clock, Woody."

"Hey, you haven't got a timer on your oven. How else was I to know when it was done?"

"You didn't have to put the clock *in* the oven." Pete grabbed a pair of jeans that were lying on the floor and used them to pull the tray out of the oven. He dumped it on the draining board where it gave a little hiss.

Now that I knew what it was, I could see that the white plastic blob had once been a digital alarm clock/radio. Pete continued to stare at his alarm clock he as if hoping that once it had cooled down, it would resume its former beauty. "Why did you put it in the oven?" he asked. "You didn't have to put it in the oven."

As he watched, the white blob gave a little rasping the noise, reminiscent of somebody with a lisp making a slightly bored raspberry. It repeated this noise twice more before emitting a final little buzz and then died completely.

"Pie's ready," Woody said.

Despite the trauma involved in the cooking, the pie tasted remarkably good. It was steak and mushroom. Woody had also prepared some pot-noodles as a side dish. I balanced the plate on my lap as I wobbled inside the inner tube. Each time I breathed, I undulated from side to side putting the plate in danger of sliding onto the floor. Cerberus watched me carefully. He'd realised the pie might land on the floor, and was readying himself to move in quickly should the need arise. Pete and Woody seemed to have their plates under perfect control, and were having no difficulty at all.

Cerberus gave up watching me and then pretended to be asleep with his head resting on his paws. Every so often I caught him watching my plate..

"Woody tells me you might know where Astrid has gone," I asked Pete.

"No way, man! Who knows? She'll be back though."

"When?"

"When she's got her head straight again."

"She's done this before then?"

"Several times. She leaves me the keys to her flat so I can keep Harvey fed and watered then off she goes. Never tells me where she's going or when she'll be back. Went for a year once." He gave up on his pie and placed the plate on the floor by his side. I noticed Cerberus' head give the tiniest of movements and his eyes opened to a barely noticeable slit as he stared at Pete's plate.

"But she always comes back?"

"Well, if she hadn't, you would never have met her, would you?" He smiled.

"Where does she go?"

"Last time she went to Morocco."

"What was that all about?"

"That was over a pensions salesman."

"A pensions salesman?" I said. "She got involved with a pensions salesman?"

"No, she's never been involved with anybody. He tried to sell her a pension."

"She ran away because somebody tried to sell her a pension?"

"All about commitment, isn't it?" said Pete.

"But a pension doesn't tie you down!"

"Yeah, but it makes you think, doesn't it?" said Pete. "You know, getting old. Roots. That's what she runs from."

"How long did she go for?"

"About three months, that time. But she won't be gone for so long this time."

"How do you know?" My insides gave a little stir at this piece of information.

"Glastonbury rock festival. She's never missed it."

"When's that?"

"Sixteenth of June."

I glanced down at Cerberus. He was trying to wriggle across the floor a millimetre at a time, while still pretending to be asleep. He was stalking Pete's plate.

"That's about three weeks," I said.

"I guess so."

"Want some wine, man?" Woody asked.

"Yeah, sure!"

He prised himself free of his inner tube and headed over to the mantelpiece. There was a big Chinese vase in the centre of it and next to that, a box of German hock. He poured wine into three mugs that looked identical to those used in the Cafe Oceanic. He handed me one.

"Thanks," I said. "You both going to Glastonbury?"

"Of course," said Pete. "Though now it's not going to be so profitable since our little catering franchise has been sunk." He glanced accusingly in my direction. "Then it's on to Stonehenge for the summer solstice. I have to scatter Cooking Fat there."

I wondered what bizarre ritual this was.

"Is that something to do with the druids?"

"Druids? No! Cooking Fat!" He pointed at the vase on the mantelpiece. "My cat, Cooking Fat! She died two months ago, and I promised her I'd scatter her ashes at Stonehenge on the summer solstice."

"Oh," I said.

Cerberus was now only about six inches away from Pete's plate and still pretending to be asleep.

"I'd like to go to that. I haven't been to a festival for over twenty years. Where do you get the tickets?"

"Tickets?" said Pete. "You don't need tickets. I'll show you how to get in. Come with us."

"Deal!"

Cerberus gave a final little shuffle and extended his paw. It landed in the middle of Pete's plate. His head lifted and looked around at us as if to say, "That's mine!"

Woody topped up the wine mugs.

"Remember you were saying about your mate building me a website?" I asked Pete.

"Yes, no problem."

"I think I need to do something about that now. I find myself a little financially embarrassed."

"You could always hire your dog out as well, you know. Say take a twenty five per cent cut of what anybody gets with him."

"Really?"

"Yeah, easy. Always get more money with a dog."

A flicker of light from a cigarette lighter in Woody's direction caught my eye. The ubiquitous joint burst into life. The thought that I would see Astrid again lifted my spirits slightly. Of course, I didn't yet know whether she would want to see me again. After all, it did appear that it was me she was running from. Cerberus had licked Pete's plate clean and had settled back down to sleep with a contented grin on his face.

We talked on into the evening. Woody kept us topped up with wine and hash. Pete seemed to have an endless supply of chocolate and cookies for when the munchies took us.

The effects of the cannabis combined with the wine, and we giggled our way through the evening. I awoke about 1.00 am, staggered back to the camper site, and collapsed on the bed.

Sunlight lancing through the gap in the blinds alerted me to the fact the day was already slipping away. I dressed hurriedly then took a trip to my bank expecting the worst. I wasn't disappointed. My account had been frozen.

I had about a hundred pounds in cash, and that was it. No credit cards or cheque book. I should have been overwhelmed with panic. In fact, that was probably what Sam had expected. But I wasn't. Something was bound to turn up. The seeds of Pete's philosophy had been growing in me. I just had to keep an eye out for the angles, that's all.

I spotted another poster for master Li's Tai Chi class in a shop window. I decided to give that a try later. I spent the rest of the morning outside the Post Office. I made twenty-one pounds thirty pence, two loaves of bread, and a tin of dog food. So, if the worse came to the worst, we were both okay for Pal on toast.

I was reluctant to spend any of my cash unless it was absolutely necessary. Guessing that the Cafe Oceanic was probably short staffed, I offered to help out over lunchtime in return for a meal. I was put to work baking potatoes and loading the dishwasher. I rather enjoyed it. Afterwards, Cerberus and I stuffed ourselves silly.

In the afternoon, Pete introduced me to his computer whiz kid mate, Nigel. We struck a percentage deal, and Nigel told me he could have the web page up and running within three days. I needed to organise myself a Visa collection account for payments. The only thorn in that particular plan of course, was the fact that I didn't even have a bank account any more. And opening one up in my own name would be an open invitation to Sergeant Treluggen to come knocking.

"I might be able to help you there," said Pete. "What do you need? Birth certificate? Driving licence?"

"That sounds like serious money to me." I said.

"I'll do it for a percentage. Let's say, twenty per cent for a year?"

We argued on this for a while before settling on ten per cent for two years. I wasn't too sure that I'd made any ground on the deal, but at least I haven't lost any. And with Pete, that made me feel good.

Chapter 19

Master Li held his Tai Chi class in an annex next to the public library. As I walked into the entrance lobby, I could smell the incense, sandalwood I thought, and heard the tinkling of the wind chimes that fluttered in the breeze from the open door.

I pushed my way through the double swing doors and found myself in a large oak-panelled hall. The lighting level was set at gloomy, and soothing sounds of flute music filled the air. Several people were already going through some gentle stretching. A stick insect of a woman in her mid sixties sat cross-legged on the floor. Her shoulder length, greying hair was tied into a ponytail. She had her eyes closed, and she hummed gently to herself.

A bearded man in sandals stood in the middle of the room. He raised his arms slowly up and down. I remember doing something similar as a nine-year-old in a drama class when I'd been instructed to impersonate a tree. Somebody at the far end of the room appeared to be trying to push the wall down. But I guessed he was just doing calf stretches. He looked vaguely familiar, and it took me a moment to place him, out of context as he was.

Sergeant Treluggen straightened up and looked around the room. At one point, he appeared to stare straight at me.

I froze.

I waited for him to pull his personal radio out and call for back up. But his eyes continued roaming the room. Then I realised why he looked different. He wasn't wearing his glasses. Remembering the thickness of his lenses, his vision was probably on a par with that of a deaf bat.

I was feeling a bit conspicuous standing just inside the doorway while others went through their warm-up procedures. So I thought it best to blend in and do some warm-ups of my own. Twenty star jumps should do it, followed by some running on the spot. It wouldn't do to stand out too much with Sergeant Treluggen in the room.

I had just finished my jumps when another group of people entered. They chatted amongst themselves and appeared oblivious to everybody else in the room. In the middle of the group was another face I recognised. He certainly looked the part with his long, flowing hair. He wore a red silk shirt and matching trousers complete with a green dragon motif.

Charlie.

I suppose I should have guessed really. Master Li. After all, there probably aren't that many Orientals named Li living in St Ives.

He gave a single clap of his hands to bring the room to order.

"Good eve'ing ev'ybody. So nice you all come to tonight." His oriental accent was as thick as the first day I had met him in the shop. I wondered if he knew any more about Tai Chi than he did about Feng Shui. Probably not.

"Tonight we do Lazy Monkey form," he continued. "This is ancient form, 5,000 years old."

Charlie made a deep bow. Everybody else responded similarly. I followed suit. He gave a big pushing of breath that sounded like "Whooos." Everybody copied this. I couldn't very well run out, so I joined in.

Charlie brought his hands down to his chest in a sort of praying position, then pressed them forwards looking for all the world like he was doing the breast-stroke. He gave a long "Saaa" sound.

So far, we had called out "Who's a..." if the next word resembled anything like "Silly," I was out of here. But it didn't. We returned to "Whooos", this time combined with a deep squatting movement. I copied the movements as best I could.

I pushed my hands out and drew them in. Stood on one leg, squatted down then up again. All the time I had this dreadful feeling that Charlie was just taking the piss, along with punter's money of course. And what we were really doing was a sort of slow motion version of a song by Black Lace.

It was quite good fun watching Sergeant Treluggen move his huge frame in front of me. He was going through a sequence of movements that wouldn't look out of place in a ballet school.

Fraud or not, I did feel better by the time I'd finished. This is more than could be said for my visit to Jim's Gym.

As soon as the session had finished, I rushed over to pay Charlie and slide out before I was noticed. Charlie refused my payment.

"Any friend of Astrid's..." he said.

The night air was still warm, and I decided to take a walk along the seafront before setting off back. At this end of town, the seafront consisted of an almost continuous row of converted Victorian houses. Each one had had its garden turned into a small gravel car park, and signs outside proclaimed 'Hot and cold, colour TV'.

I sat down on a bench outside one of these hotels to take in the view. I had only been there a moment, when a silver Aston Martin slid up alongside me. The passenger window hissed down and a blue rinsed head poked out. It was balanced on top of a fur coat.

"I say," the head said. "Would you be so kind as to direct us to the cinema, please?"

I had never liked people who begin sentences with, "I say." Why don't they just get on and say it?

"It's just round the next corner," I said, pointing to a turning a hundred yards up the road. Then a thought struck me. "But you'll never get parked. Not tonight."

"Oh, really! And why is that?"

I had to think quickly.

"The Spice Girls are playing. Everywhere is choc-a-block. You'll have to park out of town and walk in. It's only three or four miles."

"Oh, drat! Dashed inconvenient. Are you sure there's nowhere else?"

"No, but I'll tell you what. I've got an idea. My car is in for service, why don't you park in my space for this evening? For a fee of course."

"Where's that then?"

"Just here." I indicated the hotel car park behind me. "My spot's over there by the front door."

The blue rinse head bobbed back into the car to have a conversation with the driver. A moment later, it reappeared

"How much would you want then?"

"Oh, I don't know, a tenner should cover it."

"Very well." She pulled her purse from the back seat of the car and extracted a brand new ten-pound note. She passed it to me by fingertips, as if trying to keep as far away from me as possible.

"Thank 'e ma'am." I touched my forelock.

The Aston Martin swung into the drive. I thought it best to be gone quickly before the hotel porter came out. I had walked about a hundred yards before I realised what I'd done. I had worked the angles. I had pulled a scam. Better yet, I'd thought it all up by myself. This was definitely the new me; things were starting to look up.

My route home took me past the Post Office. Of course, at this time in the evening it was in darkness. A young woman stood outside. She wore jeans and a sweatshirt that told of her allegiance to Queen. She hopped from foot to foot and appeared to be somewhat distressed. I stopped to ask her if everything was all right.

"I have to send some money to my brother. His train fare home. He's in Birmingham University, and I need to send him ten pounds. But I've only got these coins, and I can't send this in the post, can I? It would be bound to get stolen. You haven't got a ten pound note you can swap for these, have you?" She tipped a handful of pound coins from her purse to show me and held an addressed envelope in her other hand to illustrate the problem.

"Sure," I said. I drew my crisp, new ten-pound note from my pocket, and we did the exchange. I checked the coins. There were ten. She slid the note into the envelope and sealed it down.

"Thanks," she said. "I'm so grateful. I don't know how I would have done this otherwise." "No problem," I said gallantly.

"Oh, hell!" she said. "I don't think I've got a stamp! Hold this for a minute will you?" She passed me the envelope as she rummaged in her handbag. "Damn it! I haven't got one. I'll have to leave it till morning now. I'll take the coins back then, you might as well hang onto the note." She pointed at the envelope that I held.

"Okay," I said. I didn't really want ten pounds in coins anyway. I fished the change back from my pocket and handed it to her. She gave me a big smile and said thanks again. She turned and set off in the opposite direction leaving me with the envelope.

I stood for a moment and watched her go until she was round the corner. The bizarre scene replayed itself in my head. When I got to the point where I gave her back the coins I had a horrible feeling gather around the lower part of my stomach. I tore open the envelope.

Of course it was empty.

She had been very quick. I just hadn't seen that switch.

Okay, so the new me wasn't completely on the ball. I'd figured out that I could generate money by my wits, all I had to do now was learn how to hang onto it for a bit longer than three minutes.

Nigel was as good as his word. Within three days, my website was up and running. I scanned the Financial Times for likely looking shares and then composed some suitable financial double-speak for him to upload. A few weeks later, the money started to dribble in. Nothing spectacular, but at least it showed that the idea was working.

Cerberus, on the other hand, proved to be a gold mine. I had him rented out sixteen hours a day, seven days a week to a variety of people. He had turned out to be quite an intelligent dog and had perfected the art of looking sad and forlorn when people walked by him.

Woody had taken it upon himself to paint a unicorn on the side of my van. It raced through a sea of clouds with a naked damsel on its back. Steam flared from the unicorn's nostrils. I wasn't too sure about that, especially as the damsel was very graphically drawn, and it did attract a fair amount of attention on the camper site. The new part of me enjoyed the rebelliousness. The old part wondered what Sam would think.

There was still no sign of Astrid, and I set my heart on meeting up with her again at Glastonbury, which was now only a week away. Pete's idea was that if we turned up at Glastonbury early enough, we could mingle with the construction crew before they sealed the gates. So Pete, Woody, and I set off in my camper van, exactly one week before the festival was due to start.

It was only 150-mile drive, so it should have been an easy journey.

It should have been.

Chapter 20

I stopped for petrol about twenty miles outside St Ives. Pete went inside to buy sandwiches as I filled the tank. He returned a moment later, and he and Woody sat in the back of the van changing the sell-by dates on the empty sandwich packets. Pete was planning on going back and arguing with the cashier, hoping for a refund.

The filler nozzle had just clicked off when the van rolled back, and onto my left foot. I screamed. Pete's face appeared at the window. He realised what had happened and dived to the front of the van and yanked the hand brake on.

The van had stopped right on my foot. I banged furiously on the side and yelled. Pete and Woody dived out and came to see what the commotion was all about. As soon as Pete saw my foot he leapt back in the vehicle and let the hand brake off again, allowing the vehicle to roll back another few inches before he reapplied it. I collapsed onto the ground to investigate my injured appendage.

"Are you all right, man?" Pete asked when he came out again.

"No, I am not all right! What the hell were you two up to in there? "

"Woody lost his sandwich."

"I'm sorry, man," Woody said. He was shifting from foot to foot like a three-year-old that needed the toilet. "It sort of slipped down between the seats. I took off the hand brake to reach it."

I pulled my shoe and sock off. I expected to see mangled bone and lot of blood. Instead, it just looked a bit red. Although swelling was starting to settle in.

"Hey, cool colour, man!" Woody said.

I prodded and poked at my foot searching for signs of anything broken.

"You need to get that looked at," Pete suggested.

"No kidding!" I said, with as much sarcasm as I could scrape together. "Where's the nearest hospital?"

"Bodmin, I guess," said Pete.

The moment I tried to put any weight on the leg, it felt as if it were being run over afresh. I hopped back into the driver's seat of the van and sat there for a moment working out just how I was going to drive. I tried pressing the clutch very gently. The pain that greeted me quickly dissuaded me from attempting that again.

So, driving was out of the question.

I twisted round to look at the other two who were sitting expectantly in the back of the van. They reminded me of the children. I half expected Woody to say 'Are we there yet?'

"I don't suppose either of you two can drive, can you?" I asked.

"Yeah, sure," Pete said.

I shuffled over to the passenger seat and let Pete slide in behind the steering wheel. He waggled the gear stick.

"Now, what is it?" he said. "Two forward, two back?"

"Perhaps we should call this plan B," I said to Pete.

Pete was having none of it. His usual over confidence brimmed forth. "Now, where's the kick-start?"

"What?" I shouted.

"Joking! Just joking. Pah! Can't you take a joke?"

"You used up your joke allowance when you parked on my foot."

He fumbled with the key and turned the engine over. The vehicle jolted forward.

"Ah, yes," he said. "It's one of those that you have to put into neutral first, isn't it? I know this sort."

He pumped feet and arms in a seemingly random manner. We jerked forward off the petrol station forecourt as if powered by pogo stick.

"You might want to try second gear in a moment, Pete," I suggested.

"Right you are then!" He pummelled the gear lever from side to side and pumped his foot up and down on the clutch a few times. The engine alternatively screamed, then crunched as we juddered forward onto the main road.

I waited until he had got into fourth gear before I spoke to him again. I didn't want to break his concentration.

"What other vehicles have you driven, then, Pete?" I asked.

"Motor bikes, mainly. Well... when I say motorbikes... I mean scooters... you know, mopeds."

"Oh, good! And you see no difficulties in making the transition to a two-and-a-half ton van from a motorised bicycle, do you?"

"All the same principle," he said as he re-engaged second gear for no apparent reason.

He seemed to settle into the driving remarkably quickly, although I still found it disconcerting when he felt the need to lean violently one way or the other each time we went into a corner. We had been driving for about five minutes when I had a horrible realisation.

"Did anybody actually pay for the petrol?" I asked.

Pete shrugged his shoulders and shook his head.

Woody said, "What petrol?"

So, that was another score on my lengthening rap sheet. This would go along with suspected armed robbery, arson, and robbing phone boxes. I had a mental image of Sergeant Treluggen having to add more paper to my file.

"Didn't anybody think to pay?" I asked.

"Hey, man. I thought it was cool! I thought you had it all planned."

"You know they'll have us on camera, don't you? And we're hardly inconspicuous thanks to Woody! It isn't going take Sherlock Holmes to figure out which way we're headed. Pull over, Pete." I indicated a lay-by coming up. "I think we need to work this out before we go any further."

"Right you are!" Pete said.

He swung the van into the lay-by. To my surprise he gave no sign of slowing down and just hurtled out of the other end.

"What happened?" I asked.

"Which one's the brake again?" he asked, staring at his feet.

"The middle one! And keep your bloody eyes on the road!"

He pressed it experimentally, and I snapped forward against the seat belt.

"That's the one," I said. "But you might find it easier if you use your right foot."

"Oh I see, I thought it was one foot for go, and the other for stop!"

The next lay-by appeared, and this time Pete managed to stop roughly inside it, although he did stall the engine.

Woody jumped down from the back. "Just doing some picking," he said.

I watched him scramble over a fence and head off into a field.

"Right." I said to Pete. "What now? We can't go on into Bodmin, and if we turn back, we're likely to meet the police coming the other way."

"I know a short-cut," Pete said. "We can cut across the moors just over the hill. I've done it before."

"Where does that bring us out?"

"About five miles past Bodmin."

As that sounded like the only way out of this mess, I reluctantly agreed. I hoped the van salesman had been honest with me when he described this as a 'Nearly All Terrain Vehicle.'

We had to wait several minutes for Woody's return. His pockets were bulging I noticed as he clambered back over the fence. But I was too agitated about staying here much longer to give it any thought.

"Hurry up!" I shouted at him.

We turned off from the main road and followed a gravel track. The twisting trail proved a challenge for Pete's newly acquired driving skill, but at least there was nothing around for him to hit.

I heard Woody clattering around in the back, and shortly after, the smells of cooking wafted forwards. I remembered the last time I'd witnessed Woody's cooking abilities, and a spark of worry flickered across my mind.

The fields rolled by on either side of us, and I began to relax and enjoy the journey. It looked as though Pete had been right, and we were well in the clear. I wriggled my toes experimentally. My foot still throbbed but probably wasn't seriously damaged. I'd get some ice when we stopped, that should sort it.

"Bacon and mushroom sandwiches?" Woody called.

I reached back to take his offering without removing my gaze from the track in front of us for one second. I handed one to Pete. He released his white knuckled grip on the wheel just long enough to grab the sandwich and shove half of it straight into his mouth. I remembered having bacon in the fridge, but I wondered where the mushrooms had come from. I figured I'd just forgotten I had them.

The sandwich was wonderful, although there was a slightly bitter aftertaste. Woody passed a can of beer round, but I didn't let Pete drink any. Much to his annoyance.

The trail continued over fields and then dipped down into a wooded area. After another ten minutes, it had narrowed and become increasingly uneven. We bounced from one pothole to the next, and the trees seemed to close in with each bump we took.

One of the trees smiled at me. I ignored it.

"What were you driving last time you came along here, Pete?" I asked as a thought struck me.

"My moped!"

"Of course you were! Why should I have thought any different?"

"Huh?"

"I think we'd better turn round. This is getting too narrow, Pete."

"No problem! It gets wider just past those traffic lights."

I couldn't see any traffic lights. I wondered if he was confusing them with the Christmas tree.

Still the track narrowed. Branches brushed at us from both sides, and men with brooms banged on the windscreen.

"Pull over, please!" I begged.

"I can't," Pete yelled at me. "They're trying to get in! We can't stop here, or they'll peck our eyes out!"

"Who?"

"The rabbits of course!"

I gripped the side of the seat as we swerved from side to side. I was in awe as to how quickly Pete had picked up this driving business. He managed to avoid both of the kangaroos and the vicar who just jumped out in front of us. It was only when we rounded the Arc de Triomphe that he finally lost control.

We bounced over the pavement and knocked some tables and chairs flying.

"Left!" I yelled. "Hard left!"

Pete obliged, and we headed for the gap underneath the Eiffel Tower. I had always thought it was bigger than this. We only just cleared the first set of stanchions, but by the time we'd reached the far side, the iron struts had closed in. We crashed in between them, and the vehicle slammed to a halt. We were wedged firmly in the base of the tower.

"I suppose we'll have to buy a ticket!" I said.

My mind was clouding over, and I felt ready for a nap. But just as I was drifting off, I recalled the bitter aftertaste to the bacon and mushroom sandwich.

Realisation struggled through.

"Woody," I called. "Where did you get those mushrooms?"

Chapter 21

I awoke with a headache the size of the Millennium Dome. Pete lay slumped against the side window. He still the seat belt around him. I twisted round to look into the back of the van. Woody was sprawled out on one of the seats. He too appeared to be asleep.

Trees pressed in against my door, and it wouldn't respond to my attempts to open it. I struggled free of my seat and clambered into the back. My foot reminded me it didn't want to be part of the walking process, so I half slid between the seats. Cerberus jumped from seat to seat, his tail going like a windscreen wiper on 'Storm' setting.

I cast my eyes over the chaos. Cooking utensils lay everywhere. What possessions we had brought had fallen from the top cupboards and were scattered over the floor. Near the cooking area I saw some brilliant white mushrooms stuck to the bottom of the frying pan.

I pushed myself out through the back door. We were in a richly vegetated wood. Birds sang, and shafts of sunlight pierced the trees. The ground was firm and grassy with two muddied tracks leading to the rear wheels of my camper. I looked back the way we had come. The track was extremely narrow; Pete had to be congratulated on getting us this far.

I pushed the branches aside and hobbled my way to the front of the vehicle. The track in front of us had suddenly narrowed. Whilst still probably passable to Pete's moped, that was about all that would get through here. The van was well and truly wedged between two large trees. The stanchions of the Eiffel Tower, I remembered hazily.

I climbed back inside and went in search of aspirin. Woody was just stirring.

"What happened?" he asked.

"Bacon and mushroom sandwiches, I think," I said.

"Oh, yeah! Hey, they were good ones, weren't they?"

"Yes, Woody. They were good ones!"

My tongue felt like a shag-pile carpet, but my leg was feeling slightly better. Could this be a new cure for a run-over foot? Magic Mushrooms? I took my shoe and sock off again. A selection of interesting colours greeted me, but the swelling seemed to have subsided somewhat. Cerberus decided to play doctor, and licked it better for me.

Pete extricated himself from the front seat. "Nice one, Woody! We'll put Tony in charge of the cooking from now on shall we?"

"I'm not too sure we'll fare any better there," I said. "I've got a first in salmonella!"

"What now?" Pete asked.

"We walk, I guess. We're not going to get this out of here without a tow truck, and there's no way we can involve a tow truck without risking alerting the police."

"You can't leave it here!" Pete shuffled his way to the fridge and helped himself to a beer.

"Why?" I snatched the beer from his hand and opened it. "Somebody going to steal it, are they? We can collect it on the way back. Things should have calmed down by then."

Woody cut down two small trees and fashioned me a perfectly serviceable pair of crutches. Pete very carefully wedged Cooking Fat's pot in the side pocket of his rucksack then we packed what belongings we could into several bags and set off up the track. Pete had assured us it came out onto the main road in about a quarter of a mile. He was about a mile adrift in his calculations, but we emerged well clear of Bodmin. We settled down by the side of the main road to try our luck at hitch hiking, although I didn't rate our chances much. Three hippies, a dog, and a pile of clutter that looked as though we had just ram raided a car boot sale.

We waited for about an hour, and I had just about given up hope when a green painted double-decker bus pulled over. It looked like it was about thirty years old, and the gaudy paint job seemed to be the only thing holding it together. Big bubble writing along the side it proclaimed as,

'The Green Machine'. And then in smaller letters underneath, 'Purity food for the soul.'

As the bus pulled over, a girl with short-cropped hair leaned out of the door. She looked to be in her mid twenties.

"Hi! Need a lift?"

We climbed aboard. The lower deck had been done out with tables and chairs, and a small kitchen took up the far end. Several posters on the walls advertised Organic lentils, Seaweed mousse, and Brown rice muesli.

"Going to Glastonbury?" I asked.

"Yes," the girl said. "You are vegetarians though, aren't you? We don't allow cannibals in here."

"Oh, yes!" Pete said. "None of us would ever eat anything with a face. Would we? In fact, Woody's a vegan!" He looked around at us and winked.

"Right!" Woody and I said in unison.

"Smashing! the girl said. "I'm Star, and this is Fallow." She pointed to the driver, another crew-cut girl in blue dungarees. Fallow smiled.

I heard some scrabbling noises, and what sounded like squawking drifting down the steps from the upper floor. I looked quizzically at Star.

"Chickens," she said, helpfully.

"You've got chickens upstairs?" I asked.

"Yes," she said. "Four of them, plus two goats and a goose."

My eyes scanned the posters again, and I found one that advertised fresh goat's milk and free-range eggs. I thought the top floor of a double-decker bus was probably stretching the term, 'Free range' a bit far, but I didn't say anything.

Star sat on the step next to the driver, and we settled ourselves at two of the tables. Fallow wrestled with the oversize steering wheel, and we pulled out onto the road. It seemed as if she had to shift gears about ten times before we were up to a decent speed.

Woody looked at me from behind his hand. "What's a vegan?"

"Someone who doesn't eat anything from animals. Meat, eggs, milk, nothing."

"What about bacon?"

"Even bacon, Woody."

"Heavy!"

The bus rattled and vibrated as though the wheels were made of stone. But it was transport. After a while, Star came to sit with us. I hoped she wasn't going to quiz Woody on his eating habits.

"Where are you from?" she asked.

"St Ives," Pete said.

"We've just come from there. We set fire to the abattoir."

Great, I thought. That just about puts the lid on it. Here I am, St Ives's number one most-wanted, making my get-away in a 1960's double-decker bus with a farmyard upstairs and driven by two terrorists.

"You don't think your choice of a getaway vehicle was a little obvious?"

"Don't be silly," Star said. "Nobody saw us in this."

I noticed that Cerberus was doing his inching forward trick again, heading in the direction of the stairs. I planted my foot on his rope.

"You do much of this animal lib stuff?"

"Oh, yes! There's a mink farm just outside Exeter. We're going to stop there on our way up and set the poor little creatures free. You want to help?"

"Err, not me," I said. "I've got this foot you see." I pointed at my foot in case they didn't understand about feet.

"How about you two?" she asked Pete and Woody.

"Hey cool, man," Woody said. "Never had a mink."

"Yes," Pete said. "We'd love to." He had all the conviction of a politician up for election.

I watched the rolling Devon hills drift by the window. The steady drone of the ancient diesel engine soothed the alpha rhythms of my brain and sent me into a fitful sleep.

I awoke with a start. Something had changed. Silence. We had stopped. I carefully straightened my neck out from its slumped-over position. I was rewarded with a pain that stretched from the top of my head to the base of my spine.

"What's happening?" I asked.

"We're going on a mission," Woody said.

I looked up at him. His face was covered in green camouflage paint, and a green woollen balaclava covered the rest of his head. From somewhere he had found some too-small green trousers and a matching pullover. He looked like a cross between Rambo and the Jolly Green Giant. A huge smile on his face told of the joy of his anticipation.

"You're in charge of the home base, then," Pete said. He didn't appear to be dressed any different than usual. "If this goes wrong, arrange the bus in a circle and hold them off until reinforcements arrive."

"We won't be long," Star said.

"Are you sure this is altogether wise? After all, it's still broad daylight out there." I looked out the window. We were parked on the gravel forecourt of a truck stop.

"Best time," she said. "We can see what we're doing."

"How far away is it?"

"You see that small hill there?" She pointed across a field where a gentle rise led up to a small wood.

"Yes," I said.

"Just on the other side of that wood is one of the biggest mink farms in the south of England. This is the perfect way to approach it as they will be looking for people coming from the front."

She pulled a huge pair of bolt-cutters from a box by the side of the driver's seat.

"Ready?" she asked the others.

They nodded.

"Let's go save some lives then!" And off they went leaving me alone in the bus with Cerberus and the mobile petting zoo upstairs.

I watched them running across the field, the two girls leading the way. Woody ran close behind. He crouched and ran in a zigzag fashion. Pete seemed to lag behind. In only two or three minutes, they had all completely disappeared.

Cerberus gave another tug on his rope and managed to gain a few inches in his own personal quest towards the stairs. I braced my foot more firmly against the knot in the end of the rope. He turned and gave me a recriminating look.

I looked alternately through the front and rear windows, scanning the road in both directions. I expected to hear at any moment the sound of wailing police sirens. Cerberus continued to strain at his rope. The thought of what would happen if he broke free and managed to get upstairs worried me, so I tied his rope firmly to the leg of one of the seats. I gave it a checking tug.

After several minutes, I began to relax ,and my curiosity about the upstairs menagerie grew. I checked the rope once more before venturing up the stairs. A wooden gate blocked the top step, and I climbed over it. All of the seats had been removed from the top deck, and the floor was covered with straw. The resulting space was surprisingly large. The goat looked up briefly then decided that I wasn't anybody very interesting and returned to munching at the straw. The chickens and goose seemed oblivious to my arrival. They went about their business of scraping and pecking. This was a microcosm of an English farm; even the smell was authentic. I held my breath then headed back down the stairs.

I was about halfway down when I heard the noise. A clattering sound coming from the lower deck.

I froze.

It was too soon for the others to be back. That could only mean either a thief, or the police. Neither option filled me with joy. I told my legs to creep down the last few steps, but they disobeyed. So I resorted to craning my neck down in an attempt to see what was happening. The clattering continued, and my ears strained to hear anything else beyond it. The breath I had been holding fought its way free, and I blew gently through my lips. I risked creeping down one more step then stopped to listen again. I wondered why I hadn't heard Cerberus. He hadn't barked or growled. My mind cycled through the possibilities. Had he been drugged? Shot with a sleeping dart? No, that was too ridiculous.

"Fucking cooker! Why won't you light?"

That was Pete's voice! I quickly descended the last few steps. Pete was standing in front of the cooker at the back of the bus. His hands jumped from one control to another as he tried to bring it into life.

"What the hell are you doing?" I asked.

He turned round to look at me. "Oh, there you are. I'd been wondering where you were. I thought you'd abandoned your post. Deserted your fellow freedom fighters."

"Don't change the subject. What're you doing back here? Aren't you supposed to be out there helping our four-legged friends?"

"I got lost." He turned his back to me and continued fiddling with the cooker.

"What, the same way you got lost on the way to Maurice and Ivy's caravan that evening?"

"Look, I can't help it if I've got a lousy sense of direction, can I? Now, do you know anything about cookers? I can't get this sodding thing to work."

"What are you trying to cook?"

"Steak."

"What steak?"

"This, look!" He dipped his fingers into a plastic bag by the side of the cooker and pulled out a large slab of meat. It dripped blood onto the floor.

"Where the hell did you get that from?"

"From the back door of the Cafe over there. It was just sitting on top of the fridge. If I hadn't taken it, some stray dog would've probably snuck in and had it. Come on, Tony. Give me a hand to get this going."

I joined him at the cooker. There appeared to be no gas coming from the burner. I traced a red rubber pipe back to a tap on the floor.

"This looks like the problem," I said. I turned it on then pressed the ignition button again. The burner sprang into life.

Pete pulled a frying pan from a hook on the wall and dumped his slab of meat into it. It made a loud sizzling noise.

"You know you shouldn't be cooking that in here, don't you? They could be back any minute."

"Oh, stop worrying. I like it rare anyway. Take the horns off, wipe its backside, and stick it between two slices of bread. That's how I like it."

"But why now? Couldn't you have waited?"

"Forbidden fruit, I guess! I've being craving for a piece of animal flesh since we met these two fruitcakes."

"Where's Cerberus?" I suddenly realised he wasn't there. I had been so engrossed with Pete and his culinary excesses.

"I let him go. I think he wanted to go and do his business or something."

I looked out through the door; there was no sign of him. "I'd better go look for him."

"Good idea," said Pete. "Keep your eye out for the others while you're there."

I scouted around the car park and eventually spotted Cerberus sniffing at the wheel of a large truck. I called to him. He lifted his head, gave me a lop-sided look then ran away. I chased after him as best as my sore foot would allow, but by the time I had rounded the truck, he had disappeared completely. I searched around the back of the Cafe, I even stuck my head in the back door on the off-chance that he'd gone in search of his own piece of animal flesh.

Without success.

As I was looking for him across the field, I saw the others running back down the hill. I decided to deal with

Cerberus later. Top priority now was to get back to the bus and warn Pete.

Pete was just putting his slice of almost raw meat into a sandwich as I climbed back on board.

"He's upstairs," Pete said.

"Who?" I asked.

"Cerberus! He came back and ran upstairs while you were out."

"You didn't try to stop him?"

"Hey, I can't do everything." He held up the sandwich.

I ran up the stairs wondering what carnage would greet me. Cerberus was running around barking at, and chasing anything that moved. And a lot of things were moving very quickly. The air was thick with flying straw and feathers. The stench of manure kicked up by the panicking animals was overpowering. Cerberus himself was in hot pursuit of the goose. The pair of them hurtled around the top floor of the bus in a scene reminiscent of a Tom and Jerry cartoon.

One of the chickens, in a desperate attempt to avoid the mayhem, launched itself off the wooden gate and head-butted the window. It fell with a little thump onto the floor at my feet. It was either unconscious or dead. I picked it up with half a thought to trying to revive it. At that point, the goose made a bolt for the steps, closely pursued by Cerberus. I followed them down, carefully shutting the gate behind me. Although there seemed little point in that now.

I met Star at the bottom of the steps. She was just getting onto the bus. We looked at each other. Then both of our gazes turned to take in the scene on the lower deck. The room was full of floating white feathers. Cerberus lay on the floor with the now dead goose between his paws. Pete was standing next to him, his blue steak sandwich dripping blood down his arm as he appeared to be frozen in time and mid-bite. His eyes were locked on Star.

Still, Star said nothing. She turned to look in my direction, this time looking down towards my hands. I realised I was still holding the dead chicken. I noticed across her shoulder, Woody and Fallow approaching the bus.

"So," I asked. "How did the mission go?"

Chapter 22

We stood on the gravel forecourt and watched the bus drive away into the distance.

"Well I don't know what they got so sniffy about," Pete said. "It was only a bloody goose!"

"I think it would probably be for the best if we didn't hang around here much longer," I suggested.

With several hundred mink running free across the countryside it wouldn't be long before the police came to check this place out. And with my track record, and Woody still in his Rambo outfit, I didn't rate our chances very highly.

"I'll see if I can rustle us up a lift," Pete said. He disappeared inside the Cafe.

As we waited for Pete, I noticed Cerberus was paying a lot of attention to Woody's coat pocket.

"What's he after?" I asked. "You got some chocolate in there, or something?"

"No, that's George."

"George? Who's George?"

"My pet mink. Look!" He pulled a furry little creature from his pocket.

I looked at the thing in Woody's hands. "Are you sure that's a mink, Woody?"

I didn't recall ever having seen a mink before, but I had seen a rat. And this looked remarkably similar.

"It was running around with the others when we opened the cages."

"Did the other minks have pointy noses and long tails?"

"I don't know! There was just a lot of furry things running around everywhere, and I grabbed one."

"I think you should really let him go."

"No way, man! George is mine. He's my friend!"

"Oi!" Pete called.

I turned to look. He was standing in front of the Cafe, next to a man in a black leather jacket.

"Come on then, you two!" He waved his arms, beckoning us.

"You'd better keep that away from Pete," I suggested, nodding at George.

Pete had secured us a lift in the back of a white Transit van. We couldn't see where we were going and that, coupled with the erratic movements of the driver, and highly pungent chemical smell emanating from several plastic bottles in a crate, all combined to spin both head and stomach.

"So, Pete," I said. "What're your plans for getting us in now?"

"Oh, something will turn up!"

We rattled around in the back of the van like three marbles in a matchbox for another hour. Then the driver pulled off the motorway and came to a halt on the slip road.

"I'm going straight on. Glastonbury is about fifteen miles in that direction," he said, pointing east.

The first thing I noticed on emerging back into the daylight was that this appeared to be the dropping off place for hitchers on their way to Glastonbury. There were about fifteen other assorted travellers either side of the road. They ranged from clean-cut, weekend hippies with ultra lightweight, carbon fibre rucksacks and five-berth tents that you could fold up and put in your hip pocket, to the true hardcore citizen-of-the-world with his army surplus clothes and rolled up sleeping bag.

It looked as though we were in for a long wait.

"We're never going to be able to hitch a ride here," Pete said. "We'll move on to plan B."

Why did those words fill me with dread? "Which is?" I asked.

"I don't know. I haven't thought it up yet. But we need to get away from here. Let's head for the nearest pub and see what turns up."

Two miles down the road, we came to 'Arthur's Rest', a small country pub that claimed to have been built at the spot that King Arthur once rested on. If he'd come up from the motorway the same way we had, then I guess it would stand to reason that he would be tired about here.

I was all set to go inside and experiment with some mediaeval ale, when Pete said, "Wait, let's check out the car park."

I couldn't see what he was looking for. The car park was filled with the usual assortment of vehicles, cars, vans, and other commercial vehicles. The one that caught Pete's attention was a flatbed truck with a dozen Porta-loos tied down on the rear. It bore the name 'Denman's Temporary Sanitation' along the side.

"That'll do," said Pete. "Let's go buy the driver a drink... Or two!"

Despite the gloominess of the interior, it didn't take us long to locate the driver. He wore blue overalls with the label Denman's across the breast pocket.

"You two wait over there." Pete nodded at a corner table.

I couldn't make out what he was up to. It was all well and good to get us a lift to the gates, but security were not going to let us in, not when we would clearly be passengers in the vehicle.

Pete surreptitiously approached the man from behind. He waited until the driver had just lifted his pint and was raising it to his lips. Then Pete reached out and pushed the man's shoulder, causing him to spill his drink. The man swung round in his chair, annoyed. Pete raised his hands in supplication. I could see he was piling one apology on top of another. He pointed at the bar offering to buy the man another drink. Within a few minutes, they were both sitting at the table with fresh pints in front of them. For an hour, Pete continued to ply the driver with drinks. Eventually, he called us over.

As I approached the table I could see the driver was three-sheets-to-the-wind. Pete had his arm around him.

"Tony, Woody," Pete slurred. "I want you to meet my very best friend in the whole wide world. Excepting you two, that is. This is Bob."

"Hi, Bob," I said.

"Any friend of Pete's is a friend of mine," Bob said.

"Bob's got a bit of a prob, haven't you Bob?"

"Bob's a bit tiddled," Bob admitted.

"I would never forgive myself if my old mate Bob got himself done for drink-driving. The police are everywhere out there, you know?"

"I would lose my job," Bob said. He looked like he was going to cry. "I really would." He gazed into Pete's face as if imploring him for help.

"That's when I had… hic! Whoops!… I had... My wave brain. Old Tone here," he held an unsteady arm out in my direction. "Tone can drive. No sweat. Tone's a bit of a whizz with anything with wheels on!"

"Would you do that for me?" Bob pleaded.

"Well, I suppose—" I started.

"There you go! Told you he would," Pete said.

"You're the best mate a man can have, Pete." Bob patted Pete on the shoulder. "If I hadn't met you just when I did, I don't know how I would have got out of this mess."

"Hey, what are friends for? If we can't help each other as we pass along our way... Well, the world would just be a sad old place. That's all I can say."

This conversation was more inclined to make me vomit than the ride in the back of the van.

Woody and I helped the other two wobble into the car park. We stopped by the side of the truck.

"Look, Pete," I said, "we still can't all sit in the front. Two of us maybe."

"Right, yeah. Well, who then?"

"If I'm driving," I said, "I've got to sit in the front. And we need Bob. That means you and Woody..." I nodded towards the Porta-loos stacked on the rear, "have got to find somewhere to hide." I was beginning to see the upside to this plan.

We piled our kit into two of the spare Porta-loos then Woody and Pete climbed into two others with Cerberus in a fifth.

"Got a newspaper?" Woody asked, as he stepped into his cubicle.

Pete looked decidedly unhappy. I guessed that he hadn't thought the plan through to this point. I pushed the doors shut on them and tied them down. I had to help Bob up into the passenger seat of the cab. He was singing a tuneless version of 'King of the road'.

For all of its size, the truck had a remarkably light clutch and didn't aggravate my foot too much. Contrary to Pete's advertising of my abilities, I had never driven anything larger than my camper van, so I was very nervous about a vehicle of this size. But I swung out onto the main road and within a mile or two, I was driving like a pro. All I needed now was my Yorkie Bar and a CB radio.

"Breaker breaker, I've got a smokey on my handle, come back you all, ten four."

I wondered how the others were getting on in the back. I pictured Pete in his drunken stupor being bounced around inside the tiny cubicle. An evil thought crossed my mind when I saw a large pothole in the road ahead. I headed straight for it. The wheels hit the hole with a thump, and I watched in the rear view mirror as all of the Porta-loos jumped six inches into the air.

"And that," I said out loud, "is for parking on my foot."

As we approached Glastonbury the police presence became more noticeable. However, they were much more interested in parked vehicles than moving ones. In fact, every time we slowed down, a policeman would appear from nowhere to wave his arms at us and ensure we didn't stop.

I found a small car park in the centre of town.

"Just going to find us a tent and a barby," I shouted to the Porta-loos on the truck as I jumped down. I heard a muffled response but couldn't make out what it was.

The camping supplies shop was heaving. It was like a scene from 'Armageddon'. Panic buying took on new meaning. I could only find one tent and going by the picture, it was a huge affair, and outrageously priced. It consisted of two compartments and a central area. But I had little choice. It came without instructions or packaging, so I was able to haggle the price down slightly. I fared slightly better with the barbecue, having a selection of three to choose from. I parted with my visa card. I was nearing the end of my funds and hoped my web site was busy.

We pulled up at the gate to the main site entrance, our way blocked by a security guard. He wore a white T-shirt two sizes too small with 'Security' stencilled on the front. He clutched a walkie-talkie to his ear as he watched us. Bob had advised me that these people like to be called 'Guv'.

I wound down the window and called, "Afternoon, Guv!" at him.

"What you got here then?"

I wondered if this guy knew what a Porta-loo was.

"Porta-loos! Temporary toilets... Guv"

"They'll be needing those I guess," he said. "Especially if they get another outbreak of food poisoning this year." He laughed loudly, obviously enjoying his reminiscences of the previous year's festival highlights. "Do you know where you're going?"

"No, Guv!"

"Go through here," he pointed down the field. "follow this track and the shit-hole compound is down there in the far corner."

"Great! Thanks, Guv."

I moved the truck forwards through the gates.

We were in!

We bounced across the uneven grass. I did try to avoid as many potholes as I could as I was now beginning to feel sorry for the three of them in the back.

Vehicles of all descriptions scuttered about. Catering wagons, small diggers erecting fences, even a couple of cranes putting the finishing touches to the stage. Within a few days there were going to be enough people here to populate a small city. They all had to be fed, watered, and entertained.

I wondered if Astrid was here yet. Had she too found a way in without paying? I found the corner of the field we had been directed to and stopped the truck. Bob immediately scrambled down, leant on a nearby fence post, and vomited all over his feet.

As I hopped up onto the back of the truck, I heard Pete banging furiously on the door.

"Come on, you sadist. Let me out!"

I undid the ropes and the door swung open. Pete burst out like a horse from the starting gate. He leapt down from the back of the truck and was soon adding his contribution to the mess started by Bob.

Cerberus barked his demands to be let out, so I attended to him next. Woody stepped out of his cabinet with an air of composure, but the aroma that greeted me testified to the fact that he had made use of the facilities while he was there.

"Oh, Woody," I said. "How could you?"

"Hey, man. Economy of time! Saved me a little job later, didn't it?"

We waited until Pete and Bob had recovered then helped Bob unload the Porta-loos. Being especially careful of Woody's. When we had finished, Bob settled himself down in his cab for a sleep, and we set off to find a discreet corner in which to set up our tent. There were still two days to go before the festival opened, and the only people on the site were construction crew, security, and a few early traders. We would have to be careful to blend in.

We found an area where a few catering stands had set up shop. If we pitched our tent in amongst them, we should look innocuous enough.

Pete unrolled the tent onto the ground. It was enormous. It looked like a deflected hot air balloon tangled up with a do-it-yourself scaffolding set. All three of us stood watching it for a moment, as if hoping somehow it would assemble itself.

"I think I know how it goes," Pete said. He set to work slotting poles together and staking guy-ropes into the ground. Within half an hour, we had assembled what appeared to be a hang glider.

A re-think was in order.

Another half an hour. This time it looked like someone's parachute entangled in an electricity pylon. Where was Maurice when I needed him?

"I don't think this bit belongs here," Woody tugged at one of the poles, and the whole mess fell down again.

By the time we'd put it together for the third time, the sun had dipped below the horizon leaving a pink smear on the underside of the clouds.

"Well, at least this time it looks something like a tent," I said. Although the flapping canvas construction still looked nothing like the picture I'd seen in the shop. And par for the course, we had some bits left over.

We piled our stuff into one of the compartments and zipped up the flaps. It took me a while to work out how the doors operated. They seemed wrong somehow, when undone, they collapsed onto the floor.

The barbecue wasn't anywhere near as high-tech as the Thunderer 5,000, but it worked well, and the flames were adjustable, which was a bonus. Woody set about cooking a pile of bacon sandwiches for us. It struck me that apart from the pie with the side dish of radio/alarm clock, bacon sandwiches was about all I'd ever seen him eat. I declined his offer of added mushrooms, but I did accept a fried egg.

We settled back in our deck chairs to enjoy the evening air and Woody's cooking.

"Hey, man! What's he doing?" Woody nodded towards a security guard who was chatting to the owners of a nearby hot potato stand.

"Oh, hell!" Pete said. "He's checking permits."

"Woody…" I said.

"Yes?"

"Make some sort of sign quickly. I'll go stall him."

"What sort of sign?"

"Oh, I don't know. Be creative."

I waited until the security guard had finished with the hot potato stand than I intercepted him as he headed in our direction.

"Ah, there you are!" I said. "You took your time."

"What?" He was wrong footed. Good.

"Look, I reported the theft over two hours ago. Or perhaps I shouldn't have left it to you guys. Perhaps I should have gone straight to the police." The cruellest blow imaginable to a security guard.

"No, no! We're the police here. Now, just remind me, what was the problem?"

"Didn't the office brief you properly then? Our cash box... Our cash box was stolen. Surely they told you that?"

"Yes, yes of course they did. But I wanted you to say it, sort of a security check you see. Now, just confirm what was in it?"

"About twenty five pounds, a stack of receipts, oh, and of course, our trader's permit."

"Your permit, well, oh dear." The guard shook his head. "What would they want that for?"

"I assume it's gate crashers. But hey, I'm not a security expert. That's down to you guys."

"Yeah, right! Gate crashers, I expect then. I suppose I'll have to give you a temporary permit." He pulled a note pad and a pen from his pocket. "What's your trading name?"

I turned round to see what Woody had come up with. He was just propping a cardboard sign against the barbecue. A large unicorn adorned most of the sign and written across the top, in felt tip pen, were the words, "The Bacon Sandwitch Company"

"Err, the Bacon Sandwitch company. That's with a T," I said.

"Right," he said. He wrote on his piece of paper,' Temporary permit. Bacon SandwiTch Company.'

"Hope you catch the thieves," I said, as I took it from him.

"They won't get far," the guard said confidently. "Oh, by the way,"

"Yes?"

"Your tent's upside down."

We watched as the guard continued on his rounds.

"Nicely handled, man," Pete said.

I glowed inside. Praise from Pete was a gold star moment indeed. The only fly in this particular ointment was that we now appeared to be the proprietors of the Bacon Sandwitch Company, and our entire stock consisted of half a loaf of bread and three rashers of bacon.

Chapter 23

The next morning we held our first board meeting. The financial director's report revealed our finances were in a sorry state indeed. Funds were running desperately short. Pete had spent a fair amount of money plying Bob with alcohol, and none of us had very much left in our respective bank accounts.

"Well, I suppose we'll just have to make a go of the Bacon Sandwitch Company then," Pete said.

It fell to Pete to go into town and replenish our stocks. My foot, although recovering, was not up to that kind of walking just yet. Trusting Woody with the last of our resources was not even up for discussion.

While Pete was away, Woody and I tried to rectify the problems with the tent. Now, in daylight it was easier to see where we had gone wrong. The tent was indeed upside down. Once we had come to that conclusion, it didn't take us long to sort it out.

I was hammering in the last of the guy ropes when I heard a voice behind me.

"Could you do me one with mushrooms, mate?"

I turned to see the security guard from the evening before standing by our barbecue.

"Hey, cool," Woody said. "Our first customer. A bacon butty with mushrooms coming right up!"

"Woody," I whispered, "we haven't got any mushrooms."

"Yeah, man," Woody whispered. "I've got some..."

"No, Woody. We don't have any mushrooms!"

"It's cool, I've got a bag full of..."

"No, Woody, you don't understand. We haven't got any mushrooms." I winked at him. Big, exaggerated winks.

"But I've got—"

"No! No mushrooms!"

"But I—"

"No!"

Eventually, the message got through, and Woody turned back to the guard. "Mushrooms are off, man."

"Oh, never mind. I'll have one with an egg then."

Woody turned to look at me. "Have we got an egg?"

"Yes, Woody. We've got eggs."

"Cool, bacon butty with egg coming up." Woody slapped the bacon on the grill.

The guard pulled a sheet of paper from a folder under his arm. "I actually came over to give you this," he said as he handed it to me.

"What is it?"

"There's a known paedophile lives nearby. The police usually keep a watch on him, but they lost track of him two days ago. They thought he might turn up here and asked us to keep a look out. We're handing these out to all the traders."

I scanned the sheet of paper. A black and white photograph took up the top half. He looked like anybody's favourite uncle. No manic gleam in the eye, no tattoos on his forehead. Receding hair which the text below described as red, seemed to be the only thing distinguishing him from a thousand other middle aged men.

Woody handed the man his sandwich. I felt my mouth watering just looking at it. He did cook them beautifully.

"We'll watch out for him," I said, as I collected two pounds from the guard. We were now stockless, and I was starving hungry.

We had just sold my breakfast.

Pete returned about two hours later, bringing with him about twenty packs of bacon, five loaves of bread, and a sack of coal for the barbecue. And the same amount of money as he set out with.

"How did that happen?" I asked.

"Oh, we've entered into an advertising deal with Lindy's Late store."

"An advertising deal?"

"Well basically, Woody puts up a sign saying Lindy's Late store, purveyors of fine organic bacon. Or something like that."

"And they went for that?"

"Why shouldn't they? Over the next three days, a quarter of a million people are going to see that sign. A few packs of bacon is small feed for that.

Throughout the next twenty-four hours we built up a good customer base from the construction crew. The following evening, the site started to fill. A constant flow of people oozed through the gates, like a broken kaleidoscope oozing its colours across the ground, spreading out across the site. They brought with them their own sounds. Guitars, tom-tom's, Ghetto Blaster's, all adding their own layers to the constant chattering and shouting.

I found the smells really triggered my memories. A unique blend of incense and barbecuing.

And there was still no sign of Astrid.

My eyes constantly raked the procession of new arrivals. My heart quickened each time I caught a glimpse of blonde hair. Several times I thought I'd seen her and was just about to call out when I realised I was mistaken.

The Bacon Sandwitch Company proved to be a surprise hit. Pete had almost a full-time job trotting into town keeping our stocks up, while Woody and I did most of the cooking.

When the music started, business died dramatically for a while as everybody flooded to the main arena to see the opening bands.

We took it in turns to man the stall, allowing each of us to enjoy the events.

In the early evening of the first day, the 'Beautiful South' took to the stage, and the area around the trader's stands was suddenly devoid of people. I had never been a lover of their particular blend of folksy pop, so I volunteered to look after the Bacon Sandwitch Company, while Woody and Pete headed for the main stage.

I hadn't seen a customer in over an hour, and I was stretched back in my deck chair, eyes closed, soaking in the sounds and smells.

"Can I have a bacon sandwich please, Mister?" A small voice snagged my attention.

"Sure," I said. "With the ketchup?" I sat up and turned round to face my customer. Instantly, every cell in my body tingled. "Simon?"

The boy jumped back with a start. His eyes searched me, struggling for recognition.

"Simon, it's me. Dad!"

He squinted, as if trying to peer through a haze. The last time he had seen me had been nearly three months ago. I had been Mr Respectable then. The epitome of the London office dweller on holiday. But now... I mentally imagined what he was looking at. My long hair was tied back in a ponytail, and I had a thick beard and sunglasses. My jeans were torn at the knees, and I wore a T-shirt with a phallic parody of the Nike tick and the words 'Just done it' underneath.

Perhaps it was understandable that he didn't recognise me. I pulled my sunglasses off.

"How's Natasha, and mum?" I asked.

He looked as if he were cast in stone. Pale and immobile. Only his mouth moved.

"They're... They're over there." He finally managed to raise a hand and pointed towards a nearby stall selling leather goods.

I followed his pointing finger. I saw the back of Sam's head as she rummaged through a rack of leather belts. Natasha was nowhere to be seen.

"How are you keeping?"

"Okay." He was still looking apprehensive.

I dropped onto one knee and held my arms open. "Come here."

He paused for a moment then his eyes filled with tears, and he ran the last three steps throwing himself at me. His arms tightened around my neck. I thought he was going to cut off my breath. I held him close.

"I missed you, Simon. You, and your sister."

We had never been a close family. I couldn't remember the last time I'd hugged Simon. It had been a long time, anyway. Too long.

"When are you coming home, Dad?" he said, into my shoulder.

"I don't think that's going to happen, Simon. Your mother and I are... Or perhaps it's just me... we're not the same people any more. We want different things. That doesn't mean I won't be seeing a lot of you both. I will. I just need to get settled."

He pushed himself back from me and studied me afresh. "You look cool, Dad!" He smiled. "Where are you living?"

"Ah, well. Mostly in a camper van." I wondered if my van was still there. Though I doubted anybody could move it even if they found it.

"Great! Can I come and live with you?"

"Perhaps you can come and stay for a while. Once we get your mum used to the idea. Go call her over, will you? "

"Sure, Dad." He ran over to Sam. I watched as he tugged at her arm. She broke her arm free from his grip and flapped him away. He tried again. This time she made shooing movement with both hands. Even from this distance, I could hear him shout, "It's Dad!"

Her head whipped round like a bird in search of danger. Her eyes scanned back and forth and must have passed over me several times before coming back to lock on to me. She kept her eyes focused on me while she called for Natasha. Her left hand reached behind her and Natasha emerged from around a rack of leather bags. Sam grabbed her hand, and they walked slowly across towards the Bacon Sandwitch Company's headquarters.

"Hello, Tony."

"Sam."

"You look... different."

"Yeah, I changed my hair style. Like it?" I said.

"No, I meant... even with the more obvious changes, you still look different. More... more relaxed."

"I am different. I am more relaxed."

Natasha hugged closely into Sam. I reached out for her. She shrank back.

"It's all right, Natasha darling," said Sam. "It's your daddy. He just looks a bit strange that's all. Why don't you give him a kiss?" She eased Natasha towards me.

Natasha took hold of my offered hand then seemed to overcome her nervousness. She pushed herself against me and kissed my cheek. She stepped back to look at me properly. Her nose wrinkled. "You smell funny, Daddy."

"Out of the mouths of babes and innocents," Sam said.

"So, how you keeping, Sam?"

She wore a navy-blue tracksuit with brilliant-white trainers. She looked as though she had just been diverted from her afternoon jog.

"Oh, I'm fine," she said. "How's your... erm... your... friend?"

"You mean Astrid?"

"If that's what her name is."

"I haven't seen her for a while, actually."

"That little fling didn't last very long then, did it?"

"No, it didn't, did it."

"Mum?" said Simon. "Can I go and look at the hippies?"

"Yes, dear. Take Natasha with you, will you? But don't go too far. Stay where I can see you."

"I got your letter," I said.

"Good." She paused. "Tony, I don't think there's any way back from this. I don't want you to waste time pleading—"

"I agree."

"I mean, I know that by now, you probably realise what a dreadful mess you've made of things. But you can't expect just to come running home. After what you did—"

"Yes, I know!"

"It's no good arguing. I've been thinking about this. And it's better if we go our own separate ways."

"Absolutely!"

David Luddington

"Now, I can see you're upset. But it's for the best. We—"

"I agree!"

"It's no good you going on— You agree?"

"Yes!"

"What do you mean, you agree?"

"Sam, what are you doing here?"

"I just thought... I thought I'd take the kids for a day out."

"You have never been to a place like this in your life. You came here looking for me, didn't you? "

"Yes, I suppose."

"I realise you've probably been working on what you were going to say to me for several weeks. Am I right?"

"Well..."

"Let me make this easy for you. You draw up the papers; I'll sign them. You can divide up everything in any way you like. I'll trust you. Just leave me enough for a lobster boat. That's all I ask. A lobster boat and access to the children whenever I want. Agreed?"

"If that's what you want, Tony. I'll arrange things then."

So that was it then. Twenty years coming to a conclusion. I felt I a need to say something profound.

"Would you like a bacon sandwich?"

Once I'd broken through her barriers, we chatted comfortably for several minutes until Woody returned. I introduced them.

"Woody, this is Sam my... my soon-to-be ex-wife." I smiled at Sam.

"Hey, cool," said Woody. "Does that mean you're available?" He gave Sam a big wink.

"It means I'm going to rip your genitals off if you come any closer to me. You horrible little creature."

"Ain't she just the sweetest?" I said.

"Hey, fiery, man. Fiery's cool."

Simon and Natasha returned from their wandering, and I managed to persuade Sam to let them come with me for a while. We agreed to meet back at the Bacon Sandwitch Company in one hour's time.

I grabbed the children, one in each hand, and we ran off into the crowds, leaving Woody and Sam in charge of the stall.

"You want to go to the fair? Or do you want to watch the music?" I asked, as we ran.

"Fair," they both answered in unison.

"Me too!"

I didn't have much ready cash with me so I needed to play the angles a bit. We wandered around the fairground while I surreptitiously gathered the names of various ride operators. When I had accumulated a few such names, we set off for the galloping horses roundabout.

We waited until the ride was just about to start then I leapt up onto the platform and said to the man collecting the money, "Joe wants you, over on the dodgems."

"Oh, right! Thanks!" And off he headed.

We jumped onto our horses, and the ride started.

We raced our mounts around the roundabout, pretending to gee them on, as if racing each other. When that turn had finished, we pulled the same stunt on the other rides in the fair.

For half an hour, we rode up and down, around and round. Spun in circles, or bumped in cars. By the end of it, I was feeling happy, hungry and ill at the same time. An interesting combination.

The next vote was for whether we should have candy floss, toffee apples, or hot dogs. It was a three-way split, with no chance of resolution, so we opted for all three. Both Simon and Natasha managed to create a fascinating blend of toffee, spun sugar, and tomato ketchup down the front of their clothes. I dipped the bottom of Simon's T-shirt in a mug of lemonade and tried to use that to dampen the mess in order to clean it off. It didn't help very much. Just spread it around a bit.

Natasha said she wanted a donkey ride, and while we were heading in that direction, I noticed a man with a small crowd gathered around him. We stopped to see what was happening. He was playing 'Find-the-lady', the ancient three-card trick. Pete had once explained to me how this worked, and I was keen to observe it in action. Once I knew the trick it was easy to see, and I pointed it out to Simon.

"You see, Simon, when he uses one card to turn over another, he actually switches them. It's so smooth, you can hardly see it unless you know what you're looking for."

I gave Simon a one-pound coin to have a go. Within a few minutes, he had accumulated ten pounds. Two minutes later, he had been asked to leave.

We took Natasha over to the pony ride area. I gave her the three pounds indicated by the sign then settled on a wooden bench to watch. She stood for a while on the edge of the enclosure. I wondered for a moment if she was frightened. Then, when all of the ponies except one had a rider, she went over to the man collecting the money and tugged at his arm. I couldn't hear what was being said. She pointed across the field. The man looked up and nodded at her then he ran off in the direction she had indicated. Natasha smoothly seated herself on the last pony, and they started around the paddock.

That's my girl!

As the ride finished, I went over to meet her. She jumped off her pony and landed in a fresh pile of horse manure. I helped to wipe her shoe as best as we could on the grass.

I checked my watch, we had five minutes to get back. We were just setting off in the direction of the Bacon Sandwitch Company, when I noticed a group of trees in the far corner of the site.

"Come on," I said. "Race you to the trees!"

We ran across the field, each of us taking the occasional tumble before we reached our destination.

There were only half a dozen trees, rugged and gnarled with all manner of interesting branches. Ideal for climbing. We chose a large oak tree, and I helped push the children up into the lower branches. Once they were safely ensconced, I clambered up to join them. We sat astride a thick branch, enjoying the view across the festival site.

After a while, we resumed our climbing up into the higher levels of the tree. We shuffled outwards along a branch until it dipped alarmingly, threatening to dump us on the ground. We moved back to the trunk, then climbed as high as we could before we ran out of solid footing. At one point, Simon slipped and scraped the side of his face against the trunk of the tree. He just laughed.

Eventually, I decided we'd best head back. Battered, bedraggled, and bestained, the three of us raced across the field back to Sam.

Sam spotted Simon's scraped face from twenty metres away. She ran to him, scooping him up.

"Oh, you poor little dear. What's happened?"

Simon pushed her away. "Nothing, Mum," he said. "We had a great time. Can I live with Dad in his camper van?"

"Oh, yes please!" Natasha echoed.

Sam shifted her gaze to Natasha's dress, obviously trying to work out just what each of the individual stains represented. She clucked around her brood and scrubbed at faces with a spit-laden handkerchief.

"How could you, Tony?" she muttered. "It's one thing allowing yourself to sink to this level, but it's quite another to take the children down with you. Look at them! I leave them with you for five minutes, and look... They look like refugees from...from…" She struggled, clearly trying to drag from her memory the places that refugees came from. "From some... poor country," she added weakly.

I ignored the rest of her tirade and turned my attention to Woody.

"How's business?" I asked.

"And that's another thing," Sam said. "Why you haven't given food poisoning to half the site, I'll never know. You have no hand washing facilities here. Those mushrooms he's been serving look weeks old. They're all funny colours!"

"Woody?" I asked. "Mushrooms? Tell me about the mushrooms." Although outwardly calm, my insides were showing the first signs of panic.

"They're the ones that I... Oh... Yeah...No mushrooms, right?"

"What have you done?"

"I'll tell you what he's done," Sam said. "He's probably started a salmonella epidemic so enormous it will make the Great Plague look like a mild case of excema. Thank goodness the children didn't eat any."

"Sam?" I said.

"Yes?"

"Shut up!" In all of the millions of words that I must have spoken to Sam over our twenty years, I don't think I'd ever put those two words together before. The effect was startling. Her face drained of colour, and the whole of her body became immobile. With the exception of her mouth, which made little opening and shutting movements as if the batteries were running down.

"Woody, how many bacon and mushroom sandwiches have you sold?"

He thought for a moment. "Three," he said.

Well, not the end of the world anyway. Three hallucinating hippies in a crowd of 250,000 were probably not going to turn too many heads. But Woody hadn't finished.

"They all had one, you see. One each."

"Who did?"

"The BBC film crew. They were filming us... The traders. They filmed me making their sandwiches." He looked pleased with himself. So he should be. He was going to get his fifteen minutes of fame. Not only had he poisoned a BBC news crew, but they had film of him doing it as well.

That'll be one for 'You've Been Framed'.

Sam was still quiet, and I turned to look at her. She was just finishing off straightening the children's clothes. I noticed her eyes were red. She'd been crying.

"Sam... I..." I started without thinking through what I was going to say. She saved me the trouble.

"Forget it, Tony. Anything you want to say from this point on can be said through court. Come along now." She gathered the children together and marched off with as much dignity as the pot-holed field would allow.

It seemed that our marriage had taken one more step down the path marked 'Irredeemable'. But I had more pressing things to worry about. Like how to prevent Woody's expertise appearing on the late evening news.

At that point, Pete showed up.

"How's things going then? Have I missed anything interesting?"

Chapter 24

Against our better judgement, we left Woody once more in charge of the Bacon Sandwitch Company. But not before removing all of the mushrooms. Pete and I set off in search of the BBC film crew. We needed to retrieve that film.

It didn't take us long to track them down. Their van was parked near the main stage. It was not difficult to spot. The satellite dishes sprouting from its roof could be seen from hundreds of yards away. It was a large van, painted grey in colour with the blue BBC logo along the side.

As we approached, I heard the sound of laughter inside. The back door was ajar, and I crept up to peep inside. Although the truck itself was a huge vehicle, the inside appeared cramped. Banks of equipment lined the walls. Screens flickered, tapes whirred, and lights blinked.

If I'd had any doubts at all about the potency of Woody's mushrooms, they were dispelled as soon as I saw the state of the pride of the BBC. One of them sat crouched in the corner, sucking his thumb. Another man was leaning over the mixing desk, carefully and methodically pulling the tape out of a pile of videocassettes on the desk. He was already knee-deep in tape. It swirled around him like brown stringy fog. The third crewmember was putting on his own private strip show at the far end of the studio. He was down to his Y fronts, and bumping and grinding like a Soho lap dancer.

I wondered if the tape I needed was one of the ones curled around the engineer's feet. But I couldn't take the risk. My best guess was it was still in the camera. They wouldn't have had either the time or the wherewithal to begin editing it before the effects of Woody's mushrooms caught up with them.

Pete tapped my shoulder. "Well?"

"They're all in there, but I can't see the camera."

"Shit," he said. "How're we going to get it?"

"It might not be that difficult. They're not entirely on this planet at the moment."

"Paris?"

"Paris!"

I peered in again. The lighting level was low inside compared to the bright sunlight outside. I blinked to help my eyes adjust. It didn't take me long to locate the camera. It lay on a small bench alongside the mixing desk. The only reason I hadn't spotted it at first was because it was half covered in unwound videotape. I stepped quietly but confidently into the vehicle and headed for my prize. I had to turn sideways to slide past the man pulling the tape.

"Wait," he said, holding his hand up.

Oh hell! I froze.

He dipped into his pocket, extracted a ten-pound note, and stuffed it into my hand. He said, "Get me another beer, please?"

He returned to his mission of playing cat's cradle with their last two days' work.

I reached across and picked up the camera. For all of its size, it was surprisingly light. I turned to leave, but Pete blocked the way. He had pulled the door shut behind him.

"Shush," he said. "There's people outside."

I listened at the door. We both jumped with a start when somebody knocked on the outside.

"What do we do?" whispered Pete.

"Bluff it out," I said. "Come on." I hefted the camera onto my shoulder and stepped out of the door.

Two young men in jeans and T-shirts hovered anxiously outside.

"Aren't you ready yet?" the first one asked. "They've been waiting for twenty minutes."

"Oh, right!" I said.

"Come on then," the youth said. "The band is ready to go onstage."

I glanced at Pete. He looked as horrified as I felt.

They walked closely alongside us not allowing us a chance to escape. We came to the backstage gate, and they flashed security passes. We were ushered through by two bulky security guards.

The logo on the back of the youth's T-shirts indicated that they were roadies for 'Young Love', a particularly clean cut boy-band who were riding high in the charts with 'My Heart Sings'.

They led us up the steps to the rear of the main stage then motioned for us to wait. The announcer was already on stage. He was apologising for the delay to the start of 'Young Love's' set and he assured the audience they were now ready to go.

He raised his arms high in the air, "Are you ready for them?" he yelled.

The roar from the crowd indicated they were ready for them.

"I can't hear you! Are you ready for them?"

The resulting noise was painful, like an express train rattling through a tunnel.

"Well, here they are. Winners of the New Musical Express Best Newcomer's Award. Number three in the charts at the moment, please welcome... Young Love!"

Five shiny faced youths with washing powder commercial T-shirts bounded past us and onto the stage. One of them knelt down at the front of the stage. He reached his arms out to the audience and started singing a particularly vomit-inducing ditty about lost love.

The announcer returned to the wings to see us.

"You the film crew?" he asked.

I nodded.

"Well, they're all yours! Bless their cotton socks."

Pete nudged me in the arm, "Go on then! You're the cameraman."

"Great, thanks."

As I stepped onto the stage, one of the boys spotted me. He came over and sang directly into the camera. I pointed it at him and looked through the viewfinder. The screen was blank. My fingers groped across the control panel, pressing at every button they could find. Eventually, the viewfinder sprang into life and the boy's face appeared in glorious close-up. So close in fact, I could see his tonsils. I hadn't a clue how to widen the shot. I didn't even know if it was recording. I just pointed it at him and let him sing his little heart out.

I panned around the stage and did a sweep of the audience. The boys continued to come to the front of the camera, vying with each other as to who could look the most wholesome. They all looked identical to me. Smiley faces, unnaturally white teeth, and neatly gelled hair. They each wore combat trousers, white T-shirts, and trainers.

They were just launching into their second number, 'True to You,' when I felt a tap on my shoulder. I turned to see Pete.

"Can I have a go?" he asked.

"What do you mean, can you have a go? We shouldn't even be here."

"Oh, come on. You've had a long enough turn, let me have a go?"

I shrugged and passed him the camera.

"How does it work?" he asked.

"How the hell do I know? Just point it at them!"

"Is it on?"

"I think so."

Peter leapt around the stage with great enthusiasm for his new role. He moved from one band member to another and several times lay down on the stage to point the camera upward at them. At one point, he even planted the camera on the top of his head, and spun round, lighthouse fashion. The group lapped it up. They responded to his energy and played up to him. As the intensity of their performance increased, so did the excitement of the audience. The whole of the arena was on its feet. Arms swaying in time with the music. It would be a big shame if the camera weren't recording this. These lads were giving the performance of their lives.

The set lasted half an hour, and Pete filmed every note and every droplet of sweat. The boys finished and stepped into the wings. The audience still cheered, clapping rhythmically, demanding an encore. Pete stood at the front of the stage. He kept the camera focused on the audience and waved one arm in the air keeping time with their chanting. Encouraging the frenzy to new heights.

At one point, I noticed him focusing the camera on a small scuffle going on to left of the stage. He seemed to hold onto them for a long time, before returning his attention to the main audience.

'Young Love' returned to the stage amidst a terrifying noise, and impossibly, as their backing tape played the first few notes of 'My Heart Sings,' the noise level increased even further.

Pete jumped around the stage once more with seemingly endless energy and with a degree of mania completely out of keeping with the ballad he was supposed to be filming. Even when 'Young love' had finally finished their set, Pete was still trying to whip them up. I heard him talking to the lead singer.

"Smash your kit up!" he said.

"What?" replied the singer.

"Smash your kit up. All the bands do it these days."

"Are you sure?"

"Yeah! They'll love it!"

"Pete," I called. I needed to put a stop to this.

"Wait a minute, Tony"

Pete returned his attention to the lead singer, who after a bit more coaxing seemed to get the idea. He ran over to one of the speakers at the edge of the stage and gave it a good kick. His colleagues quickly picked up on what was happening and joined in attacking the other speakers. The feedback screamed through the dying sound system, almost drowning out the pops and fizzes of short circuiting electrical equipment. Sparks flew, and acrid smoke drifted across the stage, stinging my eyes.

The band members were yelling and whooping, thoroughly enjoying this new finale to their performance. The audience on the other hand, appeared to be in stunned silence. "Teen Magazine" had recently voted this particular group as the "Nicest Guys in Pop".

This was not the behaviour expected of them.

Before long, it dawned on the individual members of 'Young Love' that the audience was not with them on this one. One by one, white T-shirted, formerly Mr. Nice Guys, turned to face Pete. The still-life tableau on the stage could have been a painting. Everything was motionless, with the exception of the smoke, which curled around the dying equipment.

The audience stared at 'Young Love'.

'Young Love' stared at Pete.

Pete turned to look at me.

"Tony," he said.

"Yes?"

"Run!"

We both made a dash for the steps that led from the rear of the stage. We darted through the crowded backstage area and out the security gates. Pete held on to the camera with no less passion than a mother holding her newborn baby.

"We can't go back to the BBC van," I called to Pete as we darted through the crowds. "That's the first place they'll look. We'll have to hide in the tent."

We ran a circuitous route until we were sure nobody was following us. Then we made our way back to the tent. We both dived inside and lay flat on our backs, panting.

Woody poked his head through the tent flaps.

"Get it?" he asked.

"I think so," I patted the camera. "I hope it's in there."

"Let's have a look then?"

I picked up the camera and turned it around in my hands. I hoped to find a big button marked 'Play'. There wasn't one of course. There were a hundred and one other controls but very few I could understand.

"Hey, I know this one!" said Woody. He took the camera from me, and a series of coloured lights blipped into existence on the front of the machine. Something inside whirred and a moment later there was a loud click. The viewfinder's screen showed a scene of the area surrounding the Bacon Sandwitch Company. A wide angle shot around the various traders then came to rest on our stall. The screen flickered, and there was Woody, spatula in hand and grinning like a politician as he prepared his hallucinogenic menu.

"Where did you learn to do that?" I asked Woody. "No, on the other hand, don't tell me."

Woody fast-forwarded the tape, and there were the shots of 'Young Love.' Some of them were quite inventive. But in the main, even the computerised picture steadying couldn't keep up with Pete's frenzied camera work. The whole thing resembled one of those late 60's art house movies. There were some interesting moments. At one point, we had a beautiful close-up of the inside of Jason Brightly's nose. Surprisingly hairy for a seventeen year old, I thought.

The view then changed to the audience and homed in on the scuffle I'd seen Pete filming during the break.

"Oh yes, I'd forgotten that," Pete said.

"What's happening there?" I asked.

"Look, that guy there," Pete pointed out a small figure. "Familiar?"

"I don't know. It's too far away."

"Do you want me to zoom in?" asked Woody.

"How can you do that?" I said. "It's on a film."

"Digital isn't it?"

Woody's fingers worked a small dial and immediately the picture enlarged. Once more, I was forced to reassess my mental image of Woody. Each time I thought I had the measure of him, he'd spring a new surprise on me.

"There! That's him!" Pete said.

"Who?" I asked.

"The paedophile they're looking for. Look!"

He was right. The close-up left no doubt. I felt a chill in my stomach as if I'd just swallowed a tray full of ice cubes. The man was reaching for the hand of a child who sat on the ground.

Their hands touched.

The child stood up.

"Pete," I said. "You should have done something, not just filmed it."

"No, wait," he said. "Look. Watch."

The boy resisted, pulling back against the man's grip. They struggled momentarily then another, larger boy kicked the man in the groin. The paedophile doubled over and slinked away into the crowd.

"Good for him," I said. "That was a close one! But we've got to hand this over to the police."

"We can't do that," said Pete. "Not only are you wanted by the police, there is video evidence here of Woody poisoning the BBC!"

"Yes, but if we don't do something, he's going to try it with some other child. He might even have done so by now!" I thought of Simon and Natasha out there somewhere. I hoped Sam had taken them home by now.

"Give it to the security guard," Woody suggested. "Then we leg it!"

We pondered this for a while. I was reluctant to leave until I'd found Astrid. That was the whole reason I was here. But I really couldn't see a way through this. If we handed the tape in, we were going to have the police after us for theft of BBC equipment and poisoning people. As well as probably inciting a riot. If we didn't hand it in, the paedophile was free to pursue his nefarious ways.

We couldn't let that happen. It seemed Woody's was the only option open.

"We could rub Woody's bit off," I suggested. "That would solve one problem. Can you do that, Woody?"

"No worries!" He fiddled with the controls for a few minutes. "There!" he said. "All gone."

We reviewed the tape. He had edited it perfectly.

"Well", I said. "That's it then! We'd better make a move."

Chapter 25

Even though I knew that each moment's delay allowed that monster more chance of escape, I still couldn't stop myself from working unnaturally slowly as we folded the tent. We finished packing up our stuff and jammed it into the various bags.

My foot was much better by now, which was just as well as we had far more kit on this part of our journey due to the tent and barbecue. Financially, we were fairly solvent. The Bacon Sandwitch Company had done us proud.

We dropped the videotape into the security guard's office on the way out, and explained what was on it. The senior guard tried to insist that we stay and talk to the police, "For continuity of evidence," he said. We explained that wasn't possible.

Just as we were leaving the site, I stopped and looked back, hoping beyond reason to see Astrid. I would have stayed there for much longer had Pete not tugged at my arm.

"Come on, Tony. She'll show up at Stonehenge anyway, for the summer solstice. That's a much smaller area. You're bound to see her there.

We walked about a mile to find the main road that would take us to Stonehenge. With the amount of kit we were carrying, it was an arduous walk. We covered it in silence. I used the time for thinking.

I didn't feel concerned about the way things had turned out with Sam, and I was pleased with the new bond I had found with the children. But I was disappointed at not finding Astrid, and as the summer solstice was still nearly a week away, I just had to put that set of feelings on hold for the moment. I felt frustrated knowing she was probably only a couple of hundred yards away.

I also decided I wanted my van back. Life would be much more convenient all round if I could retrieve that. I raised the subject with Pete when we came to a halt on the main road.

"I am going back for the van. It's better if I travel alone. It's almost impossible for the three of us and Cerberus to get a lift anyway. I could probably be there and back in a day. Providing I can find some way to get it free."

"What about Cerberus?" asked Pete.

"Best if you take him," I said. "I'll travel faster that way. With luck, I can come back and catch up with you."

I gave Cerberus a 'good-bye' tickle behind his ear, and set off down the road in the direction of Bodmin. I found a straight patch of road with a well-positioned lay-by, and I set my kit down.

For an hour, I watched the cars go past, totally ignoring my outstretched thumb. Eventually, a red BMW veered wildly into my lay-by. The wheels locked as it slid to a halt. Little puffs of dust swirled around its tyres.

The passenger door swung open.

I walked over, and poked my head inside. Clouds of cigarette smoke filled the interior and made me wince. The woman inside appeared at first sight to be in her mid thirties. But as the smoke drifted out of the open door and my vision cleared, the telltale signs of youth reconstruction became apparent. Jet black hair a bit too jet, duskily tanned skin a bit too dusky, and the eyebrows just a bit too surprised. I estimated she had a few years on me.

"Hi, Sweetheart, looking for a ride?" She patted the leather passenger seat.

"Er, yes. Thank you! What shall I do with this?" I pointed to my bags.

"Pop them in the boot, Luvvy. It's open."

"Okay," I went round the back and opened the boot. A hastily packed Louis Vuitton suitcase was the only other item in the boot. Only the straps held it closed, and various items of intimate apparel were trying to escape through the open zipper. I slid the case to one side to make room for my muddy rucksack and three plastic carrier bags. I pushed the lid shut then climbed into the passenger seat.

She was wearing a black leather skirt and a red silk blouse. Gold adorned every finger, wrapped around both wrists, and dangled from her ears.

"All set, Sweetheart?" she asked as I closed the door. She gave a wriggle in her seat, and the skirt rode a little higher on her stockinged legs.

"Yes fine," I said.

She flicked at the gear lever in an almost dismissive fashion, and instantly, I felt the seat push into my back. I heard, and felt, a pile of grit being kicked up by the wheels as it spattered on the underside of the car. We hurtled out of the lay-by and onto the road. I wasn't aware of her checking to see if the way was clear.

"Where are you going then, Sweetness?"

"Bodmin," I said.

"Ah, Bodmin," she mused. "I could do Bodmin. Okay, Bodmin it is!"

She drove like a rally driver, accelerating into corners, and straightening out the bends in the road.

"Thank you for picking me up," I said.

"My pleasure," she said. "I feel safer having a man in the car with me"

I wasn't too sure I understood the logic behind that statement. I might have been just the sort of person she wanted me to protect her against! But I wasn't going to argue. An air-conditioned lift all the way to Bodmin was more than I could have hoped for.

"That's a lot of luggage you've got there," she said. "You must be very strong to carry that around."

"Oh, it's not that heavy, really." I half shrugged and grinned boyishly. "You get used to it."

She smiled at me and at the same time pulled out to overtake a truck on a blind corner. Much as I like being smiled at by attractive women, I would still rather she kept her eyes on the road. As we overtook the huge vehicle, I couldn't help myself, and my fingernails dug into the side of the soft leather seat.

"I expect you work out, don't you?" she asked.

"Well, I do belong to a gym in St Ives."

We raced along the country roads, scaring rabbits and pedestrians alike. Each corner either pressed me into the door or threatened to throw me across her lap.

My right foot pumped at an imaginary brake as we slid to a halt at the entrance to the motorway. She waited until the junction was almost clear then hurtled straight across into the third lane of the motorway. Her manoeuvre was accompanied by a selection of car horns. I stared at my feet. The view out the front was far too frightening, and drivers making obscene gestures took up the view from my side window.

She brought the speed up to 120-mph then flicked on the cruise control. In order to maintain this speed on the crowded motorway, she had to weave like a football player making a run for the goal.

"What's your name then, sweetheart?"

"Tony," I said.

"That's a good, strong name. I'm Harry." She obviously noticed my quizzical expression then continued, "Its short for Arabella."

"Hi... er... Harry."

"What are you doing in Bodmin then, Tony?"

"I left my camper van there. I'm going to get it back."

"Oh, you've got a camper van! How wonderful! I suppose you go off for weekends in it, do you?"

I noticed that every time I spoke to her, she very politely made eye contact with me. This of course meant that she was also losing eye contact with the motorway. I tried to keep my answers as brief as possible.

"No, I live in it."

"Lovely!"

I pretended to go to sleep in order to allow her to concentrate fully on the more important task of keeping all four wheels in contact with the tarmac. It also meant that I wouldn't be aware if the Grim Reaper came for me any minute. I decided that was probably a bonus.

After a while, pretending became unnecessary. I lapsed into an uncomfortable sleep invaded by spasmodic visions of roller coasters and bacon sandwiches.

The snap of the seat belt cut into my shoulder and jolted me awake. I chased away the last tentacles of sleep and gave my groggy head a shake.

"What?" I said, very eloquently.

I looked out the window. We were parked in a disabled bay outside the main block of the motorway services.

"I'm just going to powder my nose," she said. "Do you need to go?"

"No," I said. "I'm fine."

She climbed out of the car, and her skirt rose even higher, displaying a fine glimpse of stocking top. I had a feeling it was intentional. As I watched her walk through the entrance, I noticed she was surprisingly tall and walked with an air of supreme confidence.

My head leant itself against the window. My eyes defocused. I half dozed until she returned to the car.

The car door slamming shook me awake. Her left hand held two open bottles of coke. She handed one to me, and I drank half of it in one. I hadn't realised how thirsty I was. I noticed a slight after-taste and wondered if it was one of those diet versions.

We set off once more. As one of her hands held a cigarette and the other the bottle of coke, she had to guide the car out into the flow of traffic using her knees. We continued south, and the motorway started to clear. I was less in fear of my life. Harry finished her coke and threw the empty bottle across her shoulder into the back seat. She pressed a button above her head, and the sunroof slid open.

Her hand settled on the gear lever. The wind buffeted the inside of the car, but the warm breeze was exhilarating.

"I love the sunshine, don't you, Tony?"

"Oh, yes," I said.

"I read once in Cosmo that sunshine does something to a part of the brain. Makes you feel all randy."

"Oh!"

"Does it make you feel all randy?"

I slowly drank the rest of the coke in order to hide my embarrassment and gain thinking time.

"Ah, well... I suppose it does, sometimes." I tucked the empty bottle down by the side of my seat. I glanced across at her and noticed that since her return from the services, there were two more buttons undone on her blouse. It could have been an oversight, I supposed. But I was willing to bet it wasn't.

The miles continued to unroll behind the car, and as they did so, the turn of conversation became weirder and distinctly more personal.

"You look like you could please a woman, Tony."

This was getting out of hand. Her fingers made a gentle rubbing movement on the gear lever.

"Er, yes, well... I suppose."

She ran her fingers through her hair and pushed it back from her face.

"My husband couldn't, you know."

"Is that so?" I said. I was feeling rather warm despite the breeze from the open sunroof. I noticed for the first time the hypnotic smell of her perfume. I think it was a Chanel something or other. But I'd never been too hot on those. "It's always a shame when that happens." Bland empathy. That was the best solution.

"He had no idea about a woman's needs."

A sign flashed by, 'Bodmin 21 miles'. Should I ask to get out now? I could be standing by the side of the road for hours. I decided to risk this a bit longer.

"Some men are like that," I said. For some reason, I became aware of my heart working. It seemed to be thumping much harder than usual.

She held the open part of her blouse between thumb and forefinger and flapped it to and fro. "Warm, isn't it?"

"Yes," I had to agree it was getting warmer.

"I bet you know what a woman wants."

"Yes," I said. "I know how to do ironing." I figured that should defuse this. I just had to keep this up until we got to Bodmin. A delicate balance. Too many signals one way, and she'd stop the car and throw me out. Too many signals the other way, and she'd stop the car, throw me out, and climb on top of me.

She squeezed my thigh. "I love a man with a sense of humour! My husband's idea of a joke of was to belch the national anthem." Her hands stayed on my thigh, fingertips stroking gently.

Against my will, something was stirring in my groin. My body was about to betray me. She rubbed her legs together, and even above the drone of the car engine, I heard the wonderful rustling noise that only stockings can make. The problem in my nether regions was growing.

"It's so hard to find a good man," she said. "And as they say, a hard man is good to find!" She moved up her hand to explore my embarrassing area. "And my, you are a hard man!"

I didn't know what was the matter with me.

I thought about football.

"My husband had problems, you know?" Her hand returned to stroking my thigh.

I thought about the Queen.

"He was so useless down there, I had to buy him some Viagra," she continued. The pressure from her hand became more intense and her fingers probed higher again.

I thought about the Queen playing football.

"Did that work?" I asked.

"Oh, that worked all right! Marvellous stuff. I haven't seen anything quite that magnificent since we watched the space shuttle launch in America last year. It just didn't do me any good, that's all."

"Why, what happened?" I was desperate to avoid the inevitable and the longer I could keep the conversation going the more chance I had.

"He went off to some floozy he'd been seeing. No wonder he could never get it up with me!"

"Oh, how dreadful." I said.

The penny was starting to drop. The funny tasting coke. My independently-minded nether regions. I had been doped. She'd laced my coke with Viagra. I needed a way out of this. I couldn't let this situation reach its logical conclusion; I would feel I was being unfaithful to Astrid. Strangely enough, I didn't think about being unfaithful to Sam. Although Astrid and I had only ever spent one night together, it was her I would have been cheating on.

"I gave him a triple dose the other day, you know."

"Oh," I said.

"You should have seen it! Like a tree trunk! If it had been New Year's Eve I could have taken him along to Trafalgar Square, stuck a star on the top of it, and they'd have all danced around it singing Auld Lang Syne!"

I could understand how that would happen. My jeans were already giving a very good impersonation of a tent.

"I bet he was pleased," I said.

"Pleased? He was over the moon! The trouble was he decided it was too good to waste on me. He took it into town to share with his floozy. He didn't come back till the following morning. The damned thing was still standing to attention!"

I was wondering how much she had slipped into my coke. Would I have to put up with this for the next twelve hours?

"So, what are you doing?" I asked. "Divorce?" If I could keep the conversation on this level, I might survive until Bodmin. I estimated I only needed about another ten minutes.

"No, I waited until he had fallen asleep, then I got the garden shears and cut it off!"

"Oh, shit!" I said. "Is he all right?"

"I don't know. I called an ambulance, then left him to it. I went straight to the Post Office, to post his pride and joy to his floozy. She could keep it! The bloody thing was still standing up. I had to get a bigger envelope!"

That was it! I needed out of here now! A nymphomaniac I could just about handle. But a psychopathic nymphomaniac was too much.

"I mean, how could he do that to you?" I managed to splutter. "He should have been so grateful. I only wish I was allowed to take Viagra." Hook baited. I hoped she'd take it.

"What?" Her head snapped round in my direction. "What do you mean you wish you were allowed to take it?"

"Oh, I have a heart condition. It would be quite serious if ever I took Viagra. It would probably kill me. There have been all sorts of reports about people dying with this condition."

She continued to stare at me, and despite the fact the skin on her forehead was severely over-stretched, she still managed to wrinkle it. We veered across the road towards the back of a truck in the slow lane.

"Er, truck!" I said, pointing through the windscreen.

"Huh?" She turned back and swerved the wheel violently. "So, it would kill you, huh?" Her voice had taken on a strained but light-hearted tone.

"Yes," I said. "Any sort of exertion ,and it would just go pop!"

The sign said, 'Bodmin 2 miles'. That meant the entrance to the woods I wanted was only about a mile away.

"Strange thing," I said. "Just talking about this is making me feel ill. I've gone all dizzy."

"Do you want a paracetamol?"

"Just a bit of fresh air, I think. If I have a little lie down I'll probably feel better shortly. Don't want to put you to any trouble. Just drop me off at the next lay-by. I'll be all right soon. In an hour or so, I expect."

"Right, okay then."

A minute later, a lay-by loomed up ahead.

"There," I said. "That'll do."

She swung the car in with such force I was again thrown against the door and nearly head butted the windscreen when she managed to defeat the BMW's anti-lock braking system.

A royal marine in full uniform was standing in the lay-by on the opposite side of the road. His kit bag was by his side, and his thumb out expectantly. He was watching us while keeping half an eye on the traffic heading in his direction. I clambered out of the car, puffing and blowing and clutching my chest for good measure.

"I'll be all right in a minute," I said. "Thanks for the lift!"

"Oh, right you are then. Take care."

I think she meant it.

I went round to the back to retrieve my luggage. She was driving away before I'd even closed the boot. She swung the car 180 degrees across the road and pulled up alongside the marine. I saw a hand reach out of the passenger door towards him, beckoning him over. He disappeared into the car remarkably quickly. I wondered if she'd actually pulled him in. The wheels spun, and when the dust cleared, she was gone.

I was alone in the lay-by. Just me and my erection. That was a close one, I thought.

Chapter 26

It didn't take me long to find the woods, and then my van. It was still there and surprisingly enough, intact. I dumped my kit inside, checked everything over, and made myself a nice cup of tea.

It was good to be home.

I surveyed the interior of my residence. Compact and bijou is what the estate agents would call it. Easily capable of sleeping both the children and myself. I thought back to the fun I'd had with them during that brief hour or so around the fair and climbing the tree. I had spent so long in the past just bringing them up that the idea of fun had always taken second place. Too often, second place meant no place. Maybe in the future there would be more time for fun.

Time, at least, was something I appeared to have in abundance these days, whereas in my previous life it had always been a constant race against the clock. I now found I was seeing new things, hearing new sounds, even experiencing new smells. And all because I had time to take these things on board and not just race across them in the mad headlong rush towards the next deadline. I had gone in search of the Hippy and found instead a New World. A world with more hours in the day, a world where the idea of communicating with somebody still meant talking to them while sharing a drink or a joint and not just sending them an email or sticking a Post It note on their PC screen.

I just needed somebody to share this with now, on a deeper level. But for that to happen, I needed to shift this van and get myself to Stonehenge. What was needed was a friendly farmer with a tractor.

I locked up the van and set off up the track. My errant member was still rubbing against my jeans as I walked. I wondered how long I was going to be stuck with this. I walked for about a mile then came to a fork in the track.

The left-hand track was blocked by a five-bar gate. It had a wooden sign nailed to the top bar saying 'Ponderosa Farm'.

Remembering how as a lad I used to vault these gates by grabbing hold of the top and swinging my legs over, I decided to give it a try. I was okay until about the halfway point when a nail caught in the top of my jeans. My legs couldn't complete their graceful arc, and for a moment, I dangled upside down from the top of the gate, suspended by the nail. I was just trying to work out how to disentangle myself when a loud ripping noise made the decision for me. I fell on my back on the ground, the puff knocked out of me. I lay there for a moment going through a mental checklist of the various parts of my body. Everything seemed in order, although I did notice a bit of a draught around my upper thigh. I sat up to investigate. The nail had ripped the top of my jeans and my little soldier had popped out for a breath of air.

I pulled everything back together as best as I could, brushed myself down, and set off up the track again in search of the Ponderosa.

The farm consisted of nothing more than a collection of ramshackle buildings with a cob stone farmhouse in the centre. The stink of manure was overwhelming. I spotted an ancient tractor in the courtyard as I strode up to the front door. That'll do, I thought.

I pulled the piece of rope that was attached to the tail of a wooden woodpecker and he rapped firmly on the door for me. A woman's voice called from inside, "Be with you in a minute, my lover."

After about a minute, the door swung open to reveal a small, well-rounded woman in her fifties. I noticed a rack of keys on the wall behind her. The smell of baking drifted through the door, temporarily masking the delightful country fragrances. The woman's hands were covered in flour, and she wiped them on her apron as she spoke. "Oh, hello! What can I do for you then, lover? You looking for work?"

Her eyes raked my body and stopped at the groin area. I didn't want to put my hands down to explore in case she got the wrong idea.

"I've got my van stuck. I was wondering if somebody could give me a hand to get it free."

She said, "Oh, yes." But I don't think she actually heard what I'd said. Her eyes were still firmly focused on the bulge in my jeans that was my proud advertisement for Viagra's capabilities.

A man, who I presumed to be her husband, appeared behind her.

"What's up, duck?" He was tall and muscular. His leathery face testified to years working on the open land.

"Huh?" Her eyes were still transfixed.

The farmer, realising that his wife's attention was still elsewhere followed her gaze. Now they were both staring at my groin. The farmer was the first to recover.

"'Ere, what're you doing? You some sort of pervert? Come round here frightening my missus with a thing like that!" He pointed at the bulge.

Okay, so it was obvious now they had noticed. I reached down to cover the offending protuberance.

"No, it's not like that. I…"

The farmer continued, "Got an idea what he wants. He wants his backside full of buckshot. That's what he wants." He looked up at me. "Don't you go away now, mister, I'm just going to go fetch my twelve-bore. Come round here getting all excited at the sight of my missus."

I decided not to obey the farmer's request that I remain there. Instead, I turned and ran towards the track. I expected any second to hear the sound of gunfire. This time, when I reached the gate I cleared it in one smooth, balletic movement.

I returned to the camper and settled down to sew up my jeans with the complementary sewing kit I taken from the Fisherman's Steps hotel. Sewing had never been one of my strong points, and by the time I'd finished, I discovered that I'd sewn my shirt to my jeans, and I needed to start all over again.

To put plan B into operation, I was going to have to wait for nightfall. I switched on the television then searched the cupboards for food. I found a loaf of bread and a tin of beans. As I had never been partial to the particular shade of green the bread had taken on, I decided to just stick with the beans.

The early evening news from the BBC carried a report from Glastonbury as to how their own film crew had been drugged then robbed of their equipment. Another one for the scrap book.

The evening painted the trees with dark shadows, and the crickets started their nightly chirping. My errant member had returned to normal, but I was left with a dull ache. I put on my dark coat, checked my torch, and headed for the Ponderosa. I relied on the fact that farmers, being early risers, would also be early to bed. My hunch proved correct. The building was in darkness. It had been my intention to creep up to the window adjacent to the front door and climb in through there. I discovered creeping was out of the question. There was so much cow muck all over the courtyard that each time I placed my foot down it made a loud squelch, and when I drew it up again, it made a sort of schlooping noise. I squelched and schlooped my way to the front door.

I was banking on one of the keys on the rack just inside the door belonging to the tractor. The side window was ajar, as I'd remembered it, and I clambered through. I found myself in a small, dark cloakroom. I also found my foot in the toilet bowl. Well at least that would wash off the cow muck. I tugged my foot free of the toilet bowl. It came out minus the shoe. The choice that faced me now was a simple one; continue the mission with just one shoe, or put my hands down inside the farmer's toilet to retrieve it. Easy. I left my shoe there.

I opened the door a crack and peeped out. The hall was in darkness. My shoe clopped and my wet foot slapped as I made my way over to the key rack. I flashed my torch across the array of keys and gathered up everything that looked as if it could remotely be used in a vehicle. I slipped out of the front door.

The cow muck squelched through the toes of my bare foot as I ran across the courtyard towards the tractor. I climbed up onto the seat and quickly located the keyhole on the control panel. I found the right key on the fifth attempt and stuffed the remaining keys in my pocket. One of the advantages of taking all of the vehicle keys was that I couldn't easily be chased. The key turned freely, and I tried it a few times before I realised there must be a separate ignition button. The engine roared into life as soon as I found it. There was no doubt this was going to wake up everybody.

I fumbled with the controls in a frantic effort to engage first gear. Lights started to come on in the farmhouse. The tractor gave a violent jolt as I found the correct gear. I nearly fell off the back. The machine swung easily through 180 degrees, and I headed for the farm entrance. The huge rear wheels made light work of slicing through the cow muck. Unfortunately, It threw most of it straight up in the air where it fragmented into a black rain before descending on my head.

I risked a glance across my shoulder. The farmer was silhouetted in the doorway; he was bringing the shotgun to bear. I hunched over the wheel and pressed my foot to the floor. The tractor was too noisy to hear if any shots had been fired.

I couldn't figure out how to work the lights, so I had to steer with one hand holding the torch. Consequently, my manoeuvrability was severely hampered and I must have collided with every fence post and pothole going. But the tractor was reasonably forgiving and rumbled on happily.

I clattered the tractor through the gate I'd left open earlier, then along the track and backed it up to the rear of my van. A few minutes later, I had a rope connecting the tractor to the rear towbar on my van. I let the brake off the van and jumped back onto the tractor. I eased the tractor forward and took up the slack in the rope. But it went no further. I increased the power until the wheels started to slip.

But still my van wouldn't pull free.

Damn it! I really needed the van to be driving as well. But I couldn't be in the driving seat of two vehicles at the same time. Or could I? I could prop the accelerator down on one of the vehicles. But which one? If I blocked the one down in my van, when it broke free it would pile straight into the back of the tractor. The damage could be massive. No, better if I had propped down the accelerator of the tractor and I drove the van. That way, when it broke free, I could use the brake in the van to hold back the tractor until I had time to shut them both down.

I found a piece of wood the right length to reach from the tractor's accelerator to the seat. I tied the steering wheel in a locked forward position before jamming the wood against the accelerator. The tractor once more took up the slack in the rope and came to a standstill. Its wheels strained against the ground. I jumped into my van and started the engine. As I eased the clutch back, there was a loud scraping noise along the sides, and the van tore itself free from the trees. The wheels bit into the mud. We were moving. I let the vehicles roll another few metres to make sure we were well clear then jammed my foot on the brake. I expected both vehicles to come to a halt.

They didn't.

We continued forward at the same speed. I pulled on my hand brake. Still nothing. I now had absolutely no control over the speed or direction of the two vehicles. I really needed to get back on the tractor in order to shut it down. But I couldn't see how that would be possible. I didn't want to go anywhere near those huge wheels while that thing was in motion. There was only one thing for it; I was going to have to cut the rope.

I switched off the engine of the van, put it into a forward gear, and applied the brake. I was still being dragged along behind the tractor, but once I'd cut the rope, it should come to a standstill. I didn't want it rolling back into its previous position. I clambered into the back of the van to retrieve my carving knife from the drawer then jumped down and attacked the towrope.

It was surprisingly difficult to cut through, especially as I had to keep pace with the tractor. But when I'd cut about half way through, the strain told, and the remaining strands snapped. The rope twanged back in both directions with a loud crack. The noise of the tractor's engine suddenly increased, and it then continued on its merry way up the track.

I jumped back in my van and re-started the engine and set off in reverse in pursuit of the runaway tractor. After about fifty yards, I found a place to turn around.

I had to drive carefully to avoid wrecking my van on the numerous potholes or tree trunks that littered the path. Before long, I'd lost sight of the tractor.

After a few more minutes, I came to a sharp left-hand bend in the track. The tractor had gone straight ahead, cutting a swathe through the undergrowth. I still couldn't see it but I didn't feel like following it up there. I continued along the track.

I emerged onto the main road and turned right to head back towards Stonehenge. I'd travelled about 100 metres when I saw blue flashing lights in front of me. A police car was stopped in the road. I drove slowly and carefully. I didn't know what was ahead, and I didn't want to get pulled now. As I drew nearer, I noticed that the front of the police car was all smashed in. I drove past. The policeman was standing by the front of his vehicle. His head alternately moved from the damage on his car to watch a tractor rumbling across the field on the opposite side of the road.

I stared fixedly ahead and drove on.

About five miles down the road I stopped off at a Little Chef Restaurant. Most of the tables were already occupied, but I found a vacant one near the middle of the room. A young waiter came to collect my order. Despite his undoubtedly superb training, he couldn't help himself, and he wrinkled his nose when he picked up the aroma of cow dung that surrounded me. Much to his credit though, he didn't say anything.

A few minutes later, my order arrived. I had ordered such a huge amount, that I was surprised they'd got it all on the one plate. Bacon, eggs, fried potatoes, beans, tomatoes, sausages, all piled high in front of me. I attacked the food with great enthusiasm. As I ate, I kept one eye on my fellow diners. Wrinkled noses and funny looks abounded.

I finished my meal and pushed the empty plate to one side. Although I was absolutely stuffed, I picked up the menu and surveyed the sweet selection.

A tall man with a white shirt and dark tie watched me from behind the counter. When he realised I was planning round two, he came over to talk to me.

"I'm afraid I'm going to have to ask you to leave, sir," he said.

"What? But I wanted a sweet! And maybe cheese and biscuits, coffee."

"Sir, I have no wish to cause offence, but you're disturbing my other customers."

"How's that then? I haven't said a word!"

"It's your... Shall we say... Aroma."

"Oh, I see. I'm not good enough for you, huh? Just because I work on the land to produce your food for you, so that you can sell it at a huge profit, you don't want me in your middle-class restaurant. Is that it?"

"No, sir. It's not like that. If you'd just keep your voice—"

"Well I'll have you know that I think this is prejudice. If I wore a tie," I flicked the end of his tie with my forefinger, "you'd let me sit here for another hour with my coffee and biscuits. But because I work with my hands, you want to grab my money and throw me out as quickly as you can."

"No, sir. It's not like—"

"Well I hope you're not expecting me to pay for this. After the way I've been treated!"

"No, sir. Of course not." He was becoming flustered. The whole restaurant had stopped eating and was now watching us.

I picked up a napkin and patted at the corners of my mouth. "All right then." I let him escort me to the door. "I'll be contacting my MP, you know," I told him, as a parting shot before he closed the door in my face.

I returned to my van. A free meal in my stomach and a nice warm shower. All was well with the world.

Almost.

I dumped my muck-laden clothes into a plastic bin bag and tied the top tightly to keep the smell in until such time as I could find a laundrette. Having dealt with both the inner and the outer man, I felt ready for the road once more.

Twenty miles later, I was just turning off onto the A303 that would take me through to Stonehenge when I saw a lone hitch-hiker standing by the side of the road. Time to return the favours.

I pulled up alongside him. He looked familiar. It was the marine that Harry had given a lift to earlier. As he climbed into the passenger seat, I could see the telltale bulge in his trousers, a sure sign of Arabella's handiwork. He didn't speak and just sat down with a big sigh, eyes wide and staring forwards. I thought these guys were supposed to be tough.

Eventually, he recovered the power of speech. "You'll never guess what just happened to me," he said.

Chapter 27

We travelled through the night, and dawn was just doing its bit on the horizon when I spotted Woody and Pete. They were sitting huddled near a bus shelter; their kit piled around them. We were still about twenty miles away from Stonehenge. I pulled over alongside them.

"Want a lift then?"

Cerberus leapt up at my open window and tried to lick my face. Why do dogs have to do that? Can't they be content with yapping and wagging?

They piled inside and nodded hello to my passenger.

"Nearly gave up on you," said Pete.

"Something came up," I said.

After a few more miles, we came to the turning for Stonehenge. I dropped the marine off so he could continue his journey. He gave me a salute as we drove off, and I returned it. Veterans of the Arabella conflict. Brothers in arms.

We completed the final leg of the journey in a little under five minutes, and I pulled into the field adjoining the Stonehenge site. Already, a fair sized campsite was growing up around the monument. High fences had been erected to keep away all but those with special passes. The police presence was subtle, but noticeable.

"Well, here we are," I said.

There was still some twenty hours to go before the solstice dawn. I was desperately tired and torn between the desire to sleep or satisfy my curiosity as to whether Astrid was here. Pete said he would scan the site and keep an eye out for her. So I gave in to the call of sleep.

Hot breath and a wet tongue broke through the veils of sleep. It was still too early in the waking process to open my eyes, so instead, I just pushed at the lump that was settled on my chest.

"Bloody dog, get off!"

"Woof, woof," said a voice. Moist lips planted themselves on mine.

I figured this probably wasn't Cerberus, and I hoped to goodness it wasn't Woody. That meant... My eyes dragged open. Astrid's face came slowly into focus.

"Hi there, you!" she said.

"Astrid! It's you! It's really you!"

"Yes, I knew that."

"No, what I mean... How did you find me?"

"Tony, you're in a van painted like a unicorn. How hard can that be?"

"Right," I said. "No more talk then." I wrapped my arms around her and pulled her down on top of me. I held her there tightly until I was sure that she wasn't going to disappear into the ether when I properly woke up. No, as the last of sleep left me, she was still there.

"Where've you been?" I asked. "I've been looking for you."

"Yes, I know. I saw you at Glastonbury. You and Pete. I watched your performance with 'Young Love'."

"Oh, that," I said. "All to do with mushrooms."

"I came looking for you, but you'd gone. I don't know what you've been up to this time, Tony, but there were police all over the place next day."

"Where did you go?" I asked. "Before Glastonbury, I mean. You just disappeared."

She sat up on the edge of the bed and turned so that her back was slightly towards me.

"Yes, I know, I'm sorry. My fault, not yours, Tony. I have a bit of a problem. Getting close to people that is."

"Yes," I said. "Woody did try to explain."

"Bless him!"

"But I never asked for anything." I sat up and put my hand on her shoulder. She placed her hand on top of mine.

"I know," she said. "It's just me, that's all. You see... my father ran out on us when I was very young. Mum said it was because we smothered him. Ever since then I've been afraid of close contact. I suppose I should be in therapy really." She turned and smiled at me.

"Perhaps we should both go together, we could get a discount." I said.

"You don't need therapy, you idiot!" She punched me playfully on the shoulder.

"No? Look at me. Six months ago I was a stockbroker living in a smart suburb, with two cars, two kids, and a cupboard full of tranquillisers."

"You've got a point there. You make me look the model of normality."

"Hey, don't push it. I was just trying to cheer you up, that's all!"

She laughed again, and we held each other tightly. Before long, we were tugging at each other's clothes, loosening belts and setting free our desires. We made love with a passion and eagerness that left us breathless. Well, I was anyway.

I must have dozed off again. I snatched myself into wakefulness as soon as I realised what had happened. My arm reached out, searching for Astrid.

The bed was empty.

Not again! Throwing the bedding to one side, I sat up. Astrid was standing with her back to me as she made tea. She was still naked.

She heard me stir, and turned, "Hi! You're awake then?"

"Thought for a minute..."

"No, you're stuck with me now. Like a stray cat, show it a bit of kindness, and you can never get rid of it."

I glanced down at Cerberus, curled up by the door. "Or a dog," I said.

"Are you calling me a dog?"

"No! I meant…"

"I know, I was only teasing. Get dressed, there's some people I want you to meet."

"Oh? Who's that?"

"Two very good friends I met at Glastonbury. Star and Fallow."

About a hundred or so vehicles of all different descriptions were parked in the field next to the site. Most were in a fairly dilapidated state. Stonehenge at the summer solstice was a true Mecca for both travellers and mystics. Already, a large number of people had started to accumulate around the fences.

I'd never seen Stonehenge before, except in pictures, so I was keen to take a look. As I approached the stone circle, I was surprised at how small it was. But the stones themselves were massive, towering over the heads of the people who stood nearby. Dwarfing them with their presence, these monoliths were twice the height of anyone there and around two metres wide. I marvelled at the feat of engineering that resulted in these massive behemoths being balanced across each other like the first layer of a house of cards.

We found Star by the main gate. She was holding up a placard that read, 'Why only the Druids?'. She spotted Astrid as we approached. I watched her face brighten then immediately darken again as saw me.

"Oh, it's you," she said.

"Hi, look I'm really sorry about what happened. I was trying to catch the dog when —"

"It's all right. I forgive you."

I hate it when people do that. Why can't she be pissed at me then get over it? I can deal with that. But this forgiving business…

"You see, I hadn't realised that Cerberus had doubled back and when –"

"No, really. I forgive you! Astrid explained what you lot are like."

"She did?" I looked at Astrid.

"When Star told me what had happened, I knew it could only be you three!" Astrid said.

"Oh."

"Where's Woody?" Star asked. "I think Fallow's quite taken with him."

"He's around somewhere," I said. "But does Fallow know he's not really a vegan? I mean, I don't want any more… um… misunderstandings."

"Yes, Astrid also explained about his passion for bacon sandwiches. But I think Fallow feels she can convert him"

"He does do a nice line in mushrooms, though," I suggested.

"You've got a point there, Tony," said Astrid. "Perhaps we'd better go find him before he sets up shop selling mushroom sandwiches to the police. We'll catch you later, Star."

"Sure, I'm not going very far." She raised her left hand slightly to show that it was manacled to the chain link fence. Emily Pankhurst lives.

"What have the druids done to piss her off?" I asked Astrid, when we were clear.

"Oh, that. Every year, English Heritage, who owns Stonehenge, allows only the Druids to enter the Sacred Circle on the night of the solstice. They don't usually let any of the New Agers in."

"Why's that?"

"I think they figure they don't want the stones covered in obscene graffiti, or something."

"Well, that's absurd," I said. "But anyway, I suppose the druids were there first."

"That's what everybody thinks," Astrid said. "But they weren't. The stones have been here for 5,000 years; the druids only appeared on the scene a couple of hundred years before Christ. Star's claim is that the stones belong to the history of the English people. Not just some small bunch of crackpots who like to go around dressed up in sheets."

"So, will chaining herself to the fence do any good?"

"It did last year. They removed the barriers for the first time in many years. The trouble is, there were rumours around earlier that protesters were planning to invade the site again this year. Which is why they've sealed it off now."

We found Woody by the macrobiotic brown-rice stand. He was talking to Fallow.

"Hey, you've met again then?"

"Yeah," Woody said. "They forgave me."

"Me too!" I said.

"Anyway," Fallow said. "Woody's joining us. He's a vegetarian now."

I nodded at the bacon sandwich clutched in Woody's hand. "And how does that work then?"

"Oh, I'm allowed to eat bacon, man."

"It's a big step," defended Fallow. "You can't expect him to do it all at once."

"Right," I said.

She held on to Woody's arm with both hands.

He smiled. "Fallow wants me to paint their bus."

"Great," I said. "Have you seen Pete?"

"No, last time I saw him he was selling stones to the tourists."

"Selling stones?"

"Yeah, had them convinced they were chippings off the Slaughter Stone."

"He'll get himself arrested."

"Oh, don't worry about him, Tony," said Astrid. "He can look after himself. Come and show me the stones."

"What?"

"You told me you'd never seen them properly. Let's go play tourist!"

For some reason, that idea appealed greatly. I bought two tickets from the ticket office. I actually paid for them. Full price. No haggling. For the price of the tickets, we were also entitled to join the guided tour. As we waited for the

guide to start, I bought us both an iced-lolly. The afternoon
sun set to work on the ice creams, and within a few minutes,
my hand was a sticky mess. Astrid appeared to be having
similar trouble. We finished them, and I went into the toilets
to clean myself up. I usually tried to avoid these places if I
could. The washrooms were always swimming in water and
covered in graffiti. I could never understand what possessed
somebody to rush into one of these places armed with a
spray can, and paint the word, 'Penis' on the wall.

I caught up with Astrid just as the guide had started his
tour.

He pointed out the original layout of the stones that
dated back to around 3,000 BC. He showed us where they
had been added to over the centuries. The huge, blue granite
slabs that had been dragged hundreds of miles from Wales.
Each one weighing many tons. He went into great detail
about how the stones had originally lined up with the sun on
the summer solstice. But now, they were a fraction of a
degree out due to a slight shift in the Earth's axis over the
last millennium or so.

We held hands as we listened to his speech. And
although he had probably used the same words a hundred
times before, he still sounded excited and fresh. His
enthusiasm spilled over and intoxicated us all. I slipped my
arm around Astrid's waist as we listened. I felt like a
teenager on my first date.

When the tour had finished, we made for the Tea Shop
where I bought us two huge ice cream sundaes. We sat
opposite each other. The table wobbled as I put the glasses
down, and we both laughed. The place was crowded with
tourists. I noticed a family at a nearby table. The man had
neatly trimmed greying hair and was dressed in smart casual
clothes. He clearly felt uncomfortable. His two children
squabbled over their glossy guidebook, each calling on him
for judgement. The mother, very prim and in her late
thirties, seemed detached. Almost as if she were somewhere

else. Both parents had 'Help me' written across their foreheads in big black letters.

"Astrid," I started.

"Yeees?" Her voice was full of apprehension, as if she knew what was coming.

"Where are we?"

"Err, Stonehenge?"

"Yes, I know that. What I mean us... We?"

"Still trying to fit me into one of your little boxes, huh, Tony?"

"No, not really. I just want to know... If we... do we…"

"I'm not going to run away again, Tony, if that's where you're heading." My relief must have been visible as she gave a big grin. "But that's the only promise I can make you. Could you say anything different?"

"I could say that I have never been happier in my life than when I spend time with you."

"What about your children? Sam?"

"The more time I've spent apart from Sam, the more I've come to realise that we were hopelessly wrong in the first place." I swirled my spoon around the empty sundae glass. It made a pleasant chinking noise "But the children, they mean the world to me."

"You'll carry on seeing them though, yeah?" She took my hand. I didn't know if it was out of affection or because the chinking of the glass was driving her potty.

"Sam says I can see them as often as I like. They could come and live with me for a while."

"In your van?" she teased.

"Or on my lobster boat. C'mon, let's go find the others."

We found Pete in amongst a group of travellers on the far north end of the camp. He was showing them how to do the three-card trick, and in exchange, they were keeping him topped up with cannabis.

The travellers represented all generations. From small children through to grandparents. They welcomed us into their group, and before long, I was listening to stories of past Stonehenge battles with the police. It seemed they not only enjoyed the confrontations, but actively sought them out. They felt they were striking a blow against the claustrophobic oppressiveness of modern society.

As late afternoon turned into evening, more and more people poured into the site, and as they did so, the police presence increased noticeably. There was even a small contingent of mounted police patrolling the area.

After a while, Fallow and Woody joined us. They looked as though they had been together all their lives. They were a natural couple. Woody kept up a constant supply of joints, and our hosts kept their curiously strong, rough cider flowing in frightening quantities. It was an acquired taste. To begin with, it tasted musky and oily. But after several large cups, I tasted the apples and found it much more palatable. Even enjoyable.

The evening clouds darkened the sky, and the combination of cannabis and cider released inhibitions, loosened tongues… and provoked bravado.

Chapter 28

My recollection of the events that followed was somewhat hazy to say the least. I remembered a film crew coming round and interviewing us. They asked me if I had ever been on any other protests before. Which I felt was somewhat strange, as I hadn't realised I was on one now. I remembered lots of cider, and I remembered Woody asking what we could do about the bloody druids. Had it not been for the cider, I'm sure I would have heard loud warning bells at that point. I remembered more cider.

What I do remember, is waking up in a sitting position and finding myself unable to move.

The sky was still dark, although touches of orange were just scraping the underside of the clouds. So dawn must have been on the way. My back was pressed against something hard and cold with my arms stretched behind me. I tugged at them. I had five or six inches of movement, nothing more. The clinking sound that greeted my efforts informed me that I was held fast with chains.

A steady droning sound filled my ears, and shadowy shapes moved in front of me. I screwed up my eyes and shook my head slightly trying to clear the fog that was both inside and outside of my head. The shadowy shapes resolved into groups of people in white cloaks, and the droning sound became recognisable as human voices. Singing, humming, human voices.

The sight of huge, black shapes silhouetted against the night sky filled in the remainder of my Swiss-cheese consciousness. I was in the centre of Stonehenge, chained to one of the stones. The Druids were preparing for some sort of ceremony. I wondered just how much I had managed to piss them off last night and wondered whether they still practised human sacrifice. But no, surely not. In a public place, with large numbers of press around? Surely not. This was the twenty first century.

I tried desperately to remember how I'd come to be there. I certainly couldn't recall any sort of struggle. I had a vague recollection of climbing a fence. And spray painting something. Yes, I'd actually spray painted! One thing was for sure, if I ever got out of this, I was going to give cider a miss from now on.

I looked around. It was still too dark to see anything more than shadows. So, whatever work of art I had a created, wouldn't show up for a while at least. The smell of incense lay heavily in the air and mingled with that of wood smoke. I saw that the Druids carried incense baskets. Swinging them from side to side, leaving little trails of smoke in their wake. The lead Druid carried a branch of what looked like mistletoe in one hand, and a sort of shepherd's crook in the other.

I remembered being helped over the fence. So I hadn't been alone. Woody, and Fallow. That probably wasn't a good sign.

I looked to my right. The dark monoliths stood impassively. It was almost as if they were looking back at me saying, "We've seen all this before. 5,000 years of history and you guys are still chaining each other to us stones."

I turned to my left. A dark shape huddled at the bottom of the next stone. I squinted my eyes, trying to focus. That lump spoke. "Hey, man. You're awake. Cool!" Woody said. "We showed them, huh?"

"Yeah, Woody. I guess we did."

Beyond Woody, the next stone also had a visitor. A quick glance assured me the remaining stones were vacant. I looked back to the third one. I asked Woody, "Fallow?"

"Yeah," he said.

"Just remind me, Woody, what were we actually trying to achieve?"

"I think you wanted to show Star that you cared about things. You kept telling her how sorry you were about the chicken."

"Oh, and the…er, chains... Who's got the key to these chains?" I held my manacled arm up.

"I don't know, man. They're snap-lock padlocks. We threw the keys away long before we got here. You said you didn't want anybody bottling out."

"I would say that, wouldn't I. Did I mention anything about Plan B?"

"No! You said you wanted to show the world how you felt."

"Oh, right. Well, I think we've done that, don't you? Perhaps we can go home now?"

"No way, man. They won't let anybody in to cut us free until the ceremony's over."

"Great. How's Fallow?"

"Asleep. I think she over-did the cider."

"Yes, it can have that effect."

I relaxed back against the stone and resurveyed my surroundings. Pre-dawn continued to paint the sky the colours of fire. Very soon, the sun would peep above the horizon, and the Druids would reach the culmination of their ceremonies. With it would come the TV reporters, the newspapers and magazines. And in the middle of all of that, Cornwall's most-wanted had chained himself to the centrepiece of the celebrations. There was probably very little hope of this going unnoticed.

I wondered how Astrid and Pete had let me do this. But then I supposed Astrid would have felt that it was my right to express myself in anyway I saw fit, and Pete would have thought it was all one big joke anyway.

"Hey, Fallow," I called. "You okay?"

She stirred. "What's happening? Where am I?"

"We're doing a protest, remember?"

"Oh, yes."

One of the Druids came over to me. He wore a white cloak and a conical white hat with a flap at the rear. "Will

241

you shut the fuck up?" he whispered. "You're disturbing the ceremony."

That's not very nice language for a Druid, I thought.

"Sorry," I said. "You haven't got a set of bolt cutters under there, have you?" I nodded at his cloak.

He swirled his robes around him and walked away.

Sunlight continued to creep across the sky, and people stirred outside of the circle. Photographers jostled for position. Each one wanting to be first with his flash if the rioting kicked off again this year. Still the shadows lay heavily around the stones, so I didn't think they'd noticed me yet. Now, if I could just Houdini the lock and tunnel my way out of here before the sun came up properly, I might be all right. Otherwise, I was in a little bit of trouble.

I also needed to take a leak. Correction, I desperately needed to take a leak. I didn't know how much cider I'd drunk the previous night, but it was making its urgent presence known now. A Druid stood with his back to me, not three feet away. He hummed and chanted.

"Pssst," I said.

He turned and scowled at me. Teeth clenched. "Shush."

"I'm sorry," I whispered. "It's just—"

"Why can't you lot just leave us alone?" he hissed. "You do this every bloody year."

"Sorry, I need—"

He made a point of moving away out of earshot.

I needed to deal with this quickly, or there was likely to be an accident. I stood up. The chains chinkled and clanked. The Druids, who had just reached a silent portion of their meditations all turned to look at me.

"Sorry... Sorry..."

One by one, they turned their heads back to the chief Druid who was holding his arms up to the point on the horizon from where the sun would shortly emerge. If I could just get round behind the stone, it might be less public.

I shuffled sideways. The chains scraped along the stone with a sound reminiscent of fingernails on a blackboard. Hooded heads turned back in my direction.

"Sorry," I said. I waited until their heads had turned away again then continued with my shuffling, scraping and clanking. The Druids did their best to ignore me, and eventually I managed to shuffle round to the rear of the stone. There were still people within viewing distance, but that couldn't be helped. I managed to pull enough slack in the chain to twist around, allowing my right hand to reach the important place. I pointed my face as best as I could towards the stone and unzipped. Blessed relief came. The flow splattered noisily on the stone and splashed on the ground below. Before I'd realised what I was doing, I'd let out a loud sigh. Several flash bulbs erupted, and people giggled from the fences. I finished then zipped up. I needed to sit down again, but I couldn't sit down where I was. There was now a puddle at my feet. I would have to move back round to the front of the stone.

Chinkling, sliding, scraping.

As I came back into view of the Druids, I noticed they'd all stopped their meditations and were looking in my direction. If there was ever a time when they'd all wished they'd retained the human sacrifice part of their ceremony, I was sure this was it.

"Sorry."

They went back to their humming.

I slid my back down the stone to sit on the ground. I felt something hard underneath me. At first I thought it was a rock, but then it hissed at me and I felt a wetness seeping through my trousers. I jumped up. "Oh no! Look at that!" I said, without thinking.

The Druids stopped once more to look.

A dented paint spray can lay on the ground. Around it, the grass was stained red. I presumed that colour also matched the seat of my jeans.

I wondered what we'd painted.

A low murmur from the crowd attracted the chief Druid's attention. He spun his head quickly back to the horizon. The solstice sun had snuck up while he wasn't looking and now sent shafts of light in our direction. He spoke his incantations quickly. He obviously had some ground to make up.

"Blow the fanfare, man" he shouted to another Druid who held a long trumpet. "The bloody fanfare, quickly!"

The herald blew a long tuneless note on his instrument, and the chanting increased.

The sun flared across the fields in front of Stonehenge and lanced through the gap in the eastern aspect. Shafts of bright sunlight hit the stones that Fallow, Woody and I were chained to.

A loud "Oooh!" came from the viewers outside the fence.

Midsummer had arrived.

"Hey, Tony!" Pete? I thought. I twisted my head round to the right. Pete was pressed up against the chain-link fence. The crowds squashed in behind him. He was waving his hand in my direction.

"Tony," he called.

"What?" I asked.

"Shush," said the Druids.

"Cooking fat!"

"What?"

"Cooking fat. In your pocket."

Cooking fat in my pocket? His cat! In my pocket?

"Yeah," he continued. "You promised me. Last night."

I stretched a hand towards my jacket pocket. My fingers found a large cylindrical object.

"What the hell...!"

"Shut up!" called several druids in unison.

No wonder Pete hadn't tried to stop me. He'd delegated responsibility for scattering cooking fat's ashes at dawn, to me. In fact, if I could only get my cider-addled brain to work, I would probably remember that this was all his idea in the first place.

Out of a feeling of duty to the cat, rather than to Pete, I decided I'd go for it. The chain cut into my wrist as I stretched for the pocket again. I extracted the ceramic urn. I noticed one of the Druids had grown bored with the ceremony and was watching me with great interest. I smiled at him. He just stared impassively. Probably wondering what this idiot was up to now. By wedging the container between my knees I was able to unscrew the lid. I dropped the lid on the ground, where of course it clattered noisily across the loose stones. I retrieved the container with my right hand and shook it as much as the chain would allow. A gust of wind picked up the cloud of dust and blew it straight in the direction of the Druids. I would never have believed that one cat could make so much ash.

I heard Pete yell, "Wooohooo! Way to go, man!" Causing thirty druid faces to turn just at the moment the cloud of dust reached them.

Black dust settled like soot onto white cloaks and startled faces.

"Sorry," I said.

And then the sneezing started.

I could never really see the point of this druid business. But even I was beginning to feel sorry for them now as they struggled to complete their ceremony. Hurried incantations mingled with sneezes and coughs. The once pristine white cloaks now looked like a collection of Dalmatian dogs.

The noise levels increased rapidly. Photographers craned and clicked. The cameras were pointed in our direction, not at the Druids. Chattering and laughing overtook the Druid's gentle chants. People pointed at us. Why? I twisted to look across at the others, hoping to see what had pulled everybody's attention.

The coming dawn had illuminated the stones beautifully. It was as though they were floodlit. Above Fallow's head, in red spray paint, were the words 'Save the chickens'.

So that was it. Not as bad as it could have been. At least we hadn't said anything rude about the Druids.

I noticed the crowds were not only looking at Fallow's stone though. They were also interested in Woody's and mine. I leaned forwards as far as the chains would allow gaining enough angle to see what Woody had written.

'Save everything.'

Okay, still not too bad. Slightly obtuse, but then that was Woody. But what had I written? Seeing behind and above me proved more difficult. I twisted and tugged at the chains, freeing enough slack to move. At first, I still couldn't read it properly. I was too close. But by leaning back on the chains I was eventually able to see my handiwork. In bold, red spray-paint I'd delivered my single word message to the world…

'Penis'.

Chapter 29

With the coming of the full dawn, the ceremony reached its conclusion, amidst much chanting, fanfaring, and sneezing.

The Druids filed out through the gate, and a posse of large police officers filed in. They divided up, with several men approaching each of us; one officer in each group armed with a set of bolt cutters. The transition from padlock and chain to handcuffs was so swift I didn't even notice it happen.

"Am I being arrested, then?" I tried to put on my best 'Offended innocents' voice.

"What do you think?" was the curt reply from a particularly large policeman who held the crook of my elbow and guided me towards the gate.

"Well, what's the charge?"

"We'll start with urinating on a public monument, shall we? Then see what comes up from there." He proceeded to recite the statutory warning in a bored monotone. We were ushered through the gates. A pathway had been created through the crowd by two lines of policemen. I felt like Moses going through the Red Sea. The open doors of a white police van waited for us at the far end of the human corridor.

I was just being forcibly guided into the back of the van when I heard Astrid's voice, "Tony, Tony!"

I turned my head. She bobbed around behind a line of blue uniforms, waving her hands.

I put on my Humphrey Bogart voice, "Wait for me, sweetheart."

She laughed and shouted, "I'll bake you a cake!" and gave an exaggerated wink.

I smiled. I didn't actually feel much like smiling. With the dawning of the sun, had come the dawning in my mind of just how much do-do I was in. My only hope was that communications between the Wiltshire constabulary and St Ives police station were not good.

The van doors slammed shut, and I felt the oppressive efficiency of a well-oiled organisation closing around me. These guys were used to this. They did this every year. Except that most years, there were hundreds of arrests, this year there were only three. That meant that the ratio of police to arrestees was particularly high.

Fallow still looked defiant. "You see what happens when you eat too much meat, Woody?" She spoke to Woody, but the words were directed towards police officers. "With the amount of hormones they put in meat these days, is it any wonder that they can't help stomping around like testosterone-overdosed gorillas?"

"Now, miss," said one of the policemen, "there's no need for that."

"You can't silence the will of the people, you know!" she said.

"Power to the people," confirmed Woody.

"Yeah, the people," I said, not wishing to be left out but also not wanting to draw too much attention to myself.

It was not only the police who had over-staffed this event, but also the press. As we were the only three arrests, the focus was well and truly on us. The view through the windows of the police van was just a forest of cameras. Popping flashes sparkled in front of my eyes. Fluffy microphones thrust forwards, searching for quotable snippets.

We swung out onto the main road in the middle of a convoy of four police cars. Lights flashed, and sirens whooped. The word 'overkill' came to mind. But then, I suppose 300 policemen who had been expecting a royal rumble needed to vent their exuberance somewhere. I was just the unfortunate target.

The ride to the police station took less than fifteen minutes. Within another ten, I'd been processed, finger printed, and deprived of my pocket-possessions along with bootlaces and belt. I was then dumped into a cell. I spent the next four hours mulling over the curious twists in the path that had brought me to this place. The officer, who had charged me, eventually came to collect me. We sat opposite each other across the battered wooden table in a stark interview room.

"Apart from urinating in a public place, and littering an ancient monument, you'll also be charged with causing a disturbance, vandalism, and probably gross indecency if we can make it stick. On top of that, I understand the Cornish police are fairly interested in you, as you appear to have jumped bail following an arson investigation, and are suspected of attempted armed robbery in a clothes shop, stealing petrol, and robbing phone boxes.

I knew they wouldn't make all of the charges stick, but there would be enough left over to guarantee I was in big trouble. He religiously copied down, long hand, my pleas of innocence and convoluted explanations. I was then returned to my cell. An hour later, I was once more being interviewed in connection with the theft of BBC camera equipment. I'd thought for a moment I'd got away with that one.

Twenty minutes into that interview, a young policewoman entered the room and whispered in the constables ear. He looked up at me. "Your solicitor's here."

"Huh?"

"Interview suspended sixteen thirty-eight." He stopped the tape recorder and left the room.

The policewoman waited with me until my solicitor arrived. The door opened, and Sam walked in.

"Sam! What?"

"Hello, Tony. Saw you on the lunchtime news. Thought you might need a bit of help." She turned to the policewoman, "I would like to be alone with my client now, please."

"Am I glad to see you," I said, as soon as we were alone.

"So, that's some charge sheet you've got there!"

"Sam, I'm sorry about everything. You know I would never have wanted it to come to this. Not this way. Things just got sort of... out of control."

"So it seems." Her eyes never left the charge sheet.

"How are the kids?"

"They're fine. Missing you. It seems you made a bit of an impression on them at Glastonbury." She looked up at me. "Simon said, Dad's cool, isn't he, Mum?"

I saw she had trouble getting the word 'Cool' out. It seemed to stick in her mouth, like dry cracker biscuits.

"Sam," I reached across and took her hand.

"No, Tony. My turn. Listen. Ever since we met I've tried to push you, bend you, to be something you're not. You're not, and you never will be, a city shark. Yet that's what I tried to force you to become. I'm probably more responsible than Grahame for your breakdown. When I first met you, you just wanted to cruise along. Not planning further ahead than the next party. And I think somewhere that's still the person you are today. I just want you to take the road that makes you happy. I don't think us staying together is going to achieve that, for you or me. We're just too different."

I squeezed her hand. A film of liquid ran across my eyes making it difficult to see. Damned hay fever! "Thanks," I said.

"Right, now," she said. It was as if somebody had just flicked a switch inside her head and re-engaged the Sam that for a moment had been exposed. "Let's see what we can do about this lot." She tapped her forefinger on the charge sheet. "I want you to tell me, word for word, exactly how all this happened. "

She listened attentively to my every word. Much more than I think she'd ever listened to me in the past. Every so often, she stopped and asked me to repeat something, or explain in more detail. She scribbled copious notes as we went.

An hour later, she knocked on the door requesting the return of the interviewing officer.

"My client is now prepared to make a deal," she said as the officer sat down.

"He is?"

"I am?"

"Yes. He is!"

"You know the police don't make deals, ma'am."

"Well, let's discuss the options then, shall we? You have a selection of hit-or-miss charges here. None of which are going to hold very much water in court."

She went down through them.

"Robbing phone boxes. Do you actually have any evidence that my client was the person responsible for blocking the return coin chute?"

"Well, that's the Cornwall police."

"Stealing petrol. If the garage would like to check their video they will notice that it wasn't my client driving the vehicle at the time. Urinating on a public monument. We will argue that as the area was fenced off at the time that will be tantamount to being on private property. Therefore, the charges would have to be brought privately by English Heritage, and not the Crown Prosecution Service. And I think English Heritage will be unlikely to pursue that."

Boy, she was good!

"On the other hand," she continued. "My client is preparing to take action against the clothes shop on the basis that he was only trying to pay for the clothes, and yet he was chased by an over-zealous security guard. Causing much personal distress."

"Distress," I echoed.

The constable looked as bemused as I felt.

"But my client is civic minded. As long as you are prepared to stop this petty nonsense," she waved the charge sheet in the air. "He would like to help you on another matter."

"Oh, really! What's that?"

Yes, I wondered. What's that?

"I believe the Somerset police have in their custody a paedophile who they are going to have to set free very shortly."

"I understand they have somebody, but I wasn't aware they were going to have to set him free," the constable said, sucking the end of his pen.

"Lack of continuity of evidence," Sam said in a tone of voice that indicated it should be perfectly obvious. "They have nobody to prove that the videotape they hold has not been tampered with. And a clever solicitor," she paused and smiled. "Will be able to exploit that loophole. On the other hand, my client was witness to the film being recorded. He can prove continuity and give evidence that the tape has not been tampered with. That will be enough to ensure a conviction. So, do we have a deal?" She sat back with a tight-lipped smile on her face.

An hour later, I was free, and just as important, once again in possession of belt and boot-laces. I took Sam for a drink in a nearby pub to say thank you.

I had never realised before quite how good she was at her job. I think we both learned a lot about each other that day. And with that knowledge, came a new respect and an understanding that we were, and always had been, completely wrong for each other.

Epilogue

So, that's it. As I sit here listening to the waves lapping on the side of my boat, I wonder if it would have been any different had I not picked up the tobacco tin that day. Does the whole course of our lives really depend on such minor detail?

The nights are drawing in now. The big orange sun is sitting on the edge of the sea. A golden path runs from the point of contact on the horizon to the stern of my boat. It almost looks as if I could walk along it, across the sea to the sun. What would I find there?

I'd left the whole dividing up business to Sam. She is a solicitor after all. And I couldn't see the point in paying her to write letters to herself. And in the end, I trusted her. One thing our relationship had never been short of, was trust. She'd set up endowments for the children, opened a bank account for me with the remains of the settlement, and even bought me this boat. It's not really a lobster boat though. It's a bit big for that. But what the hell. I still go out and lay the pots.

"Tony, Tony!"

Astrid's calling me from below deck, so I'm going to have to go in a minute. We've just spent all day cleaning up the mess the kids left. You wouldn't have thought they could cause so much chaos in just three days! But it was great seeing them again. They've gone back to Sam now, but they seemed to thoroughly enjoy themselves while they were here. Simon fell in the water twice, and I think I've managed to ruin all of Natasha's clothes by letting her play with the lobster pots.

Sam's taken up with Martin Braithwaite now. And I think that's how it should have been in the first place. But then...

We're having the others over for a meal on-board tonight. I'm doing the cooking.

Now, if I can just get this barbecue to work...

That's funny, I can smell gas...

The end.

Lightning Source UK Ltd.
Milton Keynes UK
10 December 2010

164171UK00001B/5/P